Praise for *TRUE VOWS*

"What better way is there to prove romance really exists than to read these books?"

—**Carly Phillips**, *New York Times* bestselling author

"Memoir meets romance! In the twenty years I've been penning romances, this is one of the most novel and exciting ideas I've encountered in the genre. Take a Vow. It rocks!"

—**Tara Janzen**, *New York Times* bestselling author of *Loose and Easy*

"An irresistible combination of romantic fantasy and reality that begins where our beloved romance novels end: TRUE VOWS. What a scrumptious slice of life!"

—**Suzanne Forster**, *New York Times* bestselling author

"The marriage of real-life stories with classic, fictional romance—an amazing concept."

—**Peggy Webb,** award-winning author of sixty romance novels

LIFE . . . ROMANTICIZED

Julie Leto
HARD TO HOLD

Health Communications, Inc.
Deerfield Beach, Florida

www.hcibooks.com

Library of Congress Cataloging-in-Publication Data
Leto, Julie Elizabeth.
 Hard to hold / Julie Leto.
  p. cm.
 ISBN-13: 978-0-7573-1534-3
 ISBN-10: 0-7573-1534-8
 I. Title.
 PS3612.E82885H37 2010
 813'.6—dc22

2010027061

Publisher: Health Communications, Inc.
       3201 S.W. 15th Street
       Deerfield Beach, FL 33442–8190

TRUE VOWS Series Developer: Olivia Rupprecht
Cover photos ©Brooke Fasani/Corbis
Cover design by Larissa Hise Henoch
Interior design and formatting by Lawna Patterson Oldfield

To Michael and Anne, for proving that true love

isn't something you just read about in storybooks.

To Alison, Judith, Olivia,

and Michele, for sharing the ride.

To Anne-Marie Carroll, for so many things,

I can't even begin to list them all . . .

but in this case, for her eagle eye.

Dear Reader

WELCOME TO TRUE VOWS!

Since I've been reading and writing romance for . . . well, longer than I care to admit . . . I know that it's a rare and wonderful experience when something entirely new breaks into our beloved genre. That's what TRUE VOWS is—something new! Non-romance readers sometimes scoff at romance novels because they think, "That stuff never happens in real life." These books prove that it does happen . . . and when it does, it's wonderful.

To those of you who are seasoned romance readers—thank you for taking a chance on this new concept. I hope the books will appeal to that part of you that embraces the incredible power of love in the face of conflicts both big and small. To those of you who are new to the genre, but who love a good true-life story— welcome! I hope TRUE VOWS will satisfy your expectations and hook you permanently into reading more of this wonderful genre.

Working with Anne Miller and Mike Davoli to bring a romanticized version of their courtship to the page was a joy and an honor. I can only hope that I've done justice to this amazing couple. Anne is the kind of heroine I like to write about. She's strong, independent, and ambitious, but also nurturing and creative. Mike is the quintessential romantic hero—confident, successful, smart, and funny. And he cleans! I mean, really, what more could a woman want?

Like the real people they are, they aren't perfect. Their romantic road had some speed bumps, which is what made this such a great story to tell. I can report, however, that the happy ending you will experience at the end of the book is entirely real. And Sirus really is as charming in person as she is in the book.

Lastly, I want to give a shout out to Michele Matrisciani, Olivia Rupprecht (aka Mallory Rush), Veronica Blake, Peter Vegso, and the entire team at HCI Books for giving me the opportunity to be a part of this ground-breaking project. It's been a challenge and a joy.

I encourage you to visit the official TRUE VOWS site, www.truevowsbooks.com, to interact with the couples and novelists, learn the latest news on the TRUE VOWS line, read about the next books in the series, and even have the opportunity to tell HCI Books your true love story for a chance to be the subject of a future TRUE VOWS book.

Happy reading,

Julie

P.S. I'd love to know what you think about the book once you're done reading! Please visit my website, www.julieleto.com, or my blog, www.plotmonkeys.com, to let me know what you think!

One

"YOUR PROBLEM IS THAT YOU'RE TOO PICKY."

The blissful bubble built by Jeff Tweedy's poignant lyrics and masterful acoustic guitar burst as if pricked with a pin. Anne Miller turned to her friend, Shane Sanders, and speared her with incredulous indignation. Just before the concert had started, Shane had been ruminating on all the reasons why Anne should not have been in Albany's Egg theatre without a date. And now, a split second after the last bit of applause had died away, the discussion had popped up again like an earthworm.

"Drop it, Shane."

Shane smiled, then rested her head on the shoulder of her latest boyfriend, James. Or was it Jamie? Jim? Anne wasn't sure. Convinced she needed to expand her circle of friends, Anne usually tried harder to get to know new people. With Shane's dates, however, she rarely had the chance to keep track.

Shane pursed her naturally pink lips and gave Anne a hard once-over. "You're very attractive. Men notice you all the time. And you're smart—probably smarter than you should be where guys are concerned. You've got a career, a great family, and wonderful taste in friends."

"You should date me," Anne quipped, before lowering her voice to add, "maybe then your relationships would last more than twenty-four hours."

Shane sneered, but without any real malevolence. "You're too messy. You'd drive me nuts. Seriously, sweetie, if you want a guy to share all your fabulosity with, you're going to need to lower your standards."

"My standards are just fine," Anne said.

"Really? Then why is it that we sold that seat beside you rather than filling it with a guy you might get lucky with later on?"

"So you could spend the entire night trying to fix my love life, why else?"

Shane rolled her eyes at Anne's sarcasm, but dropped the topic as they gathered their bags and coats. One of these days, Shane would come to the same realization as Anne that worrying about her social life—or worse, obsessing about it—was a lesson in futility.

If she was destined to meet someone, she would. Efforts on her part to make this happen sooner rather than later only resulted in frustration. A year ago, she'd bought an extra bedside table and had emptied drawers in her armoire in anticipation of meeting someone special. But the emotional *feng shui* had just left her with extra storage space—a fitting metaphor for her heart. And yet, for someone who rarely put things away, the act remained utterly useless.

"Don't you feel the least bit anxious to meet someone interesting?"

"I meet interesting people every day," Anne said. "And relationships happen when they happen. In the meantime, I'll just leave the getting lucky part to you."

The walk home to their State Street apartment building would be brisk, so Anne snuggled into her jacket with anticipation of the frigid November air. The crime desk had been especially brutal this week at the *Albany Daily Journal* and even the cold was preferable to air that had been recirculating inside a courthouse since the 1970s.

When Jamie suggested they stop for drinks on the way home, Anne agreed immediately. A couple of margaritas on a Monday night was a rare and wonderful treat.

Shane shuffled behind the line of music lovers moving toward the outer aisles. "What happened to you wanting to meet new people and broaden your horizons?"

Anne sighed. "And here I thought the promise of margaritas would deter you."

"I just want you to be happy. You've been working like a maniac lately."

"Crime doesn't sleep, so neither do crime reporters."

"Good thing, because if you're any indication, crime reporters all sleep alone."

Anne gave Shane a playful shove. "You've got a one-track mind. I love my job. I love exposing the dark underbelly of society and exploring the road to justice."

"Too bad you don't meet too many cute single guys on that road," Shane said.

Anne winced. "My job is the last place I'd look for dates."

Criminals notwithstanding, Anne did not want to date another reporter. For one, reporters on high-powered career tracks were fascinating, but they moved a lot—chasing down not only stories, but better jobs in bigger markets. She had her own aspirations in that arena and wasn't quite certain she wanted to balance her professional goals against someone else's. Not, at least, in the same industry.

The only other nonfelonious people she encountered in the

workplace were overworked cops, underpaid prosecutors, bail bondsmen, and the downtrodden families of either victims or suspected criminals.

Not exactly a smorgasbord for potential mates.

Anne didn't want to date just to get out of the house. She had friends for that, both male and female, and dabbling in casual dating had long ago lost her interest. She wasn't exactly on a husband hunt, but she was done wasting her time on guys who had no intentions of settling down.

Okay, so maybe her standards were too high.

"If you're not meeting guys at work and you won't let me fix you up, then exactly how are you going to find the man of your dreams?"

"Dream men I have," Anne said. "A little Jack Bauer, a little David Boreanaz, and my sleeping hours are covered."

"That's not how sleeping hours are supposed to be covered," Shane replied, wiggling her eyebrows.

Maybe not, but Anne would rather fantasize about sexy men doing delicious, sexy things to her while she was asleep than waste any of her premium waking hours on a guy who didn't float her boat.

Anne started to followed the people on her left toward the exit, but Shane grabbed her hand and tugged her to the right, following James. They filed into the open area that would lead them out of the auditorium. "Maybe over margaritas, I can convince you to go out with my cousin."

"With tequila, you just might have a shot," Anne said, though she doubted it. The last girl Shane's cousin had dated had worked as a stripper. Somehow, she couldn't imagine him finding her thick and naturally wavy dark hair, curvy figure, and cherry red–framed glasses appealing.

A break opened in the crowd. They were slipping through rather quickly when Shane stopped short, causing Anne to crash into her. She opened her mouth to apologize when Shane spun around, her light brown eyes bright with excitement. "Or, I could introduce you to Michael."

Anne slapped her forehead. Keeping up with Shane's unending list of single male relatives and cast-off guy friends, not to mention her train of thought, required more brain power than Anne possessed this late on a Monday night.

"Who's Michael?"

Shane swung Anne around so that she bumped shoulders with a guy who'd been headed toward the same exit as they were.

A twinge of something warm reverberated through the lining of her jacket.

Something like attraction.

"I'm Michael," said the guy she'd crashed into.

Anne stepped backward, nearly trampling over a couple of girls who looked way too young to be out on a weeknight. She mumbled her apologies while her gaze connected with the most intense blue eyes she'd ever seen.

The grin that reached into their turquoise depths wasn't bad, either.

"This is Anne," Shane said, practically bouncing on her toes with excitement. "She lives in my building. Isn't she beautiful?"

There was a special place in hell for people who insisted on fixing up their friends—a place only slightly less horrifying than the dungeons reserved for those who sprang arresting-looking guys on their neighbors with no advance notice. Anne forced a laugh over her clumsiness. "Sorry. I didn't mean to run you over."

Michael dug his hands deeper into the pockets of his jacket, his grin lighting his eyes to a color that was almost hard to look at.

"The experience wasn't entirely unpleasant. How'd you like the concert? And yes," he said to Shane. "Yes, she is."

Not unpleasant wasn't the best compliment she'd ever gotten, but how he handled Shane's audacious question put her on notice. That he'd agreed she was beautiful was special. That he'd done so with such smooth skill impressed her even more.

Since they'd stopped to talk, a bottleneck of people surged behind them, pressing them forward through the exit. Despite the chaos all around, Anne answered Michael's question about the concert. By the time they spilled into the lobby of the Egg, they both agreed that Tweedy had been on form and worth the ticket price.

They'd moved on to her explaining how she and Shane lived in the same apartment building not far from the venue when Anne asked, "So how do *you* know Shane?"

Michael and her neighbor exchanged a quick but meaningful look.

"Oh," she said.

"What do you mean by that *Oh*?" Shane jerked up the zipper of her coat against a sudden gust of wind coming in from outside the auditorium.

Anne glanced at Michael, who looked a little perplexed, an expression that added a dash of adorability to his attractive face.

She'd assumed that Shane and Michael had dated sometime and though the odds had been with her, she was, apparently, mistaken. She covered with, "Did you go to school together?"

The moment brimmed with a layer of tension, but Michael tilted his head in the direction of the moving crowd and answered, "Actually, we met at a concert. She hooked up with a friend of mine."

Anne smiled. "She has the tendency to do that."

Michael laughed. "Pretty girls often do, but then you'd know all about that."

It took a split second before she realized he'd just paid her another compliment, though this one was definitely better than the first.

"Did you just call me pretty?"

From the indentation in his cheek, she could tell he was trying hard to waylay a smile. "You sound shocked."

"I guess I am," she confessed.

"I can't imagine why."

Though a blast of cold air swirled around them as they poured outside into the open, Anne had to admit—if only to herself—that this guy was good. In the course of a very short conversation, he'd warmed her insides like a strong, hot toddy.

"Hey, let's go to Bomber's. They make that Italian margarita," Shane said, "and they're on the way home."

Anne cast a sideways glance at Michael and realized he was not alone. Flanked by a tall, slim guy with dark brown hair, they shared a comfortable rapport that told Anne they'd been friends a long time.

"Hi, I'm Anne," she said, holding out her hand.

He accepted. "Ben," he said.

"Did you date Shane, too?"

Shane bopped her on her shoulder. "You're going to give Jamie the wrong idea about me."

"He probably has the wrong idea about you already or he wouldn't be so anxious to get you tipsy on tequila," Anne suggested.

This comment initiated a squeal of protest from Shane. Several bawdy jokes then erupted from Jamie. After Ben joined in, Anne fell back a few paces and walked beside Michael again, who was tucking something into his pocket.

"Going to your car?" she asked.

He shook his head. "Ben has a house a couple of blocks from here."

"You're roommates?"

"If you call camping out in someone's attic being a roommate. I just moved back to Albany after a stint in Portland. A leasing agent found me a place, but I haven't seen it yet. It isn't easy finding an apartment that takes dogs."

"You have more than one?"

The question lit Michael's face as if a spotlight had just been turned toward him. "No, just one, but she's a beauty."

And with only a little bit of prodding, Anne had him talking about his pooch, a Weimaraner named Sirus, which he clearly adored. Anne couldn't help but think there was nothing more appealing than a man who loved his dog. In fact, the more he spoke about chew toys and his dog's predilection for pancake batter, the more Anne wondered if, for once, her unnatural ability to bump into things hadn't worked in her favor.

They reached Bomber's Bar five minutes later. Patrons mingled outside, waiting for space in the crowded pub. Jamie and Shane headed inside to look for a table, but Ben waited by the door for Anne and Mike, whose conversation kept them a few steps behind.

"So how do you feel about margaritas?" Anne asked.

"More of a beer guy myself, but I've been known to toss back tequila for a good cause."

"It's Monday night," Anne said, a little more brightly than she wanted to. The sudden, anxious feeling in the pit of her stomach was only slightly more disconcerting than the flush currently burning her cheeks. "That's reason enough in my book."

Mike shoved his hands in his pockets and rocked back on his

heels, bringing his forward momentum to a screeching halt.

"Aren't you coming in for a drink?" she asked.

He gave a big sniff, his eyes glassy from the sharp, night air. "I can't, but thanks."

She didn't try to hide her confusion. She didn't exactly expect the guy to drop down on one knee after talking to her for fifteen minutes, but his reluctance to join them for a drink took her by surprise. Geez, her radar was really off. She could have sworn he had at least a passing interest in being friendly.

"More margaritas for me, I guess," she said, moving toward the door.

When he called her name, she turned, gasping as he wrapped his arms around her and pulled her into a quick hug.

And by quick, she meant quick. They made contact for less than a split second, and yet in that fleeting moment, heat suffused from his body to hers. The only reason she registered the warmth was because she missed it the moment he was gone.

"It was really great to meet you," he said.

"Yeah, you too," she replied.

She exchanged a smile with his friend Ben, who looked equally confused by Mike's refusal to come inside, then shoved through the crowd to catch up with Shane and Jamie. And here she thought she was starting off the week with an interesting prospect. Instead, she'd just gotten a hug from a guy who obviously didn't want to give her the time of day.

Two

"YOU'RE AN IDIOT."

Michael Davoli glanced at Ben and tried to come up with a sharp or clever retort. Unfortunately, nothing came to him. He'd just walked away from a chance to hang out with a vivacious goddess of a girl just because his nose was runny, his eyes were itchy and blinking with even more rapidity than usual. *Idiot* described him perfectly.

"Tell me something I don't know," Michael muttered.

Ben took the invitation with relish. "Where to start? That chick was into you, man."

"Maybe," he said, not entirely certain. She was certain friendly and bubbly, but for all he knew, she was that way with everyone. Which, in a significant way, made her all that more appealing.

"She was cute," Ben said.

"Definitely."

"So why are we walking in the wrong direction?"

Mike pulled a handkerchief out of his pocket and blew his nose. The action covered the insistent twitch in his neck and shoulder. Damned allergies. Damned Tourette's. His condition only worsened when his immunities were down. He'd suffered through the concert on massive doses of antihistamine, which he'd counteracted with two triple espressos and his strong will to hear Tweedy play. The music had, as usual, given him an outlet for the pent-up energy spawned by his disorder. And he'd met a hot girl whose curves, even beneath a bulky winter coat, had invoked a completely different kind of energy—the best kind.

But he was on the downside of his caffeine high and not only did he not want to sneeze all over Shane, her new squeeze, or the pretty, vivacious Anne while they sipped tequila and lime, he also didn't want his meds to cause him to pass out in front of a girl he wanted to impress.

"Man, I feel like shit," Mike admitted. "Maybe another time."

Ben shook his head and muttered under his breath. Though Michael should have known better than to invite further conversation on the matter, he couldn't stop himself from saying, "What?"

"Like you don't know."

Mike stopped walking and shoved Ben in the shoulder to stop his forward momentum. "What don't I know?"

"You've got to get over her, man."

"I just met her."

His retort popped out, despite the fact that he knew that Ben wasn't talking about Anne. He was talking about Lisa. Ben made his point clear by giving him that "you're a fucking idiot" look that always washed over his face whenever the subject of Mike's ex came up.

"This isn't about Lisa," Mike said.

"Are you sure? You've been living at my place for two months. You haven't gone out on a single date."

"What are you, my *yenta*?"

Ben snorted. "I'm just saying that a guy who hugs a girl five seconds after he's met her, but then turns around and walks away, is seriously screwed up."

As much as he'd like to spout an instant denial, Mike continued toward Ben's place without saying a word. He had just moved back home to New York from Portland, and one of his goals for returning had been to rejuvenate his love life. As the campaign coordinator for the Quality Education Initiative, he had a stable job. Though he was currently homesteading in Ben's spare attic room, he had a great lead on a new place. He even had the world's most perfect dog. Finding a woman with whom to share his bounty would be icing on the cake.

But despite Ben's pathetic assessment of Mike's love life, he hadn't been entirely lonely since his return to his home state. He might not have invited anyone special on a one-on-one, nice-restaurant, movie date, but he'd hung out with friends and their pretty friends-of-friends. Even tonight, he'd almost experienced another spontaneous, wholly accidental fix-up. He hadn't seen Shane in years and yet the very first thing she'd done when they'd met up again was introduce him to her very attractive, witty, and interesting neighbor.

The fact that he hadn't gone into the bar or, now that he thought about it, asked for her number had everything to do with his stuffy head and nothing whatsoever to do with his former girlfriend.

"Lisa is ancient history," Mike said before they crossed the street.

In the wake of Anne's bubbly personality, Mike had trouble even conjuring an image of his ex. He and Lisa had been young when they'd met. They'd dated exclusively for five years and after awhile, he'd simply assumed that she would be with him for the long haul.

But she'd had other ideas. He hadn't proposed, but the idea of marriage had occurred to him—shortly before she'd left.

Rationally and logically, she'd made the right choice. But emotionally, he'd been blindsided. While he couldn't blame her for wanting to embrace all the opportunities a woman could have if she wasn't tied down to her first real boyfriend, her departure had soured him on relationships for a very long time.

But he'd moved beyond that hurt now. He'd come home to New York to take his whole life to the next level. He had the job and the friends. Now, he just needed the right mate. And yet, the first time he met a potential contender, he walked away because he was tired and couldn't breathe.

Ben was right. He was an idiot.

The minute Anne opened the door to Villa Italia Bakery on Broadway in Schenectady, the glorious scent of freshly dusted powdered sugar hit her like a cloud of pure delight. Inhaling, she stood in the doorway, dismissing each delicious odor until the roasted, piquant scent of espresso rose to the top note of the bakery's indulgent perfume. She'd start with a double cappuccino and decide from there what treat she'd choose. After the confusing but invigorating chance meeting with Shane's friend, Michael, the night before, she'd been restless. And although she didn't have to go into the office until the afternoon, she still had enough work to require copious amounts of caffeine.

Anne fell in line behind the crush of mutually minded sugar-fiends waiting to select from the amazing smorgasbord of cookies, pastries, brownies, cakes, and breads. She forestalled her overwhelming hunger by chatting with a few fellow regulars who, like her, took advantage of the bakery's free Wi-Fi. Once at the counter, she selected an assortment of cookies for breakfast. And because she was such a good customer, she received not only a welcome smile from the girl behind the cash register, but also extra foam on her coffee and an additional biscotti on her plate.

When she turned, she caught sight of Kate Richmond, her favorite prosecutor in the state attorney's office. Anne had meant to stop by her office today to get the latest on the Smith-Wildmire murder trial, but she'd get more out of the woman here. Free of trilling phones, needy colleagues, and stacks of case files that threatened to topple if anyone so much as sneezed, Kate might be much more forthcoming.

"Hey, Anne," the prosecutor said when Anne brushed past her table.

"Fancy meeting you here," Anne said, her singsong delivery making her true purpose more than obvious. While she wouldn't go so far as call the attorney a friend, they had become friendly over her time on the crime beat. Most people at the courthouse didn't mind talking to Anne. Unlike many of her coworkers at the *Daily Journal*, she was not yet so jaded and burned out that she couldn't bend her lips into a real smile every once in a while.

"We don't expect the jury on the Wildmire case to bring down a verdict until tomorrow."

Anne frowned. Actual court cases—as opposed to plea deals—were a rarity in the Schenectady courtrooms of late. That she'd spent time actually watching a live trial last week had been something of a twisted treat.

"Any idea why they're taking so long?"

Kate shrugged. "Maybe they like their hotel."

Anne laughed. She knew which no-tell motel the state used to sequester the good citizens doing their civic duty. If the luxuriousness of the accommodations was the deciding factor, the jury would have declared the defendant guilty in a literal New York minute.

Or maybe they'd surprise everyone and determine the scumbag to be innocent, though Anne couldn't imagine how.

"What's next up on the docket? I heard something about an indictment against a local businessman for fraud? Something to do with an investment scam that focused on the elderly?"

Kate pursed her lips, so Anne turned up the wattage of her smile until the prosecutor cleared some papers from her table and with a sweeping hand invited Anne to join her.

"It's not one of my cases."

"Yeah, but you never talk about your cases until after they're over."

"This much is true." Kate handled mostly domestic violence and juvenile adjudications, so while she was not usually forthcoming with information that might hurt her victims—or in the case of the kids, her defendants—she usually made herself available to discuss less sticky topics, like the murder case that had been playing out for nearly two years from the first arrest to the eventual trial. "What did you hear about the fraud case?"

"Not a name," Anne replied. She'd actually only overheard a tidbit of conversation last week while in the ladies' room at the courthouse, but no one in the know had verified anything she could print.

"Grand jury is supposed to finish up today. If you can be in the courthouse around two, you might just get some answers."

Anne snagged a cookie coated in thick, powdered sugar before sliding her plate across to Kate. Wedding cookies were her favorite.

"Thanks for the tip," Anne replied, smiling.

Kate downed the dregs of her latte. "I do not understand how anyone as cheerful as you can cover the crime beat."

This was the second time in two days that someone had questioned her career choice in terms of her personality. She wasn't sure what that meant—or if she liked it.

"Maybe I haven't been doing it long enough to get burned out and crusty," she replied.

"Do you want to be crusty?" Kate crinkled her nose with obvious distaste at the idea.

"Will I get paid more?"

"I seriously doubt it," Kate replied.

"Then I'll leave crusty to my editor."

"How cliché," Kate commented with a smile.

"Yes, well, there's a reason stereotypes exist in the newspaper business. Most of them are based on undeniable truths."

"Same with the court system. I'm the perfect example of the once idealistic, yet now currently overworked, public servant with absolutely no life of her own who gets more pleasure out of Venetian cookies than I do on a Saturday night."

"Welcome to my world," Anne said.

On the surface, she and Kate shouldn't have that much in common, particularly in the dating arena. Kate was in her forties, a single mom who worked long hours for a lot of personal satisfaction but very little pay. At least Anne had a job that allowed her to work from multiple locations and a daily life that didn't bring her into direct contact with crime victims or perpetrators on an hourly basis.

"Dating is the least of my worries nowadays. You?"

Anne took the opportunity to shove a particularly large sesame cookie into her mouth, giving herself time to chew over an answer. She didn't really want to talk about Michael. What was there to say? She'd only chatted with the guy for fifteen minutes and yet his haunting blue eyes and easy laugh had stayed with her long after her multiple margaritas, the chilly walk home and her restless night in bed. It wasn't as if she was fantasizing about having sex with him—not that this would be an unpleasant fantasy—but she couldn't understand how, if they'd clicked so quickly, he could find it so easy to walk away.

He *had* hugged her before he left. What the hell had that been about?

Not that she'd ever find out. Albany was not a big place by New York City standards, but the chances of her running into him again were slim. She needed to get him out of her mind. And unfortunately, cookies weren't helping.

"I don't have much time for dating," Anne replied. "Crime statistics keep rising every time we turn around."

She made a mild attempt at fake outrage, but Kate took a leisurely sip from a bottled water she'd pulled from her purse.

"Want another coffee?" Anne offered, more than willing to shell out some coin for a cup o' Joe if it meant keeping Kate around long enough to ask her more about the upcoming indictment.

"Ha! You think I'm going to sit here and have a coffee with you after you cast aspersions on the law enforcement of our dear state?"

"If it's a caramel latte, you'd probably stay until closing."

Kate grinned. "You know me very well."

Anne popped over to the counter and ordered. Once she sat, Kate immediately filled her in on the scant details she had about the fraud case, which unfortunately, were not enough for Anne to file a story.

"Why don't you come by my office this afternoon? I have a one o'clock meeting with Marshall, and he's the lead on that case. Maybe you'll be able to squeeze a few details out of him before the rest of the press get a hold of the news."

"Cool, thanks."

Anne made a note on her to-do list, which wasn't getting any shorter while she sat here. But the story she planned to file today was halfway done and other than a scheduled trip to the courthouse to check the postings and make a side trip after five to a bar frequented by the police officers who often gave her information on new arrests, she had planned an easy day in Villa Italia, using their Wi-Fi to finish up some preliminary research she was doing for an interview.

When she clipped her planner closed, she looked up to find Kate shaking her head in disbelief.

"What?" She ran her tongue surreptitiously over her teeth in case a stray sesame seed had lodged itself in an embarrassing spot.

"You," Kate said, shaking her head. "You just don't fit the image of the 'crime reporter.'"

She even added the little air quotes to get her point across.

"Why do people keep saying that? Not that I care. I've never aspired to fit anyone's image of anything."

"Still, I wonder how you pull it off. Maybe you can teach me. You write about ugly murders and violent mayhem every day, and yet you somehow manage to remain upbeat."

"Cookies help," Anne said, choosing the almond biscotti from the last few on the plate and dipping it into the foamy, cinnamon-dusted top of her refreshed coffee.

Kate nodded. "They certainly don't hurt."

"Tell that to my thighs."

"I have no credibility with my own body parts, so I don't know how I'd have any influence over yours."

"Tell me about it. I guess I try really hard to keep my job and my life separate. I'm only a reporter. I have that luxury. I don't have to talk to scumbags or deal with their slimy lawyers every single day like you do. The safety of a community doesn't rest on my shoulders."

Though the sentiment was sincere, Anne's comment won her an additional bit of insider information regarding the much-anticipated arrest of the scamming businessman. The tidbit

would give her a chance to do a little research before she headed
to the courthouse at one o'clock and would likely result in her
asking better questions. To repay the favor, Anne listened intently
while Kate ruminated over her teenage daughter's request to
attend a rock concert in the middle of the week.

"I just went to a show last night," Anne confessed.

"You're not sixteen."

"Thank God," Anne replied with a shiver. Her teenage years
had not been traumatic, but she rather enjoyed adulthood and the
freedom to go out on a Monday night without having to check
with her parents first.

"Who'd you see?"

"Jeff Tweedy. He's the front man for Wilco, one of my favorite
bands."

"I feel very old when people talk about bands I've never heard of."

"I'm sure a lot of people younger than you haven't heard of
them, either. They're not exactly mainstream. Tweedy's show was
all acoustic. Very low-key. It was at the Egg."

"I love that place. Show was good?"

"Awesome," Anne replied, though the lack of enthusiasm in
her voice startled even her.

"Doesn't sound that way," Kate said, her eyebrows high.

"No, the show was really great. But afterward . . ."

She waved her hand, indicating she really didn't want to continue her explanation, but Kate only scooted closer and leaned in.
The woman was, after all, a practiced interrogator. Anne wanted
to resist talking about meeting Michael because the outcome had
been both unexpected and mind-bogglingly disappointing.

"So who was he?" Kate asked.

Anne frowned. "Just some guy I met. We talked for a bit and
then he took off. It's no big deal."

"It's a big enough deal that you're still thinking about him."

Anne forced as much disinterest into her voice as she could manage—which wasn't much. "He had really fabulous eyes."

"Then why did you let him leave?"

"I had no choice," she insisted. "Handcuffing a guy to me isn't exactly my speed."

"Maybe it should be." Kate batted her eyelashes dramatically while she sipped her coffee. "My ex-husband was a cop. I bet if I looked, I might find a spare pair of cuffs for you to borrow. You know, in case you and this guy meet up again."

Anne laughed. She was likely never going to meet Michael again—and if she did, she doubted she'd have any interest in securing him with hardware so that he couldn't get away.

Not unless he showed her a little more attention than he had the first time.

Three

"SIRUS, NO!"

Michael slid the box of CDs he'd just lifted back onto the flatbed of his father's truck and yanked tight on the leash he'd tucked into his pocket. His sixty-five pound Weimaraner, thrown into hyperdrive by something interesting on the other side of the vehicle, tugged until Michael's shoulder ached. The sensation of her narrow tail wagging so hard and fast he suspected it might start rotating and lift her up like a helicopter, sliced at the thigh of his jeans. With the frigid February air already biting through the denim, the pain was more than a little annoying.

"Sirus, heal!"

He was just about to mutter a frustrated (yet utterly without conviction) curse of "Stupid dog," when he heard a distinctly feminine voice say, "Michael?" from the other side of the curb.

One solid yank on the leash and Sirus fell into an obedient sit. She panted, still excited to meet whoever had spotted him outside his new apartment. He was curious to find out who it was, too. The voice sounded familiar. He hadn't expected to see anyone he knew while he transferred the contents of his life to his new home. Particularly no one of the female persuasion. Yet when he caught sight of the woman, he suddenly understood his dog's enthusiasm. Bundled up in the most ridiculous green wool scarf and hat he'd ever seen—and looking entirely breathtaking in it—was Anne Miller.

"Anne, wow, hi."

Though he'd been in Albany for months, he hadn't run into the beautiful brunette since their initial introduction at the Tweedy show, and he'd been too busy with the holidays, work, and moving to track Shane down and ask about her friend. He'd made such a crappy first impression, and so far, he wasn't doing that much better with attempt number two.

Instead, he was greeting her while sweaty and dirty from moving boxes of his belongings from his father's truck to his new digs.

The fact that he'd acknowledged the newcomer sent Sirus into a renewed apoplectic frenzy. She leapt into the air. Her leash kept her tethered, but as Weimaraners seemed to have springs bred into the bottoms of their feet, the dog looked like a big gray bouncing ball hoping to greet this new person properly.

Anne laughed, which didn't much help his attempts to calm his overwrought pup.

"She's a handful," Anne said, but not without a smile.

"Normally, she's incredibly well behaved. But she's been stuck either inside the truck or in the bedroom upstairs since we started moving, so she's a little overexcited. I think she just needs to stretch her legs."

Anne nodded. "Maybe it's time to take a break."

Michael glanced up at the sky. Sunset was maybe forty-five minutes away and they still had an entire truckload to drag upstairs before the temperatures dropped and they lost their best light source.

"No time. My dad's helping me get my stuff upstairs and he doesn't want to drive back home too late."

She paused a moment, pressing her lips together as if she wanted to say something, but wasn't sure she should. Her hesitation, however, only lasted a split second.

"I could help."

Mike glanced at the heavy boxes in the truck and then back at Anne, not sure what surprised him more—that the woman who'd occupied more than a little time in his thoughts over the last two months had suddenly appeared out of nowhere or that she was offering to help him lug heavy boxes into his new place.

"I don't want you to hurt yourself," he said.

"The dog will settle down," Anne replied, bending so that she was eye level, but still at a safe distance from Sirus. The dog had stopped doing her imitation of a Slinky, but was still attempting to wriggle out of her skin.

"No, I thought you meant," he cut himself off before he made too much of a fool out of himself. Again.

He yanked the leash, calling Sirus to his side. She obeyed immediately. She responded when Mike meant business. This wasn't often, as he tended to spoil the pup rotten.

The dog's anxiety fed off his own. Despite obeying his command, the dog strained against her collar. She obviously wanted to know Anne better.

Yeah, well, she could join the club.

Mike knelt beside his pet and motioned Anne forward.

"Sirus, this is Anne. Anne, meet Sirus, the wonder pup."

"Hello, Sirus." The breathy sound of Anne's voice warmed him like a gust of summer wind. The scarf, which looked rustically hand-knit, brushed against her cheek, flushed with color. The fact that her jeans curved quite nicely around her hips as she knelt didn't hurt, either.

The inside of his mouth parched to desert-like conditions. He was very thankful he didn't have to speak again for a while. Anne had taken over the conversation, which was completely centered on Sirus.

"You're a beautiful lady, aren't you?" she crooned to the dog, holding out her hand so that Sirus could give her a good long sniff. The dog's butt and hind legs started rocking as her tail struggled beneath her. She wanted to obey Mike's sit command, but she also wanted to tackle Anne and more than likely, lick at those adorably rosy freckled cheeks.

Before he knew it, Anne was petting the dog, giving her extra scratches behind her ears. Inch by inch, the dog stretched closer.

"You like dogs?" he asked.

Okay, it was a stupid, obvious question, but with moisture absent from his mouth and his bloodstream pumping with the kind of powerful attraction he hadn't felt in a very long time, he was lucky to form even three words of coherent conversation.

"Oh, yeah," she said, dropping to her knees in front of the dog so she could scratch both of Sirus's ears simultaneously. For her trouble, the dog gave a long, appreciative swipe of tongue across Anne's face.

Lucky bitch.

"Sirus, don't lick." He stood and pulled the dog back into a more controlled position.

"It's okay," Anne said, wiping her hands over her face. Unadorned with makeup, her face glowed pink and pretty. "She's just being a dog. What breed is she again?"

"Weimaraner. I rescued her when I lived in Portland, though she's returned the favor since."

Anne arched a brow. "Now that sounds like an intriguing story."

He remembered her telling him back in November that she was

a reporter. Apparently, her instincts were well honed.

"If I want to get moved in before nightfall, I'm afraid the story will have to wait."

"I can't believe you're moving in here," she said, shaking her head, but smiling.

"I can't believe we ran into each other again," he confessed.

"Actually, the biggest coincidence comes from the fact that I live here, too. In this building, I mean."

Mike couldn't stop the grin that generated from deep in his belly and then spread through his extremities. He suspected he could take off his coat right now and not feel the least bit of discomfort.

"You're kidding," he said.

"No, I'm not," she said, standing. "There's a park right around the corner. Why don't you let me take the dog while you move your stuff in?"

"Really? My dad just took some stuff upstairs and Ben's coming over later with his car, but not having her underfoot would be a big help."

Anne slid her hand up Sirus's leash until her hand was inches from his. Just when he thought their fingers might touch, she tugged the loop out of his hand. "I'll take care of her. We'll go for a walk and then I'll bring her up to check out her new digs. What floor are you on?"

Mike had to think. Before Anne had shown up, he'd known the location of his apartment. Now the information had retreated to a remote corner of his brain, probably to escape the powerful chemical reaction brought on by Anne's proximity. Anne was beautiful. Anne lived in his building. Anne liked his dog.

He'd hoped that his move to Albany would spark a change to his life, but he'd never expected for kismet to explode with such power.

"The third. I'm in apartment 3-B."

She smiled. "I'm right below you. 2-D. Welcome to the building."

Anne took a few minutes to let the dog get accustomed to her before she slipped her hands back into her mittens, tightened her scarf around her neck, and headed to the park around the corner. She supposed running into Michael Davoli again hadn't been entirely out of the realm of possibility. They had a mutual friend in Shane. Albany, while not a small town, wasn't a teeming metropolis like Portland, where Mike had just moved from, or Manhattan, where Anne hoped to someday live. But in her wildest imagination, she never would have guessed they'd end up in the same building.

State Street was a hot property. The tallest complex in downtown, the collection of midsize apartments was inhabited by a wide range of people, from graduate students to young professionals to start-up families. She lived across the hall from a Republican state senator. But mostly, it was single, working professionals such as herself, and now Mike. Before today, she'd thought the residents' nickname of the place as "Albany 90210," on account of the romantic hook-ups, had been overrated.

Now, it was ripe with possibilities.

Mike had definitely seemed happy to see her. After a split second of surprise, they'd spoken with ease and, if she wasn't imagining it, some sexual tension. Anne didn't claim to be an expert on men and mating habits, but she generally knew when a guy was interested.

Of course, she'd caught a tremor of that vibe the first night they'd met and clearly, she'd been dead wrong about him then. Why did she think now would be any different, except for the whole close proximity thing?

Sirus the wonder pup, as Michael adorably called her, proved an amiable, if not hilarious companion. She obeyed commands well on the leash, tugging only a little when she noticed another dog or passed by the playground that was overun by with screaming and easily excitable kids. The dog only tested the strength of Anne's arm sockets once when they walked by a guy who was throwing tennis balls to his Labrador retriever. He'd offered her a chance to join in, but there was no way Anne was letting the dog off leash. That would be a great way to make a friend—lose his dog or let her get hit by a car.

No, thank you.

By the time Anne led Sirus over to a fountain to lap water from the chilly pool, they'd become lifelong friends. Or so she thought. Once they returned to the apartment building and rode up the elevator to Mike's new place, the dog lost complete interest in anyone but her master.

Amid a lot of human laughter and dog barking, whining, and sniffing, Anne met Michael's father, who was just on his way out to make the drive back home. With Ben running back to his place to pick up the last of Mike's stuff, Anne felt suddenly very self-conscious about standing in the middle of Mike's neatly stacked boxes and carefully arranged furniture—including, of course, a large and inviting-looking bed.

"I should leave you two to settle in." She side-stepped toward the door while Sirus circled through the apartment, sniffing every single object in the space as if to assure herself that these pieces belonged to her boy.

"I really appreciate you keeping her for me," Mike said, waving the dog away from a CD tower that looked like it might topple without the weight of music discs to hold it steady. "Not having her underfoot or tugging on me to play was a huge help. Why don't you stick around? When Ben gets back, we're going to order a pizza and he's going to sift through my DVD collection. He likes to make fun of my cinematic choices."

Anne smiled, seriously tempted by the offer. Ultimately, she was a "hanging out" kind of girl. She liked getting to know guys in a casual situation without the pressure of dressing up or putting on airs. A girl could learn a lot about a guy from the movies he liked enough to purchase, but for the first time that she could remember, her instincts screamed for her to refuse.

She'd met up with Mike twice. Both times, she'd felt a tug of interest. From him. From herself. Both times, fate had brought them together in circumstances that cast her in the role of the "new friend." The girl to have drinks with after a concert. The neighbor in the building who would take care of your dog.

This was not good.

The fact that she'd sacrificed her time without a second thought to puppy sit for him told her she wanted something more from this guy than hanging out with his buddies and chomping on slices of pizza while insulting or praising his taste in movies.

She had male friends. Lots of them. Many of them lived right in this building. She didn't need another guy to hang out with. If fate was setting up Michael to be in her life, she was going to exert some control over what role he played.

And *friend* wasn't it.

"Thanks for the offer," she said, traveling the distance to the door with a determined stride. "But you need to settle in. Maybe we can get together another time."

She let that possibility hang in the air for a moment, glancing over her shoulder to watch Michael's expression for any sign that he understood her subtle suggestion. She was being purposefully obtuse. But heck, if she had to spell it out for him, maybe he wasn't the right man for her anyway.

He took a step toward her, stopping short when Sirus dashed into his path and nearly tackled him with a raucous leap. Before Anne left, the last thing she heard beyond excited yipping was, "I'd like that."

Four

MIKE GLANCED AT HIS WATCH AND CURSED. He had thirty minutes before his dinner meeting with the head of a grassroots organization looking to partner with his employer, the Quality Education Initiative. Unfortunately, he had an hour's worth of work to do and his eyes were dry from the excessive blinking brought on by the added stress of today's workload. He soothed them with some drops, then shuffled papers and attempted to prioritize his tasks while wondering how he was going to walk Sirus before his appointment.

He hated leaving her home alone for such a long stretch. He lived close by and had already made it part of his routine to head home at lunchtime and take the dog to the park so she could stretch her legs and baptize the tree roots while he munched on a sandwich from the deli. Today, his trip home had been earlier than usual. He was risking his furniture and his dog's mental health by not going home before his meeting, but he'd have to make it up to her with a good long jog before bed.

Mike dove into his work, determined to skim a few items off his to-do list. He really needed to make arrangements for this scenario in the future. The QEI had already warned him that he might have to take more than just day trips for his job. He couldn't keep running the dog over to his parents every time he had an overnight in Manhattan or a long series of meetings at the State House. When he'd lived in Portland, he'd had a neighbor who looked out for Sirus in emergencies.

So far, he hadn't had a chance to meet many of his neighbors. Well, he knew Anne, but when he ran into her next, he did not want to talk about his dog.

He'd been thinking about her off and on for days, but his crazy schedule had kept him from dropping by her apartment. He hadn't run into her accidentally, either. He supposed his luck had run out in that department.

His phone chirped, shoving both Anne and Sirus out of his mind. He put out a quick fire between a local school board and his organization, and then dashed off the proposal revision and meeting agenda that two other department heads needed before he hurried to his car and battled traffic to reach his dinner appointment on time.

Both the meal and the conversation went on longer than he'd anticipated. After nine-thirty, he made excuses and was half-jogging down the hall to his apartment at ten o'clock. Instantly, he heard scratching and whining inside the door.

Damn.

He dug his hand into his pocket and retrieved his keys, but as he jangled them, he realized one was missing. He had his car key. He had his office key. What he did not have was his apartment key.

Damn, damn, damn.

The landlord had given him the keys the day he moved in, but Mike hadn't yet attached them to the same ring as those for his car and office. He'd broken routine and as a result, he'd left the keys inside his desk drawer. But with the building locked up tight for the night and no on-site security, he wouldn't be able to retrieve them until morning.

Sirus started barking. She could probably smell him through the door. His first thought was to call the landlord, but of course, he hadn't yet programmed the guy's number into his cell phone. Mike considered knocking on the door of a random neighbor, but they were likely already aggravated from the sounds of his dog going nuts. He certainly wasn't going to ingratiate himself with them by pounding on their doors after ten o'clock.

"Sh," he coaxed Sirus through the door. "It's okay, pup. Daddy's a moron and forgot his keys."

She whined a little louder, but momentarily stopped barking and scratching, though she'd redouble her efforts when the combination of her desire to see him and her overtaxed bladder threw her back into canine hysterics.

He flipped his phone and scrolled through his contact list, hoping to find someone who might be able to help him out. Ben was on a business trip. Nikki, his office buddy, was on a date and likely would have no idea how to fix this problem anyway.

Then he scrolled by the listing for his friend who had once dated Shane. According to Anne, Shane also lived in the building, though he hadn't seen her and had no idea which apartment was hers.

Still, this was a place to start.

He allowed a few minutes of small talk, filling him in on his recent move to State Street apartments and then listening to his summary of his pal's recent purchase of a new family car to replace the old van they used to go to concerts in.

When Sirus started growling, Mike had no choice but interrupt.

"Do you remember Shane? Sanders, I think. Yeah, that girl you hooked up with at the Phish concert back in New Jersey. I know you're a married man and everything, but you don't happen to still have her number, do you?"

After a vague promise to share a pitcher of beer sometime in the near future, Mike scored Shane's phone number with no guarantees that it was still valid. Luckily, the voice-mail message echoed with her voice. Unluckily, her message also said she was out of town.

He chanced a curse before the beep, then left a calm message and requested that she call him back as soon as possible. After soothing Sirus with more promises of imminent release, he tried to think of what to do next.

His neck twitched. Then his shoulder. He became aware of the increased dryness of his eyes again. Stress equaled increased symptoms of his Tourette's.

Damn. Damn, damn, damn. He really didn't need this right now.

Normally, his body could handle a little bit of added anxiety, but with the move, the new job, and now the inconvenience of his rushing out of work today without paying attention to the location of his keys, the disorder was starting to take over. He leaned against the hallway door and closed his eyes, concentrating on the muscles around his neck, willing them to relax. He inhaled slowly, and then breathed out through his mouth, the soft whooshing sound soothing the beast inside him. After a few minutes, his body calmed and submitted to the control of his brain and his will.

One crisis averted.

He turned and faced his door, prepared to come up with another solution in case Shane didn't pick up her messages. Judging by the solid quality of the door frame, kicking it in wasn't an option. He might have played varsity football back in high school, but that was a long time ago and tackling had never been his favorite activity. He'd just turned, determined to interrupt one of his unknown neighbors when he thought about Anne again.

She'd told him that she lived in 2-D. This certainly wasn't the way he wanted to see her again after last week, but he didn't have a choice. Chances were, she had the landlord's number. It was late, but as she did know Sirus, she'd understand his rush to get into his apartment before his dog exploded.

The elevator seemed interminably slow. Once on the second floor, he found her door and knocked.

No answer.

He paced a minute, and then knocked again. Was no one home in this infernal building? It was a freaking Monday night! He leaned his ear to the door and could hear what sounded like a television. Maybe she'd left the box on while she went out. Or maybe she just couldn't hear him.

He was knocking more loudly when his phone rang.

"Mike, it's Shane. You sound desperate. What's up?"

"I'm going to sound like a dufus," Mike confessed, "but I left my apartment keys at my office. You aren't home by any chance, are you?"

"I'm in the city for business meetings," Shane said apologetically. "I won't be back until tomorrow."

Clearly, she meant Manhattan. "You don't happen to have the landlord's number, do you?"

"Yeah, but he bowls on Monday. He won't answer his phone until after midnight, but you can leave him a message."

"Damn. My dog's inside. She's going nuts."

"Did you try Anne? She's fairly resourceful with this sort of thing," she said.

"Actually, I'm outside her door now. I knocked a couple of times, but she's not answering."

Oddly, Shane laughed. "Yeah, she wouldn't. Look, I'll give her a call and see if I can coax her up to your place. Trust me, she'll get you inside."

Anxious to check on Sirus, he accepted Shane's suggestion and disconnected the call, only mildly wondering why Anne would need "coaxing" in order to help him out. And still, the more he thought about Anne, the more she intrigued him. If she helped him out of yet another jam, he might have to do something drastic like take her out for a nice dinner.

As he waited for the elevator, though, he acknowledged that gratitude had nothing to do with his desire to ask her out. He should have gotten her number the night he met her at the concert. He should have invited her out last week when she'd taken care of Sirus. He'd screwed up their first meeting by refusing to go out for drinks. This second meeting, wholly accidental, could have been better. And now, for his third shot, he was going to look like a flake.

He tried not to think about it. His night was already bad enough.

"Anne, I know you're there . . . pick up the phone!"

This was the third time Shane had called her landline in the last five minutes. Was the woman nuts? Did she not know what time it was? Anne wasn't fanatical about a lot of things, but Monday nights at ten o'clock belonged to one man and one man only—Jack Bauer. Was it too much to ask to have sixty uninterrupted minutes once a week to watch the world's most gorgeous antiterrorist agent save the free world?

"Anne, I wouldn't ordinarily dare to interrupt your weekly drool-fest over Keifer Sutherland, but remember Michael Davoli? He's an actual *real* man in need of rescue and only you, my dear, can meet the challenge. Call me back!"

Even though she heard the definitive click of Shane disconnecting the call, Anne cursed. Unlike many of her friends who had VCRs that actually worked, Anne did not have a way to record this episode. But now that she knew Michael might be in trouble, she couldn't ignore the call to assist.

A commercial came on, so with a good three and a half minutes until the next segment of *24* aired, she grabbed her handset and dialed Shane.

"You have three minutes, less if you're going to actually ask me to do anything," she said by way of greeting.

"I had no idea that Jack massacring perfectly good terrorists made you this cranky," Shane quipped.

"Two minutes, fifty seconds," Anne snapped back.

"Mike locked himself out of his apartment. Or left his keys at the office. I don't remember the details, but he needs help. His dog is inside and she hasn't been out for a while."

Anne frowned. Poor Sirus.

"Did he call Joe?" Anne asked. Only the landlord had a spare set of keys to all the units. Most everyone who lived in the building gave spare keys to trusted neighbors for such emergencies. Shane had Anne's, but a lot of good it did her since her friend was out of town more often than not.

"Joe's bowling. Besides, Mike didn't have his number and I don't have it with me, either. Can't you dash down there and see if you can help?"

"Why didn't he come up and ask himself?" Anne asked.

"He did! He was knocking on your door when I called him back. I suspect Jack Bauer was torturing an enemy combatant at the time."

Anne winced. When she watched *24*, she snuggled beneath the quilt on her couch, a hot cup of coffee on the warmer, along with a bowl of popcorn or some other not-too-crunchy snack that she could eat without missing any crucial dialogue. Bathroom breaks were taken only during commercials, which might have been when Mike had knocked.

"The show's coming back on," Anne said. "I'll run up there next break."

She could hear Shane clucking her tongue on the other end of the phone. "You're choosing the fictional hunk over the real one, my friend."

Anne didn't bother to reply.

She watched the next segment, trying to concentrate on the show when all she could think about was Michael and Sirus. She really was a wonderful dog who probably didn't understand why her beloved master wouldn't come in. And what if she had to go? He'd been at work all day. If he had a dog walker, he could have called them for an extra key. With a huff, she tore off her fleece pajamas and traded them for a pair of jeans and a blue wool sweater. While Jack exchanged information with his team, Anne took a second to rush a brush through her hair and dig a stick of gum out of her bag. She tried not to think about how attracted she must really be to Michael if she was willing to risk missing even a minute of the show to help him out.

Ironically, the segment ended with a gunshot, which sent Anne scrambling to the door. She shoved her keys into her pocket and hit the stairs. She made it to the third floor in less than fifteen seconds and saw Michael outside his place, his forehead pressed against the door while Sirus whined on the other side.

"Anne!" he said, alerted to her approach by the sound of her hoofing it down the hall.

She held out her hand. "Give me a credit card."

"What?"

She didn't have time for him to catch up. Boldly, she slapped his backside. "Wallet. Credit Card. Get it."

He did so quickly, handing her a shiny new Visa that wasn't about to be so pristine when she was done with it.

She gave him a little shove to move him out of the way, concentrating only on her goal. Though she didn't have a pet to worry about, she had lost her own keys more times than she could count. She might not be organized, but she was resourceful. She shoved the thin plastic into the nearly imperceptible gap between the door and the jamb, then slid it to the precise spot where, if she jiggled the doorknob and pulled forward just a quarter of an inch . . .

Click.

The door moved inward just enough to disengage the loosened lock.

"Score!" She shoved the credit card back into Michael's hand and then dashing toward the stairs again.

"Hey!" he called after her. "Where are you going?"

She spared him a glance over her shoulder before pushing the door to the stairwell open. "Back to what I was doing before you locked yourself out of your place."

"Oh, okay. Thanks," he said.

Was it her imagination, or did he sound disappointed?

She was back beneath her blanket before she'd processed the answer. Yeah, he'd looked sad to see her go. In the part of her mind that contained her romantic fantasies, she conjured a scenario where Mike hadn't really forgotten his keys, but just wanted an excuse to see her. Unfortunately, as her brain had been engaged in untangling the plot of her favorite television show for the last half hour, her neurons quickly blasted that daydream to bits.

He hadn't needed any convoluted excuse in order to stop by.

She'd made that clear the last time she'd seen him. This time, however, she'd come across as wholly disinterested.

Too bad that was the furthest thing from the truth.

Anne settled into her pillows, grabbed the bag of chocolate-covered raisins from her coffee table and focused on the television. She'd helped him out. What more could a guy want? She resolved to stop thinking about him and concentrate only on the screen. If her real life suddenly seemed a little emptier than it had an hour before, such was life.

The next move belonged to Michael.

Five

"I DON'T KNOW WHY you bother watching Jack Bauer," Shane said with a snort. "You *are* Jack Bauer."

Anne rolled her eyes and pawed through a discount bin overflowing with skeins of soft, pastel-colored yarns. She'd finally talked Shane into joining her knitting group. Trouble was, Shane did not knit. She didn't sew. She didn't crochet, cross-stitch or engage in any hobby that fell under the "crafty" banner. Anne had promised to help her put together a starter kit, but only if Shane agreed to keep her questions about Michael to a minimum.

So far, only one of them was keeping her end of the bargain.

"How do you feel about lavender?" Anne asked, digging out a roll in variant shades of light purple and pearl.

"It's pretty," Shane said, though from her crinkled nose, Anne knew the hue wasn't to her taste. "I like darker colors. Bolder. You know, to fit my vibrant personality."

With a snicker, Anne moved to the next bin, which had a few jewel tones mixed in with bright summer colors of yellow, orange, and pink.

"So?" Shane asked.

"So, keep your jeans on. I'm looking."

Anne nearly fell forward into the cloud of cotton thread when Shane shoved her on the shoulder.

"I don't care about the yarn. Tell me more about rescuing Michael!"

"I didn't rescue him." Anne tamped down her annoyance that Michael had allowed yet another opportunity to ask her out go untaken. He'd left her a thank-you note the next morning—quite literally. A yellow Post-it with the words, "Thank you," written in neat block letters. She'd nearly torn it up in frustration. Instead, she's scribbled "You're welcome," underneath and pasted it on his door in reply. She wanted no mistakes made. The ball was now in his court.

Though even as she conjured the thought, she imagined a faded, chewed-on tennis ball not unlike the ones Sirus liked to gnaw bouncing impotently across a deserted concrete playground. Michael had had three separate opportunities to invite her on a date or at least ask for her phone number. Maybe the internal radar that alerted her to possible interest from a guy was faulty, but she'd never been so off base with anyone before. Her instincts told her he liked her, but his actions denied this with a vengeance.

"You got him into his apartment with a credit card," Shane continued, flipping over a few skeins of yarn disinterestedly. "Very impressive. But I especially like how you lit out of there so quickly. It adds an air of mystery. That's very attractive to men."

Yeah, she might have thought so, too, if she hadn't found the Post-it note.

"Trust me, this guy is not attracted," Anne said. "If he was, he would've thanked me properly."

Flowers. Chocolate. She didn't need Godiva—a Hershey bar would have sufficed.

"What did you expect him to do?" Shane asked. "Sweep you up into a sexy kiss, maybe do you against the wall while his dog ran around, waiting to pee?"

"You're so crude," Anne shoved two skeins of amethyst and plum-colored yarns into Shane's arms. "I didn't expect anything from him, okay? He's very nice, but stop trying to set us up. If the magic hasn't happened by now, it's not going to."

"Is that what you're waiting for? Magic?"

"Why not?"

Shane shrugged, raising her yarn-holding hands in surrender to Anne's rather over-emotional challenge. "No, no. I am a total, one-hundred percent believer in magic. It just seems like there's already been a lot of the stuff twinkling around you and Michael. I'm not exactly sure how much more you could possibly want."

"Are we going back to the *my standards are too high* argument again?"

Shane dropped the yarn into a basket. "What do you think?"

Anne beelined to the aisle that held an assortment of knitting needles, not because the idea of stabbing Shane through the eye with one right about now didn't have its appeal, but because she wanted to finish this trip quickly and get on to the drinking part of the evening.

Though her mother had taught her to knit back in junior high, she'd only recently rediscovered the hobby thanks to the cold Albany winter nights. When a couple of friends had shown interest in taking up the craft, too, they'd moved to a neighborhood bar where they sipped wine and created hats, scarves and squares for afghans. More often than not, the wine took center stage and they became a drinking club with a knitting problem rather than the other way around. Anne had been looking forward to bringing Shane along for the fun, but the evening was going to be a bust if her friend insisted on talking about Michael all night long.

"Look, can we stop talking about Michael, please? He's not interested. I don't know what magic you're talking about, but I certainly haven't seen any evidence."

"Number one," Shane said, hardly taking a breath before she launched into her counterattack. "You happen to go to a concert with me, and we run into a cute Jewish boy named Michael, who I haven't seen in years, but just so happens to be at the very same concert."

"Coincidence," Anne snapped.

"Hm," Shane hummed. "Magical coincidence. Number two—"

Anne speared her friend with a warning look, but Shane continued, wholly unfazed.

"—Of all the apartment buildings in the city, Michael not only moves into the one you live in, but he happens to be in the act of transferring his worldly possessions into the building at precisely the same moment that you are walking by. And number three—"

"Please don't tell me that his forgetting his keys is magic, too?" Anne begged.

"Well," Shane said, "Michael is practically famous for his organization and neatness. His friends used to give him a hard time about it. What are the chances that a guy with OCD tendencies would forget his apartment keys at the office?"

Anne thought back to the state of Mike's apartment after he'd spent the day moving in. Now that Shane mentioned it, he did seem to have the boxes color coded and stacked in neat rows against the door. The carpets had been newly vacuumed, as if he'd taken the time to give the apartment a quick cleaning before he set up his stuff. While this was something Anne's mother might do, it wasn't exactly expected behavior for a guy moving in to his new bachelor pad.

"Maybe he's changed."

"No guy changes that drastically unless he's had a head injury, and Michael looked perfectly healthy last time I saw him. Except for the cold. Anyway, magic may not be at play in the most obvious way, but it is here and you'd be a fool to ignore it."

Anne saw a book on elementary knitting patterns and tossed it at Shane. "What if I'm not the one ignoring it?"

Shane smiled deviously. "Aha! Now, we're getting to the real issues. You want him to come on to you instead of the other way around."

"Is that too much to ask?"

Shaking her head, Shane threw Anne a pitying look that only someone of her vast romantic experience could successfully pull off. "Not all guys are players, sweetie. The ones worth having are usually the ones most wary of being rejected. If a guy doesn't fear being blown off, he's probably too confident for anyone's own good, much less his own."

"I wouldn't reject him," Anne said, then clarified, "if he bothered to ask."

"Does he know that?" Shane pushed.

Anne frowned. She and Shane had dissected her interactions with Michael enough times for both of them to know the answer. Anne hadn't really turned on the charm and broadcasted her interest. She hadn't wanted to work that hard. But was that fair? A receiver could only pick up signals if someone sent them. Sure, she'd invited him for drinks after the concert, but that had merely been polite. She'd watched his dog the day he moved in, but had summarily turned down his invitation for pizza afterward.

And last night, she'd literally given him no more than three minutes of her time.

"Okay, okay," she said after selecting the last of the supplies her friend would need. "I'll have to do something to make sure he knows I'm available."

Shane shouted in triumph. "Excellent. What are you going to do?"

Anne shook her head, her mind focused entirely on her anticipation of her first merlot.

"I have no idea."

For the next week, Mike tried to come up with a good way to thank Anne for rescuing him with her felonious skills. He had left a Post-it note that night, the least intrusive mode of thanks he could think of, as it was more than obvious that she wanted to get back to whatever had kept her from answering his knock in the first place. Though she'd taken the time to jot "You're welcome" on the yellow square and paste it back on his door the next afternoon, he hadn't heard from her otherwise. For this, he was thankful. Before he proceeded, he needed a plan.

Mike couldn't remember the last time a woman had injected herself into his consciousness so completely and in such a short period of time. Even with his ex, he'd had a slowly developing relationship. They'd shared an intense love of music and common friends. They'd hung out and over time, started doing so without a crowd. But without drama to set them at odds, they'd stayed together until the relationship fell apart.

Mike had wallowed in the loss for a while, but then he'd moved on. Or at least, he thought he had. But he couldn't deny that since then, he'd avoided serious relationships.

Now that he'd met Anne, however, the strength of his recovery surged through him. Her magical smile—or even, as he'd learned Monday night—her annoyed smirk, awakened him to possibilities he could neither ignore nor take lightly. He wanted to ask her out, but he couldn't imagine going the ordinary route to this important destination.

That simply wasn't his style.

Boring, unimaginative, "same-old, same-old" invitations popped into his mind and were summarily dismissed. Dinner. A movie. Dinner and a movie. He knew she liked music, but though he'd scoured the local venue websites for information, no interesting concerts were taking place in the next week. He had absolutely no idea how she felt about sports. He was sitting at his desk, pondering other possibilities when his phone rang.

"Michael?"

Anne.

He instantly recognized her voice. He'd been replaying their conversations in his mind for a while and yet again, she'd proved her resourcefulness. Anne had not only managed to scare up his work number, but she'd actually made the call.

Now.

Right this minute.

And he'd yet to say a single word.

"Michael, are you there?"

"Yeah, hey," he said, drawing from the depths of his inner calm. "What's up?"

"I'm sorry I was in such a rush last week," she said.

"Come on, no apologies. You saved me, remember? I'm sorry for interrupting . . . whatever I was interrupting when I knocked on your door."

"Yeah, about that—" she said, a hint of anxiety in her voice.

Unfortunately, a hint was all it took to send his mind soaring in a million naughty directions. What could possibly be so important, so diverting, so intense, that she couldn't stop to answer the door?

She hadn't been taking a shower. When she'd darted down to his apartment, she'd been dry and smelling slightly of popcorn and chocolate. Funny how he remembered that, even after a full week.

"Hey, you don't have to explain," he said.

"Good, because I'm not the kind of girl who reveals her obsessions to just anyone."

Mike shifted in his chair. The pathways through his nervous system that had shivered at the initial sound of her voice now ignited with heat. "I'd like to think I'm not just anyone."

"Well, that remains to be seen," she countered.

And before he could challenge her doubtfulness, she continued.

"Which is why I'm calling. I thought maybe if I showed you what kept me so wrapped up last week that I didn't even hear you at my door, maybe you'd understand."

Don Corleone must have taken lessons from this intriguing Jewish girl. She'd just made him an offer he'd have to be dead to refuse.

"Sounds intriguing," he said.

"Does it?"

Her voice rose with pleasure. In instant response, his entire body seized up tight. His anticipation and curiosity spiked to a point where he was hesitant to speak.

"Yeah," he managed.

"Do you like Chinese food? I always order in on Mondays. You could join me."

He cleared his throat. "Sounds like a plan."

"Okay, then," she said, a note of surprise in her voice. Was she surprised that she'd essentially asked him over for dinner or shocked that he'd accepted?

"See you at seven?"

"Right."

Before he could form another halfway coherent thought, she said good-bye and disconnected the call.

How long he sat there, stunned, he wasn't sure. It wasn't until Nikki knocked on the top of his desk that he popped out of his reverie.

"Something wrong?" she asked, her dark, sculpted eyebrows high on her forehead.

"What? No," Mike replied, but then reconsidered. On the surface, what had just occurred was extraordinarily fabulous. A pretty, funny, generous and interesting woman who liked his dog and lived in his building had just invited him to a somewhat spontaneous dinner at her place, to be followed, presumably, by the revelation of some guarded secret regarding an obsession of hers. With Nikki staring at him, he didn't dare imagine what this might be, but that she'd admitted she had a closeted obsession was enough to send Mike's heart rate into hyperdrive. "Well, yeah. I don't know."

"You know, Michael, that's what I love about you. You're always so decisive."

Nikki's sarcasm knocked just enough sense back into his brain for him to sit up straight, scoot in his chair, and refocus on the pile of work in front of him. He'd accepted Anne's invitation without even consulting his calendar. Didn't matter. If he had anything else scheduled tonight, he would cancel. There was no way in hell he was missing this dinner.

"Did you need something?" he asked.

When he'd first come to the Quality Education Initiative months ago, Nikki had been the first person in the organization to not only show him around, but also to become a friend. Idealistic, beautiful, and sassy as all get-out, she added color and unpredictability to his day.

She could also read him like a book.

"That was a woman on the phone," she assessed.

"Yes, women sometimes call me. Amazing how that works now that they're so fully integrated into the workplace."

She tossed a file folder aside and leaned against the corner of his desk. "Not that kind of woman."

He matched her penetrating stare with one of his own. He'd learned quickly that the only way to counter Nikki's over-whelming curiosity was to hold his ground. He could only imagine how easily she ran roughshod over the men in her life. Poor saps.

Kind of how he imagined Anne might run roughshod all over him, if he was lucky enough to lie down at her feet and let her.

"What kind of women do you think call me?" he asked.

"Ordinarily, business-type women. Teachers. Activists. Busy-bodies. Any number of creatures of the female persuasion are on the other end of your phone line on an hourly basis, but none of them have ever made you look both confused and cocky at the same time. By the way you were puffing up your chest, I thought if I hadn't knocked on your desk, you might have beat your chest and yelled like Tarzan. That might have been embarrassing."

He hadn't exactly been on the verge of yodeling like Johnny Weissmüller, but otherwise, she wasn't all that far off the mark. All on account of Anne's sexy voice and irresistible invitation.

"So, who is she?" Nikki asked.

"A neighbor," he replied, dropping all pretense. Having a woman as a pal sometimes came in handy—they had insight that guys simply did not share.

Nikki smiled knowingly.

"You mean *the* neighbor."

He narrowed his gaze, trying to remember precisely when he'd mentioned Anne to Nikki. Must have been the day after he'd moved into his apartment, when he was still reeling from Anne's generosity in watching Sirus, not to mention how pretty she'd looked in her green hat.

"Yeah, her." he confessed.

Nikki grinned, then made quite the aria out of singing the question, "So, what did she want?"

He cleared his throat and tried to look unaffected as he transferred file folders from one side of the desk to the other. Of course, this was a useless exercise. He wouldn't allow the papers from the left side of his desk to remain on the right side for more than ten seconds. If he did, he wouldn't get any work done for the rest of the day—a possibility that had already been thrown into motion by Anne's call.

"She just wanted to know if I could stop by so she could show me something."

"Liar!" Nikki accused. "She asked you on a date!"

"No," he corrected. "A date would be the act of leaving the place we live and going somewhere else with a specific intention of doing something together. She just happens to be ordering Chinese for dinner and gave me the option of joining her. What wine goes with Chinese, anyway?"

He opened his browser to do a quick search when Nikki reached over and stayed his hand. "If you're bringing wine, buddy, it's a date."

He waved off her suggestion. Yes, he and Anne were getting together, but he refused to consider this a date. He wasn't against a woman asking him out, but he wasn't about to let Anne derail his plan to make the first formal move. That he hadn't taken the initiative to do this up until now was the fault of his crazy work schedule.

Not to mention a barely acknowledged suspicion that she might have turned him down.

He'd been turned down before, though admittedly, not often. He didn't put himself out there often enough for his record to be ruined. Like most of his gender, he preferred to make a move only after he was relatively certain that the woman he was asking out wasn't going to run screaming in the other direction.

Then there was the reality of his Tourette's. The name of the disorder alone freaked out a lot of people, thanks to prevalent stereotypes of people who barked and cursed uncontrollably. Mike's reality—and the reality of a majority of sufferers—was completely different. And yet, he couldn't deny that his condition caused twitches and movements that he couldn't control.

As a result, he'd become cautious, especially with women. He always established friendships first and orchestrated his meetings first in large groups, surrounded by friends with whom he bonded over common interests. He got to know potential dates slowly and methodically, weighing their responses to his comments, jokes, and conversation until he knew they were definitely interested and not put off by the Tourette's.

But Anne was new to his world. Fresh, exciting, and yet unknown. She was like a beribboned and wrapped present at Christmas, a holiday the Italian-Catholic side of his family made sure he appreciated.

Well, he'd never let the Tourette's get in his way of living his life to the fullest. He wasn't going to start now. He pushed his misgivings about that to the back of his mind and concentrated on the situation at hand.

Tonight, he was going to Anne's place to learn about her secret obsession and eat Chinese food.

"Okay, maybe it's a date," he conceded. "Maybe it's not. I won't know until I get there, but I think my chances are definitely better if I bring wine."

Nikki patted him on the shoulder. "You're a good man, Mike Davoli."

"I'm suddenly a nervous man, though," he admitted.

Nikki laughed. "Good. She's got you off-kilter. That's probably an omen of good things yet to come."

Six

MIKE HAD NO IDEA WHAT ANNE HAD PLANNED, but his first thought after she opened the door was that whatever it was, he was in.

"Hey."

Her simple, monosyllabic greeting sent a ripple of sensation up his spine. His arms tensed and his shoulders tingled, but he knew this time around, his physical reaction had nothing to do with his Tourette's and everything to do with pure, unadulterated attraction. With her thick, brown hair pulled back in a jaunty ponytail, his attention went straight to her face. As always, her smile caught him first. Enhanced by a subtle gloss, her natural pink lips curved in welcome even as she stepped back and gestured him inside. Her funky red glasses matched her soft, torturously snug sweater. Finishing the look with jeans and slip-ons, she was the epitome of casual comfort.

The fact that she hadn't spackled her face with too much makeup or dressed to the nines confused Mike even as it pleased him. Was this just a relaxed get-together between new friends or was she simply so comfortable in her own skin that she didn't feel the need to impress a guy?

Either way, he came out a winner.

"Nice place," he said, searching for something to say that didn't reveal the invigorating anxiety at being invited inside her inner sanctum. Not that he minded the feeling. This brand of disquiet came from new opportunities and unknown possibilities— the kind that made his blood pump to every area of his body, including those that hadn't had much attention lately.

"Thanks. It's not much, but it's home."

Except for the blue light from the muted television, a gold glimmer from a pair of beaded lamps set on either side of her couch, and a trio of tiny votive candles on her coffee table, the place was dark. Intimate. She'd set the low table in front of the sofa with an mismatched set of Asian-style plates with random chopsticks, soup bowls, and spoons. Two wineglasses sparkled beside a single votive candle, reminding him to present his gift.

"I owe you more than just a single bottle for all you've done in the last two weeks, but I had to start somewhere."

She took the wine, glanced at the label, and hummed in appreciation. "Hmm . . . Riesling with Chinese food?"

"According to a quick Internet search, it's the best. Unless you don't like white wine?"

"I prefer red, but far be it from me to contradict the all-knowing power of Google."

So he'd missed on the wine selection. She didn't seem to mind. In fact, from the way she moved into the kitchen in search of a corkscrew, her anticipation was palpable.

She filled the silence with questions about how he liked his new place and, pointedly, if he'd come up with a way to make sure he didn't get locked out of his apartment again.

"I'm not normally so disorganized," he admitted.

"I am," she said. "How do you think I learned how to pick a lock with a credit card?"

He laughed and when she gestured to the couch, he scooped up the two wineglasses and sat, fumbling a bit when he found his seat blocked by what looked like a discarded sweater.

"Oh, let me get that," she said absently, balling the sweater and then tossing it free-throw style onto a chair in the corner. From the shadows, Mike could tell this was her catch-all location for homeless items and he couldn't help but wonder just how unorganized she truly was.

The concern fled his brain the minute she joined him on the couch and poured the wine. The fragrance of the liquid splashing against the side of the glass was light and fruity . . . or else, that was her perfume.

She took a tentative sip that had him entirely enraptured by her mouth. With her eyes closed and her face relaxed, she allowed the mouthful to linger on her tongue before she swallowed and then smiled. "This is nice."

"Yeah," he said. "Yeah it is."

She opened her eyes. They were large and brown and full of humor; she watched him until he realized he had not yet taken a taste from which to make his assessment. Thankfully, the moderately priced white actually was flavorful and crisp.

"I ordered lo mein, dumplings, stir fry, egg-drop soup, and a couple of other things. I wasn't sure what you liked."

"I'm sure I'll like whatever you bought," he said.

She sent him a quelling look. "Unless it's something you really don't like."

"Well, I'm not much of a beef or chicken or pork guy," he said, taking a risk with being honest. "I prefer fish or shellfish."

"Good," she said, "because the sweet and sour shrimp is to die for."

She popped over to the kitchen, sliding her hands into what looked like homemade mitts. From within the oven, she pulled out a cookie tray loaded with take-out cartons. Apparently, she'd ordered enough food for the entire week.

"So, how's Sirus?" she asked.

Mike's insides warmed even before she leaned over with the tray and tilted her chin to indicate she wanted him to transfer the containers onto the table. He tried—and failed—to keep his gaze focused only on the food. Her curves spoke to a hunger inside of him that wouldn't be sated by Chinese dumplings.

"She's in heaven. The park down the street is amazing. The whole neighborhood seems great, though I haven't had much time to go exploring."

"Have you tried the Wine Bar and Bistro?"

"I saw it," he said. "But work's been crazy and with moving in and everything, socializing has fallen to the bottom of my to-do list."

"That's a sad state of affairs." She used the chopsticks to tumble a large portion of sweet and sour shrimp onto his plate.

"Yeah, but luckily, things seem to be looking up."

Mike watched and listened, amazed as she talked about the building, the residents, and the neighborhood. She made the dry cleaner sound like a must-see experience while offering him each carton in turn, warning him off the pork lo mein, but pushing him to take an extra helping of the vegetable spring rolls. He tried to remember the last time he'd used chopsticks when she jumped up and said, "Oh!" before dashing into the kitchen.

She returned with two forks. "I always forget. I like using chopsticks for lo mein, but with rice, it just makes a mess!"

The word *simpatico* sprang into Michael's mind. Their fingers brushed as he took the fork from her and a sizzle skittered across his skin. Why had he wasted so much time by not asking her out the first night they'd met?

Mike wasn't an old-fashioned guy. Politically, he was progressive. Musically, he was definitely out of the box. Even his fashion sense, when he wasn't in a business suit for work, trended toward styles most considered retro. Yet, when it came to matters of the heart, he appreciated the traditional guy asking the woman out. Or the guy, at the very least, picking up the tab.

But he'd waited too long. Lucky for him, Anne was not an overthinker. She said the first thing that popped into her head. She put mismatched plates out for guests and forgot to include forks. She seemed to live her life the same way she broke into locked apartments—with ingenuity. Her take-no-prisoners, make-no-excuses attitude was incredibly sexy.

"How's the shrimp?" she asked.

He skewered a prawn on the end of his fork and took a bite. He moaned appreciatively, which made her chuckle. From that point on, they did little but eat, laugh, and polish off half the bottle of wine and an incredible amount of Chinese food before Anne glanced at her watch.

"It's almost time!" she said.

Mike froze when she dove at him—or more specifically, across him. She snatched the remote control from the table on his left and then bounced back into her spot. Dizzy from the combined sensations of her lush body draped, albeit briefly, across his and the potent scent of her spiced shampoo, Mike took a long minute to regain his equilibrium.

"Time for—?"

"My obsession," Anne said. "I promised to show you."

She flipped the channel. Though the television had been on the entire time they'd been talking, the sound had been muted.

When she pushed the volume button, the sound blasted to nearly wall-shaking decibels.

"The neighbors must love you," Mike said.

She lowered the volume, but only marginally. "Excuse me?"

"The volume. It's a little loud."

"Oh," she said, sheepish. "I know. I'd have surround sound if I could, but with this show, I might cause a panic not unlike *War of the Worlds.*"

She refilled their wineglasses before settling into the couch, a throw pillow pressed against her stomach and her legs criss-crossed in front of her. Mike had the sudden memory of assuming a similar posture on Saturday mornings when he and his sisters geared up for their weekly cartoon mania. The glee in Anne's demeanor was contagious. Mike couldn't wait to see what program had her so mesmerized.

When Keifer Sutherland appeared on the screen, dressed in black and looking incredibly worried, Mike couldn't help but grin. "*24*?"

She glowered in his direction. "Don't even tell me you don't like this show or I might have to waterboard you."

He held up his hands in surrender. "No judgments. I'm a huge fan myself."

Her smile nearly knocked him off the couch. "Cool, though it's a shame I don't have to initiate you."

And with that last, lost possibility torturing him, they watched the show. For the next hour, she concentrated on the television with the same intensity as the life-or-death scenarios portrayed on the screen. During quiet moments and commercials, they discussed everyone's identities, what they wanted on the surface, what they wanted secretly, and how they were manipulating the people around them to achieve their goals. She kept his wineglass filled and his brain engaged, but only half of his attention was on the television.

The on-screen tension was powerful, but it was Anne who had captured him. She spoke with emotion, ate with relish, drank with gusto and watched TV as if her life depended on it. He couldn't stop himself from imagining how her take-no-prisoner's personality would transfer to other parts of her life—particularly the life she lived in her bedroom.

The thought brought him up short. He was no prude, but he wasn't casual about sex, either. Of course, he couldn't remember the last time he'd spent time with a woman he was so attracted to whom he hadn't known for a prolonged period of time before their first date. Anne presented him with new, invigorating desires—along with new, problematic decisions.

After the preview of next week's action was over, Anne pressed the mute button again.

"What did you think?"

Mike slid his wineglass onto the table and surrendering to a powerful impulse, plucked the remote from her grip and took her hands in his.

"I think there's something important that I need to tell you."

Anne leaned back, suddenly wary of the serious look on Michael's face. Okay, so maybe she'd watched the show with a little more enthusiasm than would appear "normal" to someone who had not joined the cult of *24*. At least she hadn't invited him to watch *Lost*. He'd probably be screaming for the door before the first appearance of the smoke monster.

"About the show?" she asked.

His eyebrows tilted inward, as if she'd spoken her question in a foreign language.

"What? No, the show was great."

"So, what's up?" she asked.

His hands tightened around hers, and not unpleasantly. She liked how his firm grip managed to remain gentle. Protective. She liked how his blue eyes picked up the electronic gleam of the television and reflected back with more blue than a Caribbean ocean.

"I want to go out with you," he said.

She looked around at the darkened apartment, at the glittering candles she's borrowed from Shane to make the room more romantic and cover up the fact that she hadn't dusted since sometime last month. "Isn't that what this is?"

He shook his head. "This was amazing and wonderful and really special, but it wasn't a real date, if you know what I mean."

"I'm not sure I do," she confessed.

"I want to ask you out."

"So ask," she prompted.

He pressed his lips together and in that one hesitation, a thousand scenarios for his reluctance flashed across her mind. Was he secretly married? Did he have a girlfriend? Maybe a criminal record that she could have easily discovered if she'd checked him out before she invited him into her home?

"I have Tourette's syndrome," he said.

Of all the things in the world he could have confessed, this was something she never would have expected.

His hands tightened around hers, his eyes intense and his jaw set. She couldn't tear her gaze away from him and noticed for the first time that his left eye blinked slightly more often than his right.

Anne didn't pretend to be an expert on medical conditions, but being a reporter had exposed her to a lot of information about a great many topics. She already knew that the stereotype of the

Tourette's sufferer who barked, cursed, or gestured wildly with no self-control was an extreme and not a common manifestation compared to the total number of people who had the disorder.

"I never noticed," she said.

"Really? I have mostly facial twitches, excessive eye blinking and neck movements. It's a mild case, compared to what's hyped up in the media, but when I'm really tired or super-stressed, I can even exhibit jerking movements in my arms and legs. One time in high school, I actually got punched out by a girl who thought I was getting fresh with her."

He waggled his eyebrows—and she knew the action was entirely on purpose.

"And you don't want me to think you're getting fresh?" she teased.

"Not until I actually am," he replied, his expression a little sly. "I'm on meds and I take good care of myself, so most of the time, no one realizes I have the disorder. But before I ask you out on a proper date, I thought full disclosure was important."

Anne took a minute to let the information digest, her stare caught with Michael's. For a split second, she saw beyond the brilliant blue to a deep, sincere, honest, and raw vulnerability that caught her off guard and disarmed her. This was the kind of information you shared with close friends or family, not some girl you wanted to take out for dinner and a movie.

Unless he wanted more than dinner and a movie.

After taking a fortifying breath, she smiled. "I know it wasn't easy for you to tell me, but I appreciate that you did. I'll probably have a million questions about it."

He scooted closer. The air around her instantly sparked, as if tiny sparks of electricity flashed from his body into hers. "Ask me anything."

She tilted her chin at him, but suddenly couldn't think of a single question. All the brain pathways that led to coherent thought had backed up like traffic on I-87. His pupils were dark, his breath sweet with wine, his mouth parted by a mysterious half smile.

"Do you want more Riesling?" she finally managed.

"No," he said.

And then he kissed her.

Seven

THE MOMENT HIS LIPS TOUCHED HERS, heat suffused through her body, starting deep within her belly and then flaming outward until every extremity sizzled, from the tips of her fingers to the curling flesh of her toes. Her heartbeat accelerated and she could no longer tell which flashes of light were coming from the television and which were popping from deep within her.

Then, just as quickly as someone blows out a newly lit match, he was gone.

He leaned back into the couch and whistled out a breath. "Wow."

Anne pressed her tingling lips together. *Wow* was a very good word. In her mind, a kiss like that was meant to be a prelude to more kisses, though she supposed his choice to slow things down wasn't a bad thing. At least, not in the short term.

Unable to say anything intelligent, witty, or funny, she opted to simply smile. He smiled back. In less than thirty seconds, they'd devolved from *wow* to awkward. Luckily, Michael rescued the moment by taking her hands in his and brushing a duo of soft kisses across her knuckles.

"Anne, will you go out with me?"

She couldn't contain her laughter. "I'd love to," she replied.

"Good."

They sat quietly for another minute. Anne liked his hands. The strength in his palms was offset by the relaxation of his grip on hers. He was touching her, sharing the same warmth, but not holding her in place. Then, after an inhalation that quivered with some pent-up emotion that she guessed was his half of their mutual desire, Mike starting collecting the dirty dishes.

"You don't have to do that," Anne objected, attempting to snag a spoon out of his hand.

"No," he retorted, his action becoming quicker and more insistent as he scraped the leftover food onto one plate and stacked the other dishes with the largest on the bottom. "Actually, I do. One of my best qualities is that I'm obsessive about cleaning."

"That's a good quality?" she asked. "Not that I have anything against it, but I should tell you upfront that I don't share it."

"I figured," he said, but something about his tone waylaid any self-consciousness at her peccadillo. "This mess has been driving me crazy for the last hour."

By making the problem his instead of hers, he kept her from taking a defensive posture. Anne had always made housekeeping her very lowest priority. It had driven her mother mad when Anne lived at home, but since she'd been out on her own, she'd gleefully lived her own way, preferring to do quick pickups when the clutter overwhelmed her or, like tonight, when company was coming. If she had to choose between talking late into the night with Michael or dishpan hands, there was no contest.

Mike, on the other hand, seemed downright giddy about collecting dirty dishes.

"Now, see, this is important info. The Tourette's I can live with, but neat-freak tendencies concern me," she said.

He snorted. "I try not to project my preferences on other people, so you don't have to take it personally."

"Don't worry, I won't," she said, meaning it. "I'll see what I can scare up for dessert."

In her entire lifetime, Anne had never once had a guy clean up after her—well, at least not one who seemed so happy about it. He wanted to load the plates into her dishwasher, but as she hadn't yet emptied the previous load and didn't want to bother with such a production now, she insisted that he simply set them in hot, soapy water. He complied, but only after rinsing them nearly spotless.

After that, he wiped down the coffee table and rinsed out the now-empty wine bottle for recycling. He might have dragged out her vacuum to do a light run around the living area if she hadn't suggested that they take Sirus for a walk down to the nearby café, where they could sit outside and share a slice of cheesecake and espresso. The only sweet thing she seemed to have in her cupboard was a half-eaten sleeve of Chips Ahoy.

"It's kind of cold out," he warned.

Anne shrugged. "That's what wool is for. Just give me a sec to bundle up."

She tore into her bedroom. For the first time in recent memory, she noticed how untidy it was. She had clothes on the floor, a bra bunched up on the side table and a week's worth of water glasses lined up across the dresser. As she dug into her drawer to find clothes that were functionally warm and aesthetically attractive, she wondered what would happen if Mike ended up in here at some point. Would he kiss her again or clean up first?

Not that she had any intention of inviting him into her bed so soon. They had not, as he'd pointed out, even had a real date yet. While Anne was a big fan of sex, she had to keep her eyes on the prize. Go-nowhere hookups were not her speed and Michael had the potential to be so much more. The fact that he'd shared something as important to him as a neurological disorder after they'd known each other for a short time implied that he saw her in the same light—as someone who might just go the distance.

The thought made her knees wobbly, so she took a second to sit on her bed.

Since before Anne had moved to New York from San Antonio, she'd known what she wanted—a guy in her life who would last a lifetime. She'd done the partying thing and the casual dating thing, but a serious relationship had remained elusive. Her gaze drifted to the second nightstand she'd bought.

Maybe it wouldn't be wasted space after all.

Laughing at her sudden seriousness, Anne decided that over-thinking her interactions with Michael before they'd even had a first date was more than a little premature. The furthest ahead she needed to anticipate for was the next hour or two, so she dashed into the bathroom and brushed her teeth. She then tore off her sweater, put on a snug, long-sleeve shirt and layered a heavier sweater over it. She traded her comfy shoes for lined boots and grabbed her coat, hat, and gloves. Then, as a last thought, she snagged her favorite lip balm. She hoped Michael liked the flavor of honey.

"Ready," she announced.

Mike was standing by the door, his hands buried deep in his pockets, and looking way more serious than a man about to eat cheesecake should.

"What's wrong?" she asked.

"Just wondering. About the Tourette's. Does it bother you?"

He'd risked a lot, setting such a disclosure on the table so early on. He'd either acted on impulse or out of deep courage, both of which gained her admiration.

"Should it?"

"It's not something I ordinarily disclose so early in a—"

He cut himself off, but Anne was good enough with words to know that the next one he was about to say was "relationship." She was relieved that he kept that word to himself, but at the same time, the idea that this man already had the notion in his brain thrilled her.

He leaned back against the door and held out his hand. She took it and with gentle slowness, he reeled her closer. An inch of space existed between them, but as his kiss had burned itself into her body's memory after only a few brief seconds of contact, her mouth quivered.

"I'm honored you told me," she said. "But I know what it is, and I know what I'm getting into. If your hand inadvertently brushes over my ass, I promise to ask if you meant it before I sock you. Or kiss you."

The scant distance between them disappeared in an instant and Anne reveled in the soft, tentative feel of Mike's mouth on hers again. He slid his fingers beneath the hem of her jacket and encircled her waist, his grip possessive and one-hundred percent steady.

She speared her hands into his hair, invigorated to learn that his black curls were just as thick and soft as she'd anticipated. She sighed and parted her lips, experiencing an explosion of sensation when their tongues touched, twirled, and tangled.

And then, he used his confident hold on her waist to break the kiss.

"Is it hot in here or is it just me?"

"Not just you," she said. "But maybe I am bundled up like an Eskimo."

"Let's get outside before you melt, then," he suggested.

Or before she lured him to her bed. Either way, leaving was probably a very good idea.

There had been occasions in Mike's life when he'd felt like he could take on the world. When he'd gotten into the college of his choice after struggling through high school. When he'd scored his dream job upon graduation. But none of those victories came close to the injection of elation that lightened his steps as he walked to the park with Sirus tugging at the end of her leash and Anne Miller strolling beside him. He'd already kissed her. Twice. And despite his anxiety over accidentally tugging her too hard on account of his Tourette's, he'd taken her hand the moment they'd crossed the threshold out of their apartment building. Keeping himself from touching her was as impossible as warding off the cold during a frigid February.

Though the reading on the thermometer mounted outside the bank on the corner near the park was in the teens, warmth flooded through his system—starting at the spot where his fingers tangled with Anne's. They found a bench beneath a tree and let Sirus off her leash. He commanded the dog to sit, and then reminded her to stay where he could see her before sending her off with a wave of his hand.

"Does she understand you?" Anne asked, her skepticism unhidden.

"She never goes far," Mike replied. "And she'll come right back if I call her."

"She's a smart girl," she said.

"I got lucky. Rescue dogs can be unpredictable, but she was easy to train and just wants to be loved. Did you have dogs growing up?"

"No," Anne said, her voice dripping with regret. "My parents worked a lot and we weren't home much. It wasn't fair to have a dog just to lock it up in a cage or a backyard. At least, that was my parents' argument when my brother and I whined a lot."

"They were right," Mike agreed. Since it was so cold, he scooted closer to Anne and shifted his jacket so that he could tuck his hand—and hers—into his pocket. He hadn't imagined the gesture would be so intimate, but it was. Her eyes widened for a split second before she grinned and relaxed into the curved bench.

"So you got Sirus when you were in Portland, right?"

"Yeah," he said, trying to remember the details, because at the moment, his brain was befuddled by the feel of Anne's shoulder pressed against his. "My job there was really flexible. Most days, she actually came to the office with me. I can't do that here. I'm going to have to find someone to help me with her."

At that moment, Sirus bounded out of a bush, startled, as if she'd sensed something that might require chasing should it appear in the next few seconds. With her front paws spaced out, her legs rigid and her head cocked, she looked every bit the hunting dog that Weimaraners had been bred to be.

Anne leaned in so that her voice was a whisper. "She looks so serious."

Mike inhaled the heady scent of Anne's shampoo. "To a dog, play is serious business."

With nothing to chase, Sirus spun and dashed back into the bushes, which were really no more than twigs this time of year. Once satisfied that nothing interesting lurked amid the brittle branches, she leaped out and charged down the lighted walkway to investigate the shadow and scent of a trash can.

"Speaking of *serious*," Anne said. "What's up with her name? Is it a Harry Potter thing?"

"That's Sirius," he said, referring to the infamous character, Sirius Black, otherwise known as the Prisoner of Azkaban. "She was originally named after Osiris, the Egyptian—"

"God of the dead," Anne filled in. "That's morbid."

"Which is why I changed it," Mike admitted. "I didn't get her until long after she was named and apparently, she had a lot of health problems as a puppy. Call me superstitious, but I thought naming her after a god of death was a bad omen. And since Sirius is also the name of the brightest star in the night sky, I change it to just Sirus."

The dog's scampering had started to slow and she was now sniffing the ground in search of a strategic location in which to do her business. Mike had a plastic bag in the opposite pocket of the one which he shared with Anne's hand. He supposed picking up after his dog wasn't the most romantic activity he could imagine, but Anne seemed to be getting to know the real him in all his complicated glory in one fell swoop. He'd told her about his Tourette's, he'd acted on his compulsion to clean, and he was about to make sure his dog didn't leave a deposit for some unsuspecting neighbor to step in. She was getting it all—good and bad—right from the start. He'd always been honest with the women he'd dated, but he couldn't remember ever feeling quite so voluntarily exposed.

But Anne certainly didn't seem to mind.

"So how old was she when you got her?"

"She was eighteen months old. A rescue. For both of us."

"That's the second time you've said that," Anne pointed out.

"Does it sound corny?"

"No," she replied, then laughed. "Okay, just a little. Still, it's intriguing."

Mike watched Sirus jog over to a tree, sniffing at the roots with the intensity of a police dog rooting out drugs. He'd adopted Sirus at one of the lowest points in his life, but confessing as much to Anne seemed a bit like overkill. He'd already hit her with quite a bit tonight. The date. The Tourette's. And yet, her openness was undeniable. And infectious.

"It's an old story that's been told for generations," he said, with a tad more drama than was warranted, just to drive the point home that his past, at this point, was nothing more than a distant tragedy that no longer drove his life. "A guy gets his heart stomped. He decides to fill the gap with a female who, thanks to careful breeding and training, does everything he says and never lets him down."

"I hope you don't expect unwavering obedience from all the women in your life," Anne said.

Mike snorted. "If you met my mother or sisters, you'd never have to ask."

"Not exactly shrinking violets?"

"They pretty much escaped the whole flower family. Except maybe belladonna," he joked.

"I like them already," she concluded.

"And they'd like you."

"How do you know?"

"Because I like you."

And again, they were kissing. This time, Mike didn't plan or strategize. Their bodies, leaned close against the cold, gravitated toward each other with a pull as natural as the moon and tides. Her chilly lips warmed under his, adding a layer of sweet, sensual awareness.

He traced the edge of her mouth with his tongue and she instantly let him in, twisting so that he had full access. She tasted like mint and kissed with abandon. In his pocket, their hands tightened.

And then, Sirus jumped across their laps on the bench.

"Sirus! Bad dog!" he chided, half annoyed and half thankful that his pooch had interrupted a moment that could have gotten way more intense than he'd planned before their first date.

Anne laughed and scratched Sirus's ears, which sent the dog

into apoplectic fits of happiness, punctuated with barks and whimpers whenever Anne attempted to stop.

Soon the cold was creeping in through their outerwear, so they ambled to the café. With Sirus on her leash basking in the attention of strangers, Mike went inside and ordered two cappuccinos to go, a slice of cheesecake, and two forks. They ate standing at the outdoor pub tables, making quick work of the luscious dessert before heading home.

Mike dropped Sirus off and despite the dog's protests, walked Anne back up to her apartment. At the door, he lingered, certain he wanted to kiss her one more time, but mindful of scaring her away by wanting too much, too soon.

She took the choice away from him by elevating herself onto her tiptoes and brushing a soft kiss on his cheek. "I had a great time tonight."

"Yeah, me, too."

He turned his head, stealing the full-on kiss he so desperately wanted, but pulling away before he reached the point where he wouldn't be able to stop. Anne intoxicated him. The feel of her mouth on his, her tongue flavored by the sweet dessert, was the best indulgence he'd had in a long time. If he thought too long about how her intelligent conversation, easy sense of humor and general joy for life grabbed at his insides and pulled, he might never have found the power to say goodnight.

She rushed inside. A sudden burst of energy ricocheted through his system. He could have run up and down the stairwell for at least an hour without losing a single breath, but he decided to wait for the elevator. Lingering near her, even if it was just down the hall, was a welcomed torture.

But when the mechanism finally dinged, the sound was drowned by Anne's distant scream.

Eight

NYCAM
NEW YORK COALITION AGAINST MICE

For Immediate Release
February 21, 2006
For more information:
Contact Michael Davoll
NEWS ADVISORY

NYCAM TO STAGE RAID ON SCHENECTADY COURTHOUSE: ALL MICE BE DAMNED

Schenectady, NY—Members of the NYCAM, the New York Coalition Against Mice, announced today that they will be launching a new series of raids against mice in the Schenectady Courthouse. The raids are part of a stepped up attempt to crackdown on the fastest growing crime in Schenectady: illegal mouse droppings.

This raid was scheduled two days after a massive assortment of droppings were found in an Albany high rise apartment building. The droppings carried the markings of the Schenectady mouse gang, **Magic Kingdoms Rejects**. This was the first time that the MKR had staged a dropping in the state capital.

Anne read the message in her inbox twice, and then burst out laughing. The stares from her coworkers made her cover her mouth and lean in closer to her keyboard, but she chuckled all the same. After what she'd put Michael through last night, she thought she'd never hear from him again.

Instead, he'd turned her terror into a fake press release like the ones he wrote at his job.

High on the endorphins from Michael's parting kiss, Anne had spun back into her kitchen to put the energy to good use. She'd opened her dishwasher and instantly spotted a dead mouse on the top rack. Her throat still hurt from the screaming. Only a split second later, she'd answered Mike's insistent knocking and somehow managed to tell him about her rodent invader.

Precisely how he'd gotten rid of the dead mouse, she did not know or care. He'd not only stayed late to help her rewash every dish, but he'd apparently also listened when she'd told him how she'd be spending the majority of her time this week at the Schenectady Courthouse.

The press release would make sure she didn't forget the crazy ending to their amazing night any time soon.

"I can't imagine what would be so funny on the crime beat, Ms. Miller."

The sound of her boss's voice sucked the humor out of her system with the same power as a high-flow toilet. In the dictionary, listed under the word "buzzkill," was a photograph of Pamela Toledo. She was like a female Lou Grant—only not during the lighthearted *Mary Tyler Moore Show,* but the more serious eponymous drama—and without the humanity. In fact, the only real reason Pamela reminded her of Lou Grant was because she was a newspaper editor and she looked remarkably like Ed Asner.

Anne quickly closed the window to her e-mail program, pasted on her best smile, and turned to Pamela. "Did you need me, Pamela?"

Pamela threw the marked-up copy of Anne's latest article across her desk. It floated onto the floor in a flash of red on white. "No, but you certainly need me. I guess they don't teach about dangling participles in journalism school anymore."

Anne forced her smile to remain steady. Never mind that she had graduated from journalism school more than five years ago and had since worked on several publications of equal size and scope as the *Daily Journal.* She preferred instead to picture the dangling not of a participle, but of Pamela's squirming body out of a tenth-story window.

"Right," Anne said, scooping up the marked-up copy from the floor.

"You finished with that article on the city council indictment?" Pamela asked.

"Just waiting for one more quote from the district attorney," Anne replied calmly, even though she'd reported that fact to her superior not twenty minutes ago during their morning staff meeting. "I was just about to call in. I'll make my deadline, no problem."

She stared into Pamela's scowl and silently counted to ten. Then twenty. Even after the woman cleared her nicotine-coated throat and shuffled away in mismatched montage of bad eighties business suits, Anne counted another ten, just for good measure. When the woman finally turned the corner into her office, Anne let out the breath she'd been holding with a colorful, but quiet, string of curses.

When she'd first signed on to the job at the *Daily Journal,* she'd hoped to learn a great deal from the experienced newspaper-woman before she moved up and on to a byline at either the *New*

York Times, Washington Post or *Wall Street Journal.* Instead, she'd been browbeaten, underappreciated and abused. Her ambitions, however, remained solid. She hadn't worked this hard to be undercut by someone as soulless as her current editor.

As usual, Anne would suck it up and endure—though shaking off Pamela's nastiness would be a whole lot easier to do once she'd typed a reply to Michael.

From: Anne Miller
Subject: See Them Run: Mouse Hunters Fight the
          Good Fight in Schenectady
To: "Michael Davoli"
Date: Tuesday, February 21, 2006, 1:41 PM
See Them Run: Mouse hunters clean up a courthouse
By Anne Miller
Staff writer

SCHENECTADY - With military precision, jack-booted authorities descended upon the county courthouse this morning to rid the halls of justice of the four-legged scourge plaguing local jurisprudence like an act of God. The raid, conducted by the New York Coalition Against Mice, or NYCAM, was staged after newspaper reports brought to light a mouse invasion in the aging building.

"It's become a health hazard," said spokesman Michael Davoli. "We're here to serve, protect and clean."

The sweep also included sweeping up after the mice. County court officers were seen clambering on top of desks to get out of the rodents' way. Jail inmates brought over for court appearances delighted in the mayhem. They stomped their feet, rattling ankle chains to scare up more mice. They called it their way of helping fix a problem long overdue for cleanup.

"Honestly, I'd rather be in jail some days, it's cleaner there," said an inmate who preferred not to be named. By 3 p.m., after a day when nothing got done save mouse hunting, Schenectady County

Judge K.D. literally threw up her hands, tossed off her robe, and officially closed court for the day.

Court is expected to resume in the morning, after the heroic NYCAM members take their fight to downtown Albany.

No word on how NYCAM plans to dispose of the mice.

"Really, you don't want to know," Davoli said.

"Mice in the courthouse?"

Anne nearly jumped out of her skin. God, she hated working in the office. She much preferred the coffee shop. At least there, if someone was reading over your shoulder, they at least pretended they were doing something else. At the paper, eavesdropping was an art form.

This time, Anne didn't hide her humorous handiwork. At least, she thought it was funny. She was pretty sure Michael would, too. But everyone else? Not so much. She kind of liked sharing an inside joke with a guy who was also an incredibly good kisser, not to mention rodent-warrior extraordinaire.

"While I'm sure the Schenectady Courthouse has its fair share of vermin, this is just a joke piece I'm sending to a friend," Anne explained to Billy, the intern who used her desk when she was out in the field and who, the rest of the time, followed her around in a diligent attempt to learn something.

"What are you up to?" Anne asked, hoping to deflect any other questions about her personal correspondence.

"I finished looking over the copy of Deni's piece on the zoning commission, and I was sort of hoping you'd have something more interesting for me to proofread."

Anne chuckled. "My grocery list, if I ever took the time to make one, would be more interesting to read than a report on the zoning board. I'm waiting for one last quote on this piece on the fraud trial, but if you'd like to look it over now, I wouldn't mind. I have a phone call to make anyway. I'll go down to the courtyard and you can read here, okay?"

The kid nodded enthusiastically, but she sent him to grab a Coke while she read through her e-mail to Mike, fixed a spelling error because what would he think about a writer who couldn't spell, and then clicked send. This was fun. She could only imagine what he'd send back in response. All because she'd found a dead mouse in her dishwasher.

Billy returned, so Anne pulled up the article she was nearly done with, grabbed her note pad, coat, and cell phone, and went downstairs to the courtyard that had usually been appropriated by the newspaper's smokers. The day was cold, but the sun beat down into the cement circle so she could walk around and chat with the prosecutor on the case without her teeth chattering. She had the necessary quote in less than two minutes, so she took the extra time to call Shane, who'd sent a text message instructing her to do so at her first available moment.

"So, how'd it go last night?" Shane asked.

Funny how caller ID had destroyed the niceties such as saying, "Hello."

"Up until the dead mouse, it was a very nice evening."

"Dead mouse? Tell me this is a metaphor."

"Nope," Anne insisted. "I'm being completely literal. That is what I get for emptying my dishwasher. A steamed rodent body sitting amid my utensils."

"Ew!"

Anne's stomach roiled just thinking about it again. She'd always had an aversion to rodents of all species, but mice in particular gave her the creeps. Even the stark white, lab-bred mouse that had never existed outside his tiny cage made her skin crawl, with his wormy tail and pink mouth. She shivered just thinking about it.

"The point is," she said, raising her voice in a bid to shout the picture out of her head, "he heard me scream and came running. He not only took the disgusting thing away, he reloaded the dishwasher and ran another cycle, hand-washed the dishes that wouldn't fit, and invited me to dinner at his place tonight so I don't have to go anywhere near my kitchen."

Shane was quiet, which surprised Anne. She expected a squeal of excitement—or at the very least, a hearty "I told you so."

"What's wrong?" she asked, suspicious.

"Nothing," Shane said. "Things seem fairly perfect. I think I'm jealous. Wow, there's an emotion I haven't felt in a really long time."

Anne laughed. She couldn't deny that things between her and Michael had progressed a little quickly, from that first hug on the sidewalk to the incredible kisses they'd shared on her couch, in her doorway, and later on the bench at the park. Ordinarily, any new man she kissed required a certain amount of fumbling before they got to the good stuff. Nose bumps, groping hands, and sloppy tongues that moved either too fast or too slow so that the acrobatics of the kiss took center stage from the emotional expression were par for the course.

But Michael had skipped that stage. He kissed her as if they'd been doing it for years. He'd tilted his head at precisely the right angle and more than once, he'd brushed his fingers over her cheek in a way that drove her mad.

If she didn't watch herself, she might find herself in love way too fast than was wise. She wanted a real shot with Michael—though the idea of turning down his invitation to dinner to slow the process of connection was wholly out of the question. Especially after his e-mail.

"What have you got to be jealous of? You've got Jamie." Anne said the last part with hestitation. With Shane's track record, chances were high that he was already history. When she'd knitted with Shane the week before last, the bloom was already fading off the rose.

"Eh," Shane replied. "I do and I don't. He's a great guy, I guess, but it's all so . . . physical. I don't know if he'd sit still for an hour watching a complicated television show with me, help clear the dishes, take me for a romantic stroll through a park, and then dispose of a drowned, baked, and steamed pest for me, too."

Anne willed the bile suddenly burning up her throat to return to her stomach.

"Can we please not talk about that anymore?"

"Yeah, no problem," Shane said with a snort. "It's more fun to talk about Michael anyway. Or should I start calling him Mr. Perfect?"

"It's easy to make a guy sound perfect when I hardly know him." Anne said. "Did you know he has Tourette's?"

She almost hadn't asked Shane about it, but she was the only mutual friend Anne shared with Michael and she didn't have a sense that he kept his condition particularly secret. He'd certainly disclosed it to her fast enough, as if he was giving her the chance to walk away as early in the romantic process as possible—something she could not imagine doing.

"Yeah, I think I remember something about it," Shane said. "He had a hard time with it when he was a kid, but I think he manages it pretty well now. Why, did you notice something?"

"Actually, no. He told me. But it's hard to notice anything about him but his glorious blue eyes and generous soul."

"Oh, dear," Shane said. "You sound a little smitten."

Anne smiled. "I do, don't I?"

"Why'd you ask about the Tourette's?"

"It was important to him that he tell me. But to be honest, I didn't think it was any big deal. I guess I'm afraid I might insult him by trivializing his condition, but if he has it under control, I don't see why I should be concerned."

"There's never a problem when a guy is being honest. At least, I don't think there is. It's such a rare occurrence, I don't think there are any set rules. What about Egypt? Did you tell him about your trip?"

Anne frowned. The thought hadn't even occurred to her. She and her yoga partner, Adele, had planned their vacation long before Michael had come into her life. "I will. When the time is right. First, I want to make sure this thing has legs, you know?"

Anne and Shane chatted for a few more minutes and made plans to meet up for knitting and wine the next night. Anne called a few other knitters to make the group a foursome, then headed back up to her office.

Billy had finished looking over her article. He'd made a couple of good changes and one that she decided to ignore for stylistic reasons rather than technical ones. Once she keyed in the quote she'd obtained from the prosecuting attorney, she e-mailed the finished article to Pamela—five hours ahead of her deadline— then checked her inbox for any leads on her next article.

Oh, who was she kidding? She was looking for an answer from Michael.

She wasn't disappointed. He hadn't crafted another press release, but he'd sent her a note thanking her for the laugh. And at the bottom, he'd attached a document she had to double click in order to read.

Printed over a fancy background, she read:

Invitation:

Café Davoli

Dinner starting at 8 pm (unless later is needed)

Menu

Appetizer:
Tomato, fresh basil and fresh mozzarella salad
with vinaigrette dressing
Fresh Italian bread with rosemary and
extra virgin olive oil for dipping
Angel hair pasta in marinara

Main Course:
Eggplant Parmigiana in a tomato basil sauce

Dessert
Anne's surprise
Plus an assortment of red wines.

After dinner activity TBD.

As she read, her hunger intensified, her mouth watering over the menu selections—only to have her lips instantly dry the minute she read the very last line.

After dinner activity TBD. To be determined.

Determined by whom? She could only hope that Mike would take responsibility for this call. Judging by the way her insides liquefied in anticipation of having Michael cook for her and serve her not just one of her preferred red wines, but an assortment, she figured that by the end of the night, her ability to make a good decision about what they did once dinner was done might be in serious jeopardy.

Nine

MIKE LEANED OVER THE MARINARA gurgling on the stove and took a big whiff before dipping in a hunk of crusty Italian bread. His mouth watered while he blew on the steaming sauce, readying his mouth for the explosion of flavors. The garlic was a little strong, but that's how he liked it. The salt balanced nicely against the sweetness of the tomatoes. He added an extra dash of red pepper flakes, stirred the pot, then set to his next task.

He couldn't remember the last time he'd cooked such an elaborate meal. Sure, he'd pitched in at Christmas in the family kitchen, but creating an entire meal for the sole purpose of seducing Anne's senses with good food, great wine, and clever company tested even his culinary abilities.

And yet, he couldn't wait for her to arrive.

All day, he'd been struck by the fact that last night had been much like living a romantic comedy. From the casual meal on the couch while the girl revealed her wacky obsession with a television show so antithetical—and yet, so revealing—of her personality to the witty conversation that ended up revealing more than either intended.

And then there was the mouse.

And better—the kiss.

God, the kiss.

All day, Mike had fought the memory of his lips on hers, resulting in distraction and uncharacteristically low productivity at work. Instead of finishing the press releases he knew had to be done by the end of the week, he'd worked up a fake announcement regarding imaginary mouse infestations in the building where Anne worked most often. Instead of completing his report on the new legislation making its way through the state senate regarding funding for prekindergarten programs, he'd planned tonight's menu, made a shopping list, and researched a selection of red wines to match each of the meal's three courses.

If any of his friends had witnessed his behavior, they'd call him whipped. Except Nikki. She'd helped with the wine choices. Then again, she'd been encouraging him to get whipped over someone—anyone—practically since they'd met.

Nikki was a self-avowed lover of love. She believed that the powers of infatuation and lust were limitless. He'd disagreed with her up until the moment he met Anne. If this was what whipped felt like, well, it was very, very nice.

Anne had, likely without realizing it, slid into the nerve-ending-rich area between his insides and his skin. She intrigued him. She invaded even his most mundane thoughts and had made brief but impactful appearances in his dreams. She kept his senses on edge. With her around, he had to be ready for anything—including rescuing her from dead mice.

When a knock sounded on his door, Sirus jumped down from the couch and barked. He ordered her to quiet down. Instead, she sniffled loudly at the crack between the apartment and the hallway, hunting for the scent of whomever was coming to visit.

Mike told her to sit, and then wiped his hands on a kitchen towel, popped a breath mint to counteract the garlic he'd eaten

READER RESPONSE CARD

TVA

We care about your opinions! Please take a moment to fill out our Reader Survey online at **http://survey.hcibooks.com**. To show our appreciation, we'll give you an **instant discount coupon** for future book purchases, as well as a special gift available only online. If you prefer, you may mail this survey card back to us and receive a discount coupon by mail. All answers are confidential.

(PLEASE PRINT IN ALL CAPS)

First Name _____ Last Name _____

Address _____

City _____ State _____ Zip _____ Email _____

1. Gender
- ❏ Female ❏ Male

2. Age
- ❏ Under 20
- ❏ 21-30 ❏ 31-40
- ❏ 41-50 ❏ 51-60
- ❏ Over 60

3. Marital Status
- ❏ Married ❏ Single

4. How you did get this book?
- ❏ Received as gift
- ❏ Bought for myself
- ❏ Borrowed from a friend
- ❏ Borrowed from my library

5. If bought for yourself, how did you find out about it?
- ❏ Recommendation
- ❏ Store Display
- ❏ Read about it on a Website
- ❏ Email message or e-newsletter
- ❏ Book review or author interview

6. How many books do you read a year, excluding educational material?
- ❏ 4 or less ❏ 5-8
- ❏ 9-12 ❏ 12 or more

7. Do you have children under the age of 18 at home?
- ❏ Yes ❏ No

8. What type of romance do you enjoy most?
- ❏ Contemporary
- ❏ Historical
- ❏ Paranormal
- ❏ Erotic
- ❏ All types

9. What are your sensuality preferences?
- ❏ Wild and erotic
- ❏ Steamy but moderate
- ❏ Sweet and sensual
- ❏ Doesn't matter as long as it fits the story

10. Where do you usually buy books?
- ❏ Online (amazon.com, etc.)
- ❏ Bookstore chain (Borders, B&N...)
- ❏ Independent/local bookstore
- ❏ Big Box store (Target, Wal-Mart...)
- ❏ Drug Store or Supermarket

11. How often do you read romance novels?
- ❏ Every now and then
- ❏ Several times a year
- ❏ Constantly

FOLD HERE

12. What influences you most when purchasing a book?
(Rank each from 1 to 5 with 1 being the top)

	1	2	3	4	5
Author	1	2	3	4	5
Price	1	2	3	4	5
Title	1	2	3	4	5
Reviews	1	2	3	4	5
Cover Design	1	2	3	4	5
Series/Publisher	1	2	3	4	5
Recommendation	1	2	3	4	5

13. Annual household income
- ❑ Under $25,000
- ❑ $25,000–$40,000
- ❑ $41,000–$50,000
- ❑ $51,000–$75,000
- ❑ Over $75,000

14. How long have you been reading romance novels?
- ❑ 1-2 years   ❑ 3-5 years
- ❑ More than 5 years

Comments

15. What other topics do you enjoy reading?

Non-Fiction
- ❑ Family/parenting
- ❑ Relationships
- ❑ Addictions/Recovery
- ❑ Health/nutrition
- ❑ Cooking
- ❑ Religious
- ❑ Spirituality
- ❑ Inspiration/affirmations
- ❑ Self-improvement
- ❑ Sports
- ❑ Pets
- ❑ Memoirs
- ❑ True Crime

Fiction
- ❑ Mystery
- ❑ Chick-lit
- ❑ Historical
- ❑ Paranormal

as he cooked and tasted, and then answered the door.

"Am I late?" she asked.

He was instantly struck by the scent of chocolate and sugar coming from a bright-white pastry box she held in her hands, but a split second later, his senses forgot about sweets and focused on her. Dressed in a light sweater and snug jeans, her hair pulled back loosely at her neck, she looked pretty and casual and confident. Her eyes gleamed with what he hoped was pleasure at seeing him again.

He took the box and inhaled appreciatively. "You took my dessert request seriously."

"Dessert is serious business," she replied. The minute he tried to undo the tape holding it shut, she reclaimed the treat. "But it's a surprise. No peeking."

He held up his hands in surrender. Sirus was wiggling where she sat. If he didn't give her permission to greet Anne soon, she might crack her spine.

After a slightly distrustful and wholly affected glare, Anne gave him the box again, then immediately dropped to her knees to pet the dog. He put the box of delights on top of the refrigerator and then poured her a glass of wine.

"Zinfandel?" he asked.

Her eyebrows rose as she caught sight of the trio of bottles lined up beside six wineglasses. "Are you expecting company?"

"It's just us," he replied, handing her the glass and then taking a sniff of his own. "Nikki, one of the women I work with, knows a guy at a wine store. He suggested that having different glasses for each wine would impress you. Was he right?"

"Do I have to wash dishes when we're done?"

"No," Mike answered with a chuckle.

She raised her glass in a toast. "Then I'm impressed."

He gestured her to the living room, then sent Sirus to the fluffy bed beneath the window that was her normal napping spot. He took his appetizer out of the refrigerator, removed the plastic wrap, and set the plate in front of her. He'd artfully arranged slices of fresh mozzarella alternately with thick red discs of beefsteak tomato and bright green strips of basil. He poured his homemade vinaigrette over the top, then handed her a fork, small plate, and napkin.

"This is gorgeous," she said, spearing a helping onto her plate.

"My mother always said that visual presentation is as important as the taste of the food."

"You're mother is right. Is she Italian?"

"My father's Italian. My mother is the Jewish half of my genetics."

"Right," Anne said. "I've always found that Jews and Italians have a lot in common. The overbearing mothers. The guilt over the state of the universe."

Mike handed her a knife. "Not to mention the emphasis on food."

"Best of both worlds, baby."

She oohed and aahed over his mozzarella salad and was sufficiently impressed when he confessed that he'd whipped up the vinaigrette from his own recipe. They talked about her own culinary skills, which he had to admit, he was a little surprised to learn were not deficient. She didn't like to clean, but she loved to cook. Her claims about the deliciousness of her pancakes made him wonder how to get an invite for breakfast without sounding like he was suggesting they spend the night together first.

"More wine?" he asked, bringing out the fresh Italian focaccia he'd picked up at the store, but had rewarmed in his oven.

Her glass wasn't quite empty yet, but as she dipped a hunk of the bread into a swirl of spiced olive oil, she smiled. "You have a lot of wine there. We need to pace ourselves."

"That's the beauty of us living in the same building. Neither of us has to drive."

"Good point," she said, holding out her glass. "Just half, though. I want to have room for everything and I don't want to embarrass myself by getting drunk. Unless that's your intention?"

She batted her eyelashes suggestively.

"It's been my experience that I have better luck with women when they're sober."

"Do you have a lot of luck with women?"

He'd gone to the kitchen to drop his precooked angel-hair pasta back into the salted, starchy water for a quick reheat, but stopped dead at her question.

"Define luck," he countered.

"A lot of girlfriends?"

"Define—"

"A lot," she supplied. "Okay, I guess what I'm asking is, how heavy is your emotional baggage?"

He pondered her question as he stirred the tomato-basil sauce. "I don't think I'd get charged extra by the airlines."

She smiled. "Average, then."

"You don't get to our age without a few broken hearts."

Once again, Anne's luminous brown eyes and easy manner coaxed him into revealing more than he'd ever imagined in so short a time. As he prepared the next part of their appetizer, warming and draining the pasta, ladling the sauce, and topping the small bowls with freshly chopped parsley and grated parmesan, he told her about Lisa.

Anne listened and ate, and while she shook her head when he recounted some of the more perplexing turns of the tale, she didn't criticize his ex to gain points with him. He found her attitude not only wise, but also empathetic and sincere.

"Life just sucks sometimes," Anne concluded.

"Yeah, it does."

"But I think," she said, twirling her last fork of pasta, "she seriously missed out."

"You're just saying that because of my marinara," he countered, wanting to move the conversation away from his romantic past.

"There are worse reasons to date a guy than his culinary skill," Anne pointed out.

Questions about her love life up until this point danced on his tongue, but he bit them back. He didn't really care. Anne seemed like the type who would travel light with minimum baggage, no matter the distance to the destination or the length of stay.

And this was a good thing. He wasn't looking to get serious. He cherished the time it took to become friends with a woman first, get to know her, before risking either of their hearts.

"You might want to wait until you taste my eggplant parmesan before you make any judgments."

He cleared away the appetizer dishes, teasing her mercilessly when she insisted on helping, and then cruelly jumping at her from behind when she dared open up his dishwasher.

She nearly dropped a stack of plates, but retaliated by grabbing a dishtowel and snapping him a few times in the butt before she was satisfied that his punishment fit the crime. When he spun around, she was right there, flushed from laughing and though he admittedly didn't try very hard, he could not resist stealing a kiss.

She tasted of wine and warmth. Trapped with her back against the counter, he pressed full against her, reveling in the way her curves molded against his body. She slid her hands around his neck, speared her fingers through his hair, and drew him even deeper into the kiss.

His heartbeat accelerated, pumping blood into his extremities. His fingers tingled as they clutched at her hips. His legs ached from the act of remaining vertical when other parts of his body screamed for horizontal relief.

"You taste like garlic," she murmured, smiling from beneath lazy lashes.

"So do you. We cancel each other out."

Then he kissed her again.

He might have feasted on her for hours if the buzzer over his stove hadn't cracked the sexually charged air into a thousand electric fragments. They jumped at the sound and then laughed. To give him a minute to pull himself back under control, he directed her to pour the next round of red wine while he grabbed an oven mitt.

He bit a curse when he realized his carefully stacked towers of eggplant, mozzarella, and sauce had toppled during the baking process, but he slid them as artfully as he could on to plates while Anne brought the glasses of chianti to the table he'd set beside the window.

His apartment didn't have much of a view, but the streetlights bathed the corner in a nice pink glow. He enhanced the effect by dimming the harsh lighting in the rest of the apartment. And although he suspected she might think he was a total dweeb, he lit the single candle in the center of the table.

"You should open a restaurant," she raved.

"Been there, done that," he said, shaking his head.

She put down her fork and retrieved her wineglass. "You used to own a restaurant?"

"My parents," he explained. "It was nothing fancy, just one of those places at the state fair every summer. But I learned about counting money, ordering inventory, and serving customers from

a very early age. I prefer to cook for friends and family. They're
way more appreciative."

Anne nodded. "My parents ran a business, too. Furniture. Funny
how we both have families with business backgrounds, but neither of us followed that path."

This spawned a deep and revealing conversation about why
she'd chosen to be a journalist and why he'd pursued a life in
public service. She was surprised but impressed to learn that he'd
worked on the last presidential campaign and that his current job
with a group that lobbied for educational reform stemmed not
only from his questionable experiences as a student with a dis-
ability in an often indifferent system, but also because both his
mother and sisters were schoolteachers.

"So you hated school," Anne said as she finished the last of her
wine and the eggplant parmesan on her plate, which was reduced
to a smear of sauce and flecks of onion, basil, and garlic.

He took her plate and slid it beneath his similarly empty one.
"For the most part, but I love learning. I read a lot. I'm a curious
guy, so if something interests me, I find ways to know more about
it. College was way more fun than primary and high school."

"Isn't it always? Well, don't learn anything more about cooking or I might have to eat here every night and then I'll weigh a
ton."

"Well, I wouldn't want you to weigh a ton on my account," he
said, "but you can come here for a meal whenever you'd like."

Together, they tidied the kitchen, but before either of them
could fit another morsel of food into their mouths, they decided
another walk was in order. Sirus, who'd behaved with amazing
restraint during the entire meal, leapt with the alacrity of a four-
legged pogo stick when Mike put on his jacket and grabbed her
leash. When Anne returned from her apartment sufficiently bundled, they headed out onto the streets, this time opting not for the

park, but for a quick walk around the neighborhood.

"You seem in an awful hurry to get back upstairs," Anne pointed out when Sirus made one last stop at a tree in front of the building. "Wouldn't have anything to do with the *to be determined* after-dinner activities, would it?"

He could seriously get used to being around a woman who wasn't afraid to speak her mind.

"I was thinking more about dessert," he said, matching her suggestive tone.

"Those aren't the same thing?" she challenged.

He groaned, fighting the urge to tug the leash hard and hurry the dog. Instead, he turned away from her so that she couldn't continue to torture him with her eyes.

Upstairs, he washed his hands and opened the last bottle of wine, an investment Nikki's pal had insisted would be the highlight of the evening. He poured the recioto into the glasses while Anne retrieved her bakery box from atop the fridge.

She slid her finger underneath the flaps to break the seal, then handed him the box. Intrigued, he lifted the top and immediately started to laugh.

Two mice, shaped out of sweet, ricotta cheese with ears and tail made of dark chocolate and cookie, stared back at him.

"This mouse thing has gone too far," he said.

"Wait until you taste them."

As it was nearly eleven, Mike suggested they flip on the television and catch the latest episode of *The Daily Show*. She hesitated for a split second when he informed her that unlike her, he kept his television in his bedroom, but after grabbing a cookie sheet to act as a makeshift tray, they headed into his room.

He flipped on the lights, then the television. God, there were about a thousand things he'd rather do with Anne Miller in here than watch Jon Stewart poke fun at the day's political gaffs, but he had to stem the rush of lust coursing through him. Luckily, the delicious wine and clever mice kept their mouths too busy to worry about moments not spent kissing. During commercials, Anne wandered around the room, checking out the memorabilia and pictures displayed neatly on his shelves.

"Where was this?" she asked, holding out a picture of bedraggled, rain-soaked hikers.

"Hudson Highlands State Park."

"I've been up there," Anne said. "But thankfully, it was much drier when I went."

Mike warmed his insides with another sip of wine. "That was a rough night. It poured until I thought I might never be dry again, but the next day was so clear and sunny, I ended up sunburned on my neck."

"Not a good weekend, then," she concluded.

"Actually, it was. There's something invigorating about pitting yourself against the elements. I love hiking and camping. You?"

"Oddly enough, I do," she answered. "I just don't get many opportunities to go. I used to be a camp counselor when I was younger."

In between laughing at the antics on the television and talking about their childhoods, by the time midnight came around, they were sitting on the bed, polishing off the last of the Italian dessert wine—the mice long since devoured—and going through some of the pictures and scrapbooks Mike had accumulated. He showed her family stuff first, then high school and college and then, with a brief hesitation, he took out the one book that might make or break what he had going so far with Anne.

Mike knew this was a risk, but she'd shared her obsession with *24* with him. It wouldn't be fair to keep his own mania a secret, especially not something of this importance.

"This one is about Phish," he said.

She eyed him, nonplussed. "You like to fish?"

"No, the band. Phish. Have you heard of them?"

Her expression was fairly unreadable as she scooted the scrapbook from his lap into hers. She opened the nondescript cover without a word, and then laughed at the sight of him in funky, hippie-style clothes he'd worn to a concert a couple of years ago. Tie-dye T-shirt. Baggy jeans. He hadn't even shaved. That had been a kicking weekend. Personal hygiene had been secondary by far to enjoying the music.

As she turned the pages, revealing more snapshots from the hundreds of concerts he'd attended over the years all over the country, the humor drained a bit from her face. He'd never seen a fake smile on her before—and it was neither convincing nor encouraging.

"Wow," she said. "You're really into this band."

She'd reached the section where he'd pasted articles he'd cut from the newspapers about various shows. One page was a montage of boarding passes from flights, cancelled train tickets—even gas receipts. Funny, he'd had absolutely no trouble confessing to her about his Tourette's, but coming clean about his obsession with the rock band, Phish, who had toured the country with a cadre of followers until their breakup in August of 2004, stopped him cold.

"Have you ever heard them play?" he asked.

She continued to turn pages, stopping to glance at the headlines. "I can't say that I have."

"They started as a cover band, doing mostly Grateful Dead. But they emerged into their own and their style is, well, eclectic. The music is wild and the people are wilder."

She looked up, a half-smile teasing her lips. "I never would have pegged you for a Phish Phan. Never in a million years."

"Why not?" he asked, trying not to sound offended.

With him, Phish wasn't about the lifestyle, it was about the music. He also had a personal connection to the band, having not only met the band's drummer, John Fishman, when he'd accompanied a high-school friend to an interview with the budding musician, but he'd traveled to concerts around the state with members of John's family. He could still remember the moment he'd first heard the band play—the way the notes had dropped into his soul and challenged every preconceived notion he'd ever had about rhythms, lyrics, and even life. Along his travels, he'd met fascinating people, made lifelong friends with people who understood the soundtrack of his life.

Anne had to at least understand this or she might not ever understand him.

"I guess I never realized that people who travel around the world following an off-kilter band had, I don't know, jobs and responsibilities."

"Now, you see," he said, determined to keep his sense of humor. Anne wasn't the first person to react with shock when he revealed his devotion to Phish. She certainly wasn't going to be the last. "That's a stereotype."

"Apparently. And one that I have contributed to," she confessed. "Can you ever forgive me?"

She turned the scrapbook on her lap so that he could read the page. The headline read, "Lure of Phish Powerful to the End."

And the byline read *Anne Miller*.

Ten

IF SHANE HAD WITNESSED THIS MOMENT, she would have said magic and fate had yet again come into play. What were the chances that Mike had not only read an article Anne had written about his favorite band, but that he'd also deemed it important enough to keep in one of his many scrapbooks?

Trouble was, Anne remembered writing that article. While she'd given the whole Phish phenomenon a positive spin for the masses, the circumstances under which she'd taken the assignment had been less about any appreciation she'd had for the music and more about wanting to spice up what had been a really boring week.

Prior to the concert report, she'd spent every moment the week before either in court or working on articles about teenagers breaking into cars for kicks and neighborhood disputes over noise levels. On top of having no time to breathe in an ounce of fresh air that hadn't been sullied with cigarette smoke, she'd drawn the shortest stick and ended up with a Saturday shift.

So when offered, she'd jumped at a chance to do a color piece on the invasion of Phish Phans on the Saratoga Performing Arts Center. The minute she'd met her first potential interviewee, she'd thought she'd slipped into a time warp and ended up on the wrong end of the 1970s. She couldn't imagine Mike as part of that scene, yet there he was in picture after picture, holding a beer, wearing T-shirts with pithy sayings, and camping out in a tent on what looked like a parking lot.

"Wait, you wrote that?"

He took the article and read it out loud. His voice got louder when he reached the part that read, "*But they also revolutionized the business, embracing the Internet, encouraging fans to trade tapes, and playing long, convoluted sets that captivated an audience bored by Top-40 hits. A three-day festival to mark the millennium in the Florida Everglades clogged highways all over the state—and remains, according to many fans, the pinnacle of the band's career.* "I was there!"

"No kidding," she said, trying to inject a little enthusiasm into her voice.

She wasn't sure why his fandom surprised her, except that she fully understood the breadth of what this meant. Phish Phans weren't like ordinary music lovers. They were intense, proud and committed to the point of, well, fanaticism. She'd known a few Phish Phans and nothing drove them quite so mad as a chance to travel and commune with fellow devotees.

Lucky for Anne—who wanted to spend more time with Mike, not less—the band had split up shortly after the Saratoga concert. It wasn't like he was going to be road-tripping to see them again any time in her future.

"You didn't like them?" he asked, undeniably shocked.

"I never actually heard the band that night," she confessed. "My article was just about the fans and traffic congestion."

"Well," he said, bestowing a slightly condescending smile on her that she decided not to take personally, lest it ruin the rest of their evening. "You did a great job. I can't believe I have your article in my book. It's w—"

"Weird? Yeah," she said, closing the scrapbook and covering her mouth with her hand to stifle a yawn.

"Wow, it's late," he said. "I'm boring you with all these books. Let me walk you home."

"I'm not bored," she said, and she meant it. She reached out and touched his hand and the honesty of her words seemed to relax him as if she'd just given him more wine. "I wish I had such well-preserved chronicles of my life to share with you. I have a half-dozen shoe boxes on shelves in my closet overflowing with random photographs and keepsakes, as well as a dusty stack of yearbooks, but their nonexistent organization might drive you crazy."

"You drive me crazy." He tossed aside the book that was between them, and pulled her close. "If you can forgive the fact than I'm a Phish Phan, I can overlook that you're not a pack rat like me."

"Always back to the rats," she muttered, but he cut off her joke with a kiss that was infinitely sweeter than the wine—and undeniably hotter.

Once again, Mike cued right into her body's natural rhythms. He moved like she moved, wanted like she wanted. His kiss possessed the pressure of both uncertainty and need, a combination more heady than alcohol and more addictive than chocolate. He cupped her cheeks with his hands, and as the kiss deepened, his grip tightened, as if he was afraid to move his touch beyond the safety of her face.

And yet, his longing seeped into her through his fingertips and caused a curl of arousal to sweep through her system. Beneath her blouse, her nipples tightened against her bra and her heartbeat accelerated. The mattress, so soft and inviting, dipped beneath them, but when she slid her hand down his arm, she could feel his muscles clenching to keep them upright.

When they came up for air, he didn't go far. He touched his forehead to hers. His breathing, labored and uneven, testified to a powerful want he only barely contained.

"I think I'd better walk you home now."

"Yeah," she managed, her mouth suddenly dry. "I think you'd better."

He took her hand. She stopped long enough to pet Sirus and grab the coat she'd worn on the walk, then they walked downstairs. The journey took no more than five minutes from the moment he'd pulled her off the bed to the second she'd unlocked her door. Maybe there was something to be said for long goodbyes.

"What are you doing this weekend?" he asked.

She turned, elated that he wanted to spend more time with her. "I have some work to do, but I was going to try to find someone to watch the Syracuse game with."

His eyes widened. "Basketball?"

"Yes," she said, with a mocking edge of outrage.

His smile lit those dreamy blue eyes of his to such brightness, she was sure the residual shine was going to keep her up all night long.

"Want to watch together?"

She shoved her hands on her hips, disbelieving. From his scrapbooks, she'd learned that Michael played both baseball and football in his formative years, but she'd had no idea he was a basketball fan. "Really? You follow Syracuse?"

"My father went to school there," he explained. "I grew up on it."

Even after spending hours learning everything she thought she could possibly know about him, he'd surprised her yet again. "Then, yeah, I'd love to watch the game with you."

"My place or yours?" he asked.

Anne thought it over. There were a million reasons why his

place was the better choice, but the one that made her decision for her was much more elemental.

"Yours," she said.

He did, after all, keep his television in the bedroom.

On the weekends, Anne hated to worry about the time. Watches and clocks seemed antithetical to the act of relaxation. During workdays, she kept a constant eye on the hours and minutes while she made appointments, attended hearings or escaped the wrath of Pamela by arriving early to each and every staff meeting. But aware of (and looking forward to) her scheduled date with Michael to watch the game, she'd spent her Saturday keenly cognizant of her schedule. Forty minutes before tip-off, she dashed into the bathroom to finish getting ready when she realized she was totally out of several essentials—including toilet paper.

Ugh.

She'd been meaning to hit a store for days now, but unless she was bargain hunting for fashionable togs, she really hated shopping. The whole act of walking up and down the aisles with a cart, glancing from side to side to determine if there was some unnecessary product not on her list but that she suddenly couldn't live without, bored her to tears. And yet, what had to be done, had to be done. She grabbed her purse and car keys. She'd reached the door when she realized she'd forgotten the unopened credit card offer she'd been using as a makeshift list. By the time she hit the door to the stairs, she decided to give Michael a quick call. She intended to come and go with as much speed as possible, but with traffic, she couldn't be sure she'd make it to his place at the prearranged time.

"Hey, Michael."

"Hey," he replied.

She loved how his voice seemed to drop an octave whenever she called him on the phone. Not that his natural speaking voice wasn't a sensual, sexy baritone, but even after a couple of weeks of seeing each other, the surprise of hearing her on the other end of the line evoked a natural response in him that reminded her of their kisses—deep and heavy with anticipation for so much more.

"I might be late coming over," she said. "I've been putting off a trip to Target for a week now and I'm running out of basics. I'll come up as soon as I'm back."

"Have you left yet?" he asked.

She'd just reached the lobby. She gave the couple from 4-E a wave while they retrieved their mail from the boxes that lined the wall.

"I'm heading out right now."

"Well, hold up and I'll go with you. I've got to pick up a few things myself."

"Oh, okay."

Anne waited, pacing across the tiled floor and exchanging brief greetings with her neighbors as they came in and out of the building. She hadn't been looking forward to this excursion and she wasn't sure Michael's presence while she loaded up on paper towels and tampons would improve her mood any.

She'd had a rough week at work. Just yesterday she'd had to resubmit her piece on a flasher stalking elderly women in the parking lot of the popular strip mall for Pamela three times before the irascible editor deemed it "acceptable."

Her series on the victim's advocate group currently raising funds through awareness-building events at local churches had a lot more heart, but with all her other responsibilities at the crime desk, she didn't expect to polish that article until right before the deadline.

Increasingly, her work weeks had become frustrating, infuriating, and boring. Except for her trips to the courthouse and the occasional lunch with Kate, she'd been struggling with her job nearly as much as she had when she lived in San Antonio. She'd actually loved her colleagues in Texas, but had never warmed to the social life, feeling isolated by her culture and her desire to marry someone who shared her faith. Back in New York, she had a kicking social life, from her amazing friends to her burgeoning relationship with Michael, but her workdays had become close to torturous. Luckily, she had Michael's witty e-mails to brighten her lackluster days—and even better, Michael's company to irradiate her nights.

But as they were still surfing on the crests of fresh and as-of-yet unexplored attraction, the thrill of catching a glimpse of him while he walked Sirus to the park or chatting on the phone until the wee hours even though they were only one floor away would eventually wear off.

And she couldn't think of a single thing that could take the shine off a new relationship faster than a trip to the discount store.

"Ready?"

She turned, laughing when she caught sight of him. He was wearing a long sleeved navy T-shirt with a humongous orange Syracuse "S" emblazoned on the front. Taking into consideration their plans for the night, this was not unusual. What struck her as hilarious was that she was wearing exactly the same shirt.

"You've got good taste," he said, plucking at her sleeve.

"We're going to look like dweebs if we go to the store dressed like bookends," Anne insisted. "Go change."

He barked with laughter. "You change. I like my shirt."

She groaned with frustration, grabbed Michael by the hand, and dragged him, willingly, out to her car. Scowling at him had the absolute opposite effect that it would have had, say, on her brother. Anne had been famous in her youth for her powerfully persuasive dirty looks. Whenever she cast an annoyed glare at Michael, however, his smile only deepened.

"Did you read what the sports page had to say about Coach Boeheim and his reliance on the McNamara for the offensive game?" he asked as soon as she'd pulled out onto State.

"The sports writer for the *Daily Journal* hasn't seen a live basketball game since Dave Bing played for the Pistons," Anne replied. "This team has chops. If they can get in the zone, this game's going to be a blowout and we'll be going to the championships."

Michael shook his head. "I don't know. In the last game, we were 3–for–10 on free throws in the first half and finished the game twenty points down. That kind of performance isn't going to get us into the Sweet 16."

For the duration of the drive, they talked stats and projections. Anne couldn't help but appreciate a man who could talk sports to a woman and not assume she couldn't match his knowledge on the subject. They argued over the coach's strategy in the last game and the behavior of an opposing point guard after he was fouled by an overzealous Orangeman, but the conversation quickened the drive and made the traffic seem less congested. By the time they entered the store and dislodged a cart from the cage-like train by the front door, they'd moved on to discussing Mike's projections for tonight's battle with Notre Dame after giving each other a quick run down of what they each needed from the store.

Anne left out any details regarding feminine hygiene products.

"Why don't we split up? I'll run over to the pharmacy side while you pick up that present for your niece."

"You don't want to go to the toy section?" he asked with exaggerated shock. "Come on! What's the point of having nieces and nephews if you can't use it as an excuse to check out the latest from Hasbro and Mattel?"

She couldn't resist. Rolling her eyes, she followed Mike to the back of the store where he pretended to be blinded by the overwhelming wash of pink in the Barbie aisle. He spent an inordinate amount of time scanning the Hot Wheels cars for any he didn't already have and then dragged her into the Star Wars collection so he could regale her with his best James Earl Jones imitation by repeating, "Luke, I am your father" until her stomach cramped from laughing.

She coaxed him into buying his niece a cool arts-and-crafts kit that would allow her to paint and bedazzle her own jewelry box. They were about to head to the adult sections of the store when he caught sight of a wire cage filled with inflated balls. Bearing the likenesses of Johnny Depp as Captain Jack Sparrow from *Pirates of the Caribbean* and bright red Elmos, the balls proved irresistible. Before she could stop him, he'd squeezed one out of the bin and was dribbling up the aisle as if he were channeling Eric Devendorf, one of Syracuse's best players.

"You're open," he shouted, tossing the ball to Anne.

She caught it out of instinct, but hesitated to play this game. Not that anyone was around. The toy section was relatively deserted. And since not a single red-shirted employee was milling about, there really wasn't any harm in joining his fantasy.

So she dribbled. She traveled a little on her way toward him, but feinted adequately and then threw the ball high into the air so that it arced right back into the bin.

"Three pointer for sure!" she shouted.

"There was a foul in there somewhere," he insisted.

"Want a free throw?"

"Most definitely."

Anne watched Mike grab another ball out of the bin and then back up a sufficient distance so that landing the shot would not be an easy feat, particularly since the balls weighed considerably less than a standard basketball. She'd simply made a lucky shot.

But with the shot, so sunk the memory of her absolutely horrendous week. Mike's infectious silliness had helped her shed the layer of discontent she hadn't realized she was wearing.

They declared the game a draw after a mother flanked by twin boys turned the corner into their makeshift court. On the way to the pharmacy, Mike slipped his arm around her waist and kissed her cheek.

"Glad I came along now?" he asked.

She blushed. Had her reluctance to invite him along been obvious?

"It wasn't personal. I just wasn't hyped up about having the guy I'm dating see me buy toilet paper, among other things."

He squeezed her waist and said, "Well, I can use new boxers, so we'll be even."

That they were, she couldn't help but think as they progressed into the men's section.

Even.

Balanced.

Yin and yang.

And as much as the idea thrilled her, it also scared her. Because if things didn't work out, the loss would be greater than any other she'd ever experienced. And if they made it, her life would be forever changed.

Eleven

"PARDON ME, BUT IS THIS SEAT TAKEN?"

Anne barely glanced up, engrossed in reading information on the tour's next stop. She lifted her bag off the chair beside her and gave what she hoped was a polite nod to whomever needed a place to sit.

The cool Egyptian air blew across the Nile, ruffling the guide book her friend, Adele, had bought. Anne had been to the Middle East many times, but this was her first trip to Egypt and she wanted to make sure she didn't miss anything. As Adele had gone downstairs to their cruise-ship cabin to grab sweaters for them both, Anne leaned back into her deck chair, closed her eyes, relaxed . . . and tried not to think about Michael.

Before she'd met him at the Jeff Tweedy concert and long before they'd become joined at the proverbial hip, she and Adele had planned a spring trip. A friend from her yoga class at the Y, Adele lived only a block from Anne's place on State Street and shared her love of international travel. After twisting their bodies into proverbial pretzels for an hour, they'd grab a smoothie at a nearby juice bar and chit-chatted about all the places they'd been and where they still wanted to go. When Anne had gotten a call from the local chapter of the United Jewish Federation asking her to attend a conference in Tel Aviv, she'd jumped at the chance. And since the dates coincided with her vacation with Adele, they'd included Egypt in their itinerary, highlighted by this amazing cruise from Aswan to Luxor.

The hardest part had been leaving Michael—and she wasn't sure how she felt about that.

In her entire life, she couldn't remember *ever* second-guessing plans for a vacation on account of a guy. Michael had encouraged her to enjoy the trip, even sitting side-by-side with her on the couch with his laptop to research her itineraries and stops. And yet, as each day until her departure ticked away, a piece of her heart seemed to tear off as well.

And that, more than anything, frightened her.

Michael had told her about his most painful breakup—the one that had resulted in his adopting Sirus. At the time, she'd been glad she didn't have a similar story. No dashed expectations or broken hearts in her past. Well, not like his, anyway.

Her relationships had often ended before they began. More often than not, she'd fall head over heels for some great guy who, in the end, just wanted to be friends. The last thing she wanted with Michael was a replay of that scenario. From the get-go, the mutual attraction between them crackled. They shared a love of music, sports, their apartment building, and various ethnic foods. Both career-minded and family-oriented, Michael was everything Anne could have wished for.

Except . . .

Maybe he'd been a little too supportive of her tour of the Middle East. He also hadn't been in touch much. Yes, he'd answered her e-mails and texts, but not with his usual silliness or cleverness. He'd been a bit terse. Almost cold.

"So, do you feel like Cleopatra?"

Anne turned to the man who'd spoken. She blinked a few times, trying to remember when he'd sat on the deck chair beside her.

"I'm sorry?" she asked, wanting to make sure that he had, indeed, been speaking to her.

"Cleopatra? You know, the queen known around the world as the tempting seductress who sailed down the Nile on her barge?"

Anne closed her book. "Wow, that's the best pickup line you've got?"

He rolled his eyes at his own corniness. "I'm trying to flirt in a foreign language. It's no easy feat. My name is Samir Moadab. You may call me Sam."

He pointed to his nametag, which identified him as one of the tour guides assigned to the cruise. She placed his accent immediately as native, though the country of origin listed on his tag read *Madrid.*

She shouldn't have noticed that much, but Sam was a hard guy to ignore. His fathomless black eyes, set against skin tinted to a rich burnt umber by generations of his ancestors living life in the desert sun, locked with hers, and his smile, just one curve shy of cocky, accentuated his square jawline. Sam was a hunk.

And Anne wasn't interested.

This fact, more than his physical perfection, nearly knocked the wind out of her. Before Michael, she would have at least been flattered by his attention. Before Michael, she might have flirted with him just for the fun of it.

But now, all she felt was a nagging guilt for talking to him, even though Michael was thousands of miles away and possibly losing interest in her the longer she was gone.

Well, she couldn't be pathetic about it. She had a very good-looking guy going out of his way to flirt with her. She had nothing to lose by being friendly.

"Anne Miller," she said, taking his proffered hand.

"Like the American Broadway star," he said.

She sat back, surprised. She hadn't heard a statement like that from anyone younger than her grandmother in years. "You know Anne Miller?"

"My mother loves American cinema and theater. When I went to Columbia for university, she wanted me to hang out on Broadway so I could meet the great stars. I didn't have the heart to remind her that few of them are still alive."

"Hm," she said, trying to quell any sound of how impressed she was. "Columbia?"

His educational pedigree, which she soon learned started with a degree in public relations from the University of Madrid and continued with graduate studies at both Columbia and Oxford, solidified her decision to keep talking to him. She couldn't help but wonder how a man with his background ended up as a tour guide on a Nile cruise. And if he happened to give her a few hints about great places to visit while here, so much the better.

"Academics do not exactly, what is the term, bring home the bacon? My sister works as a tour guide and she does very well financially, so since I have some very important things to save up for, I thought I'd spend my break making some extra money."

"Extra money is always good," she agreed.

She scanned the deck, wondering what was taking Adele so long. Not that she didn't find Samir interesting. She did. And that alone made her insides wriggle.

"So what brings you to Egypt?" he asked.

She smiled and with no sign of Adele coming up the stairs, she replied simply, "I love to travel."

"Do you often?"

"I used to," she said. "My job now keeps me pretty tied to one place."

She explained about her career as a journalist and her invitation to attend the Tel Aviv conference for the UJF. Sam not only listened intently, but he asked compelling questions and imparted his opinions on matters ranging from journalistic integrity to his recent adventure navigating the *Mahene Yehudah* market in Jerusalem.

"There's one place, called Marzipan, that you have to try," he insisted, leaning onto his elbows so that his face was quite close to hers. "The best chocolate rugelach you've ever had. You will be—excuse the term, but it's the only one that fits—orgasmic with delight."

Adele finally came back with the sweaters, her timing exquisite as a chill had raced down Anne's spine. She made quick introductions, hoping that Samir would now turn his attention to her rather adorable—and single—friend. His greeting didn't fall down in the charming department, but in seconds, he'd zeroed back in on Anne.

"So tell me, what sights are you hoping to see once we reach Luxor?"

"Are you offering to be our guide?" Adele asked, her tone sensual. Clearly, she recognized a good-looking guy as much as Anne had, but she had nothing keeping her back from making the most of it.

"I wish I could, but I already have a group counting on me to take them around. May I?" he said, asking for the travel guide Anne still clutched in her lap.

She relinquished the book, which he flipped through confidently as if he'd read the guide several times and had no need of the index. He produced a pencil from his pocket and proceeded to point out all the best spots for them to visit, including quite a few off-the-beaten-path restaurants and shops frequented by the locals that he sketched onto the removable map.

Anne found it increasingly difficult not to respond to his probing questions and insightful deductions. Under any other circumstances, she might have been inordinately flattered by his attention. She might have even flirted back rather than filtering every word she said through a screen of "what would Michael think if he heard me say that?"

Charming, intelligent, and knowledgeable, Sam was impossible to ignore, though she did try several times to think of a way to change seats with Adele so that her friend was the one noticing his powerfully built arms peeking out from the cuffs of his rolled-up, long-sleeve shirt instead of her. Looking at Samir's arms only made her miss Michael's arms—which made her want to slap herself silly.

"Would you ladies like a drink? I know the bartender," he said, smile dazzling.

"Sure," Adele answered.

The minute he left, Adele said, "He's totally into you."

Anne picked up her bag, stood, and forcibly moved her friend into her chair. The deck wasn't overflowing with people, so she threw her stuff on the chair now on her other side so that when he returned, Sam would have no choice but sit beside Adele.

"I'm not into him," Anne insisted.

Adele pursed her lips. "Because of Michael? He's a half a world away. You haven't even slept with him yet. There's nothing wrong with a vacation romance."

"No, there isn't," Anne said, securing every button on her sweater until she was covered up to her neck. "So you go right ahead and have one."

Adele leaned over and undid the top two buttons before Anne could swat her hands away.

"You'll thank me," Adele said. "Buttoning up only emphasizes that bosom of yours."

Anne looked down and agreed, so she undid one more button, just to be safe.

Before Michael, a fly-by romance with a sexy Egyptian man would not have been out of the question, though she wasn't one to sleep with strangers. Ordinarily, she enjoyed socializing and flirting, knowing it wouldn't lead to anything life-changing.

But Michael was in the picture. And on the canvas. And in the frame. He'd injected himself into every element of the portrait of her life—and probably without even meaning to. She couldn't help but wonder if he'd worked his way in on his own or she'd simply put him there because she wanted so much to have a man in her life.

In the past few days, his e-mails had been a little less frequent and, though she'd pretended not to notice, shorter and without his trademark humor. He'd written about Sirus's trip to the vet, but had not asked about the spa in Cairo where she and Adele had stayed for the first three days of their trip. She'd volunteered the information in her reply, but he hadn't answered before they'd left Aswan. She wanted to believe that time differences and a busy work schedule kept him from responding, but she couldn't help but wonder if in the time she'd been gone, he'd found someone new.

Or else, just lost interest.

Sam returned with the drinks and dutifully took his seat beside Adele, though he made a point to engage Anne in every conversation until it was time for them to change clothes for dinner. As they made their way to the stairwell that led to their room, he invited them to join him and his tour group for dinner. Anne had the refusal on the tip of her tongue when Adele enthusiastically accepted.

With a satisfied grin, Sam departed.

"What did you do that for?" Anne demanded.

"You said I could have him," Adele reminded her. "I can't do that unless I see him again."

Adele dressed to the nines for dinner, and yet, once they reached the table set for twelve, Sam somehow managed to maneuver so that he was sitting beside Anne and Adele was on the opposite end of the long table with a Spanish man and his brother who were on their first visit to the area.

"You know," Anne said. "I should probably tell you that I have a boyfriend."

The words sounded incredibly foreign to her, but nice at the same time. The way that Sam's eyes darkened with disappointment was nice, too. But he recovered quickly.

"Of course you do," he said. "You're quite beautiful."

"And you're quite good at this bilingual flirting."

"I try," he said, draping his napkin across his lap as the waiter brought the first course of tehina salad served with fresh baked flat bread. "And since full disclosure seems to be important to you, I'm engaged to be married in two weeks."

She nearly choked on the water she'd just sipped.

"Wow," she said. "I never would have spotted you for a dog."

He laughed and shook his head. "I'm sorry, a what?"

She explained the American colloquialism.

"Then this is not a compliment," he concluded.

"No," she replied.

"Does it help if I tell you the marriage is to a cousin and it was arranged by our parents when we were five years old?"

She narrowed her gaze, trying to determine if he was telling her the truth, but then she decided that it really didn't matter. Sam was charming and attractive and his attention shined a spotlight on Anne's feelings for Michael, which she hadn't quite realized had deepened so much and so quickly. His absence was like a constant ache in the pit of her stomach.

"Only if you accept that I'm not the type of woman who steals another woman's husband, no matter the circumstances of their engagement. So, what if, since we've *both* established that we're both unavailable, we enjoy our dinner?"

And they did. In fact, they enjoyed dessert too, and drinks in the nightclub. They crossed paths at breakfast the next morning and before she and Adele climbed into a taxi at their first stop, he chatted with their driver to make sure he not only was a great guide for the day, but also that he wouldn't try to add any unexpected charges or trips into disreputable areas.

Anne couldn't help but think that Samir's arranged marriage was going to make a very lucky woman out of his cousin.

She and Adele spent the day sightseeing and shopping. When they passed a large hotel owned by a British conglomerate, Anne used the opportunity to pick up the strong cell signal from their tower and called Mike. She'd already punched in all the numbers when she calculated the time difference and realized she was calling him at seven o'clock in the morning.

But as it was a workday, he answered on the second ring.

"Michael, it's Anne. I'm in Luxor."

Was it her imagination or did he hesitate a long time before saying, "Hey."

Anne's mouth dried. That "hey" didn't sound like the greeting that used to make her blood steam within her veins. It sounded uncertain. Maybe even disinterested.

"So," she said, pushing aside her insecurities. "What's going on?"

"Just getting ready for work."

Another pause. Didn't he know that connecting with him while halfway across the globe was no easy feat?

She turned the topic to one she knew he'd jump all over. "How's Sirus?"

When he replied with, "Fine," her heart cracked.

And until that moment, she hadn't fully realized how deeply into her system that Michael Davoli had insinuated himself.

Now, she knew it was very, very deep. And under the circumstances, she couldn't contain her rage—not only for Michael, for being so blasé about her long-distance call, but at herself for feeling so much for a man who after only a few weeks apart, no longer gave a damn about her.

Twelve

"DID YOU FALL DOWN AND HIT YOUR HEAD?"

Mike looked up. He'd been staring down into his beer, confessing his soul to Nikki, and this is how she treated his confusion? With insults?

"No," he said, annoyed.

"Then where is this nonsense coming from?"

"I wish I knew," he confessed. Ever since Anne's call, Michael had been questioning his sanity. Every moment since she'd been gone had been like a kick in the gut and yet when she'd contacted him, he'd been dismissive, even a little rude. For nearly a week, he'd tried to figure out why he'd acted so strangely, but unable to come to any conclusion on his own, he'd asked Nikki's opinion.

But from her expression, he doubted she was going to do anymore than tell him off for being such a jerk.

"You knew she was going on this trip," she reminded him.

"I know! When she first told me about the trip, I was excited for her. Even a little jealous. You know I love to travel. But I figured I'd be busy at work and that missing her might be nice after being with her so much lately. I mean, what were three weeks in the scope of my whole life? She's been looking forward to this for a long time."

119

Nikki nodded in agreement as she fished a perfectly triangular nacho out of the bowl in front of them. She scooped salsa onto it, but paused before putting it into her mouth.

"See, that's the Michael Davoli I know and love. Practical. Optimistic. Generous. This new selfish guy who blows off his girl-friend when she calls him from halfway across the world is really pissing me off."

She ate the chip with a loud crunch, chewed, and washed it all down with a swig of beer while Mike pondered her words.

Never in his life had he been so confused by his own behavior. Mike didn't consider himself a complicated guy. When good things happened, he was happy. When bad things happened, he was sad. When presented with an injustice or problem, he did what he could to solve the situation with minimal conflict and contention. His parents had always called him their peacemaker and lauded him for patience and insights beyond his years.

He'd always given his Tourette's credit for this aspect of his personality. The disorder had forced him to grow up fast and develop keen negotiation skills when dealing with teachers, class-mates, and friends who were often confused by his behavior.

But his reaction to Anne's absence flummoxed him. He'd gone from missing her like crazy to resenting her phone calls and giv-ing only short shrift to her e-mails. He couldn't blame work. Things were no crazier than usual. He couldn't put off his reac-tions on other social commitments, either. Since she'd left, he'd blown off every invitation he'd received. If not for Nikki hijacking his car keys and driving him to this Mexican joint for a serious talk, he would have been home alone with Sirus, staring at the television, and seeing nothing, saying nothing. Feeling nothing.

It was pathetic.

And it was all Anne's fault.

"I'm not being selfish," he said, remembering Nikki's last insult as he motioned to the waitress to bring them a fresh pitcher.

"What do you call it then when you treat a girl like dirt just because she had the audacity to leave you?"

He shook his head. "That's not what this is about. Maybe we just jumped into this relationship too quickly. I mean, I only moved into the building a little over two months ago. And if you count the two weeks before we actually started dating, we've only been together for four. The fact that I feel so strongly about her after so short a time . . . it's crazy."

"So you think the best way to counteract the craziness of love is by blowing her off?"

"I'm not blowing her off," he insisted, knowing it was a lie. "And we're not in love."

Nikki looked skeptical, but remained silent as the waitress brought them new drinks and refilled the chip bowl. Mike reached for a warm, crispy tortilla, but then tossed it back. He shouldn't be eating. He shouldn't be drinking. Neither activity sat well with him. Everything in his body felt off. His eyes ached from over blinking. His neck had tightened so that each involuntary twitch sent a zap a pain down his spine.

"You could be in love," Nikki said once the waitress disappeared. "At some point, I mean. She's the kind of girl you could fall in love with, right?"

"Sure," he conceded. "She's independent. Intelligent. Beautiful, inside and out. She's a little messy, but no one is perfect. But I don't want to screw things up with her by jumping in too fast. Maybe we just need to be friends for a while longer. Get to know each other better."

"Isn't that what you've been doing?" Nikki challenged.

"Yeah, but, when I'm with her, I can't help wanting more, you know?"

"So when you're not with her, you treat her like she doesn't matter," Nikki clarified. "Yeah, that makes a lot of sense."

Her sarcasm wasn't lost on him, but if Mike couldn't unravel the tangled web of his emotions, how could Nikki? Maybe he needed to get out. Not with friends, but alone. With Sirus. He should go hiking this weekend. Grab a tent and some provisions and do a vision quest of sorts. Maybe the crisp spring air, wide open spaces, and vigorous climbs through challenging terrain would help him see what to do next.

Beyond the obvious.

"Where is Anne today?" Nikki asked, her tone light.

She might not be able to read his mind, but she had instincts that were impeccable. She was backing off at precisely the right time.

"She just left Egypt," he replied. "I think she's in Jerusalem until day after tomorrow, then she comes home by Sunday night."

"You going to call her?"

"When she gets back, of course."

Nikki rolled her eyes. "Why wait? Call her now."

He checked his watch and calculated the time difference. It was after midnight. But Anne was a night owl. He could send an e-mail or attempt an instant message.

"Do you have your laptop?" he asked.

Nikki pulled the device out of her oversized bag. "Never leave home without it."

"Think they have free wi-fi here?"

Nikki pointed to a sign on the wall that claimed they did.

He had no more excuses left.

The chime on Anne's laptop drew her out of a restless sleep. She glanced at Adele's bed, but then remembered that she'd already flown home. Anne had considered doing the same, but in a fit of self-reliance, had instead stuck to her original plan to remain in Israel on her own and visit some of her college friends. She couldn't blow off seeing them again after all these years just because the guy she was dating—the guy she thought she was falling in love with—was acting like a brat.

The laptop chimed again and this time, she recognized the sound as an instant message. She opened her program and saw that someone with the screen name *KickinNik* was trying to get a hold of her. She didn't remember knowing anyone with that monicker, but now that she was wide awake, she might as well answer.

YofiToffl: Who r u?
KickinNik: It's Mike. Using Nikki's computer.

Anne sat up and dragged the laptop entirely into her lap. This was the first time that Mike had initiated contact with her in over two weeks. Though it had contradicted every instinct she possessed, she'd continued to e-mail and call him as they'd prearranged before her trip. A few conversations had been just like old times—chatty and fun. Most had been distant and cold. But after the phone call outside the British hotel, she'd resolved to stop fretting over his attitude and instead enjoy her vacation.

She'd never forgive herself if she let Michael's drama dampen her trip. But now, he was reaching out. She couldn't ignore him. She didn't want to.

YofiToffi: Glad you IM'd. Where r u 2?
KickinNik: El Mariachi's. Came for cervezas and chips. Thought about you. Don't even know if you like Mexican food.

Anne laughed. They'd sampled quite a few cuisines together since they started dating, but they'd yet to hit El Mariachi's.

YofiToffi: I like margaritas.
KickinNik: Ah, I remember.
YofiToffi: El Mariachi's has a great verde sauce.
KickinNik: That's what Nikki said. She says hello. Wants to know if you've met any hot Israeli guys.

Anne hesitated. Technically, Samir was Jewish, but he was Egyptian in ancestry and Spanish in nationality. The idea of torturing Mike a little appealed to her on a very girlish, very childish level, but she beat the mind game back. Now wasn't the time to indulge in silliness. Mike was back to his old self and she had every intention of enjoying him while it lasted.

YofiToffi: No hot Israelis. I must not put out the right vibe. Tell Nikki she'll have to come with me next time and find them for herself.
KickinNik: How about if I go with you next time?
YofiToffi: You want to find hot Israeli guys?
KickinNik: No, I just don't want to be without you for so long again.

There. There it was. Anne's eyes suddenly burned with all the tears she'd dammed behind her eyes for the past couple of weeks. She'd refused to cry—refused to give in to the intense grief of loss when she hadn't been entirely sure what was going on in Mike's head—or more accurately, his heart. She wasn't going to start now, even if one drop did spill down her cheek and splash onto the space bar.

YofiToffi: I'll be home in two days. Any plans for the weekend?
Kickin Nick: Need to clear my head. Probably a hike with Sirus. Will be out of touch. Call when you get back?
YofiToffi: Will do.
KickinNick: Sleep well.

Anne typed a reciprocal good night, and then logged off. Yes, she'd sleep well—probably for the first time in days.

Anne's plane was delayed, so she didn't reach her apartment until one o'clock in the morning on the same Monday she was due back at work. She grabbed five hours of sleep, then dragged herself out of bed, infused her system with strong coffee, and then left to deal with traffic and criminal court. She'd hoped to see Mike, or hear from him, maybe find a note saying, "Welcome home," slipped under her door or, his preferred method, stuck dead center for all the neighbors to see. But even when she opened her e-mail inbox at the office, she was disappointed.

She worried a little, wondering if he'd made it back from his hike. In the break room, she found a few copies of the weekend edition and checked the weather forecast. It has been a little chilly, but mostly clear with sunshine. Maybe she should have knocked on his door this morning. So he knew she'd made it back safely herself.

Of course, he could have easily knocked on her door. Why was it up to her to make the first move?

She went to a staff meeting, perturbed that she was unprepared for all that had happened in her absence, including a sex scandal involving local church leaders and a serial rapist operating on the fringe between Schenectady and Albany. With no sympathy for Anne's jet lag and lack of sleep, Pamela ordered her straight to the courthouse so she could file updates on both stories.

Anne entered the courthouse cafeteria around twelve-thirty in hopes of snagging a bagel when Kate waved her over to her table.

"You're back!" Kate said, rising half out of her seat to give Anne a hug.

"I am," she verified, as much for herself as for her favorite prosecutor. "At least my passport says I am. I feel like I left part of myself somewhere over the Atlantic."

"Yeah, your body clock. Sit down," she said, gesturing toward an empty seat. "This isn't Villa Italia, but the coffee isn't bad."

Anne shook her head. "I've already swallowed both Juan Valdes and his donkey since this morning. I was just hoping for something I can eat quickly."

"You have five minutes to chat," Kate assured her, checking her own watch. "You need sugar and carbonation. Sit tight."

Kate returned with a huge soda filled with ice, as well as a cherry Danish that didn't look half bad for something that had been sitting in the cafeteria since this morning. Anne picked at the filling with a plastic fork, hoping the few carbs would give her a boost to get her through the rest of the day.

Kate was appropriately curious about her trip, but aware of Anne's exhaustion, kept her questions easy and then took up the conversational slack by filling Anne in on all she'd missed in the criminal courts over the past three weeks.

"Is it my imagination, or did the criminals rejoice my leaving the country by causing more mayhem?" she asked.

Kate laughed. "Just your imagination, I'm afraid. It's a steady stream. Can you get a good sleep tonight or do you have plans with that young man of yours?"

Anne didn't have enough energy to muster a smile. Normally, any mention of Mike made her cheeks hurt. She'd drifted through her last couple of days overseas and the whole trip home bolstered by their last instant-message interaction. He hadn't seemed entirely back to his old self, but he'd contacted her—and he'd confessed that he missed her. These were both very good things. But even though she'd agreed to be the one to call him when she got home, she was still slightly disappointed that he hadn't made any attempt at checking on her first.

"I think I just need sleep," she said, pushing away her insecurities. "I'm not going to be very good company for anyone when I can barely form a coherent thought. And Pamela, of course, wants me to file both these updates this afternoon, even though three other reporters have been following the cases since I was gone."

"And I thought my boss was an old taskmaster."

"Trust me, my boss instructed your boss on the proper means to torture underlings."

With Kate's help, Anne got the quotes she needed for the articles, but not wanting to return to the office and face Pamela's impatient glare as deadline time approached, she remained in the cafeteria in order to write after Kate left for a hearing. She returned to the office long enough to put the stories to bed, then headed home. By the time she finally made it through her door, she was too tired to think. She tossed off her clothes and stumbled into bed, her eyes shut before her head hit the pillow.

It was nearly midnight before she woke. Hungry, she rummaged in the kitchen before realizing she had nothing in the cupboard but peanut butter and crackers, which she washed down with a cup of instant hot chocolate. She took a quick shower and then went back to sleep, waking when her alarm clock rang at seven.

This morning, she found a Post-it note on her door.

Hope you're home safe and sound. Sorry I didn't call yesterday. Meetings all day. Figured you were dead to the world by the time I got home. Drinks tonight? Michael.

Anne's insides warmed. A surge of adrenaline raged through her system, giving her the boost of energy she needed to punch through another busy day. She dug into her bag for a pen, jotted down a time and place and then jogged upstairs to adhere it to his door, where he'd find it when he came home.

Time swirled by in a cloud of anticipation. She finished work early, stopped by the market for a few essentials, and then went home to shower and primp. She'd missed Michael more than she'd expected to—honestly, more than she'd wanted to. She'd been looking for a man to share her life with, but years of fruitless searches had made her wary. It wasn't wise to put too much hope in a relationship that hadn't had much time to root.

But Anne didn't have the genetic makeup required to move slowly and think things to death—not in her personal life. To live life, she had to grab it. And she was going to start by grabbing Michael with both hands and hoping she never, ever had to let go.

From her closet, she selected a filmy blouse in a swirl of blues and paired it with jeans. Because the weather was nice, she slipped her tanned feet into high-heel wedges. She spent a little extra time with her makeup and even spritzed a warm, amber-based perfume onto the pulse points of her neck and wrists. She grabbed her cell phone, purse, and jacket and was headed toward the door when a knock stopped her.

Glancing through the peephole, she saw Michael.

Excited, she opened the door. She launched herself into his arms, her body primed to experience the familiar comfort of his embrace and a moment later, perhaps, the much-anticipated taste of his amazing kisses.

She got neither. He hardly moved, bracing his hands on her back to facilitate putting her at a safe distance once she broke away.

"Hi," she said, confused and a little annoyed. "What's wrong?"

He slid his hands into his pockets. "Nothing, I'm just . . . I got home early and thought we could walk to the bar together. I don't know. Maybe it was a bad idea."

Anne marched back into her apartment, her rage increasing. She was still jet-lagged and reeling from his odd behavior while she was overseas. After their last exchange, she hadn't expected to deal with his drama when she got home—not when he'd invited her out for a date.

This was not *her* Michael.

Her Michael was decisive, like the night he'd hugged her on the street corner when they'd first met or when he'd kissed her on her couch before they'd gone on their first official date. Her Michael did sweet things for her, like dispose of dead rodents and cook gourmet Italian dinners. Her Michael sent her funny e-mails and played basketball with her in discount stores and didn't make fun of her excitement over watching *24*, knitting in a bar, or Syracuse basketball.

This guy certainly looked like the man she'd kissed so passionately before leaving for Israel and Egypt, but he wasn't acting like himself at all.

"Michael, what the hell is going on with you? I've been gone for three weeks. Three weeks, I must point out, in which you barely spoke to me. Then you send me nice instant messages right before I come home, invite me out for drinks to welcome me back, and now you can barely stand to touch me?"

"Barely stand—? That's not it," he insisted, standing up straighter and meeting her gaze, though his expression was wholly unreadable.

"Then what is it? If you've got something to say, say it—but I'll give you fair warning—if it starts with, *It's not you, it's me*, you can save it for someone else, understand?"

Thirteen

OH, HE UNDERSTOOD. Loud and clear. But no matter how she'd anticipated the direction of this discussion, he couldn't change his mind. He'd thought long and hard about their relationship over the weekend and had made his decision.

Not that it had been easy. He did not doubt that Anne was a remarkable woman. Funny. Sexy. Smart. In the short time they'd had together before she left for Egypt, they'd had a great time. But when she was around—heck, even when she wasn't—the world spun around him, dipping and diving like an out-of-control roller coaster. They needed time to slow down, ease into things.

He schooled his face into a logical and reasonable expression. "I just think we should slow down for a little while. Get our bearings, you know?"

Her scowl nearly melted the skin off his skull. "No, Michael, I don't know. Why don't you explain it to me?"

Mike took a deep breath and gestured toward the couch. She sat, but instantly crossed both her arms and her legs.

Not a good sign.

He shut the door behind him. Though the possibility of a quick escape crossed his mind, he didn't want to leave Anne. Breaking up with her was not what he was doing. Not in any way, shape, or form. In fact, he was trying to keep them together.

He'd had all weekend to think about his relationship with Anne and one thing was very clear—he cared about her. Deeply. And that was the problem. He was too into her for someone who'd been on her radar for so short a time. He'd missed her too much when she was gone, and yet, he'd acted like an idiot during most of their interactions. He'd come to the conclusion that he simply wasn't ready for the kind of intimacy he and Anne were headed toward.

"Every woman I've ever dated for any period of time was a friend first. I mean, I met them that way and we got to know each other as friends before we got exclusive. You and I skipped that part—and it's my fault. We went straight into a relationship, without stopping to think. Without stopping to get to know each other. As friends."

Her scowl had not softened one iota. "So that's your usual *modus operandi* with women? Good to know. But, how exactly has that worked out for you so far?"

As she'd intended, her sarcasm sliced straight through him.

"That's not the point," he deflected.

She chuckled, but the sound was entirely without humor.

"You know what? You're right. It's not the point. If you don't want to take your past into consideration when attempting to build a future, that's your choice. I, on the other hand, have tried to learn from my mistakes."

She stood again, pacing around the small living space, making it seem even more cramped and cluttered. When she nearly stumbled over a still-packed suitcase, she kicked it out of her way. It thumped into her side table, rattling the lamp and dusty knick-knacks.

"Anne—"

She cut him off instantly. "No, Michael. You're being honest with me, I get that. But I need to be honest with you, too. My whole life, I've been the *friend*." She drew drawing air quotes around the word and sneered as she said it, as if being someone's friend was a fate worse than death. "You know all the cute boys in school? The popular jocks and the student-body president? I was always their very good friend. I was the funny girl who didn't blush or giggle, but treated them like real people. I was the smart chick who could help them with their homework and still talk to them about the latest stats for the Orioles. The whole time, I was secretly crushing on most of them but they never gave me a second look."

He scooted forward and grabbed the chance to prove his point. "See? I never knew that about you. There's a lot I don't know about you. And I want to learn it all—but without the pressure of trying to manage a committed relationship at the same time."

Anne shook her head. "That may sound ideal to you, Mike, but to me, it's torture. I won't live that way again. I certainly won't fall in love that way. I'm sorry, but I'm not looking for another guy friend. I've reached my quota. I'm looking for someone to share my life with. A partner. A soul mate. A lover. If you can't be those things, then I think you'd better go."

Mike gaped at her, but no matter how long he stared, she didn't flinch. She was furious. He could feel the anger radiating off her skin, even though he knew if he made any attempt to touch her, she'd freeze him out. Or punch him out.

He hadn't meant to, but in his attempt to save their relationship, he'd touched a very raw nerve. Maybe she needed time to think. He knew he did.

He rose to his feet, a dull ache clutching at his insides. He'd anticipated that this conversation might not go well, but he'd never imagined she'd ask him to leave. Not that she didn't have the right. He hadn't intended to dig into her past wounds. But this just proved his point. If he'd known more about her past relationships, he would have found a different way to say what desperately needed to be said.

He moved toward the door. He wanted to say something— anything. But when he turned, she flung her bedroom door shut with a definitive slam.

He didn't remember how he got back to his apartment. Might have been the elevator. Might have been the stairs. Even Sirus seemed to sense something was wrong because instead of greeting him with her usual frantic tail-wagging and excited bouncing, she sidled up with her head down and her tail tucked between her legs. He flopped onto the couch and the dog imme- diately jumped beside him and curled over his lap. She'd been his salvation when Lisa had left, but he didn't want her to play that role this time—mainly, because he didn't want to lose Anne.

Trouble was, he feared that he already had.

He raked his hands through his hair. He'd done a lot of soul- searching. He'd told her the truth. But maybe he shouldn't have hit her with his insights only seconds after she'd opened her door.

"Sirus, I screwed up."

The dog looked up at him, her blue eyes wide and trusting, as if she couldn't believe her master could do anything wrong. He scratched her ears, loving her all the more for her canine naïveté. But the truth was, while his delivery had sucked, his conclusions had been solid.

As he'd climbed the trails behind Sirus, he'd come to terms with the fact that the strongest emotion he felt for Anne was lust. He admired her and liked her and respected her, but none of those things haunted him in the dead of night or tortured him as they sat on his bed looking at scrapbooks or watching basketball. In his entire life, he'd never felt such a powerful pull to someone. His need for her transcended mere physical desires, though those were powerfully strong in and of themselves. If he didn't erect a few barriers, they might fall into something serious before either of them was ready.

Before he was ready.

This was the truth that hurt—the stark reality he'd faced when he'd been out in the middle of nowhere, influenced only by the sharp spring breeze, turquoise skies, and rough terrain. Anne could not be just a friend or just a lover or *just* anything. She was the whole package—the real deal. If he went full force into this relationship, there was only one inevitable outcome.

Marriage.

And for this lifetime commitment, he simply wasn't prepared.

Anne glanced at the label on the bottle of shiraz the waiter dropped off at their table. When she saw that it came from someplace called the Hope Estate winery, she snickered. Over the course of the last week, she'd done little but *hope* that Michael would come to his senses. Then she'd tried to *hope* that she'd forget about him by focusing on her job, her friends, and her knitting. But as none of her hopes had come through, she decided to just drink the damned wine and be done with it.

"Wow, Shane," Adele exclaimed, gently lifting the fluffy blanket Shane had nestled in her lap. "You're getting really good."

"Thanks," Shane said, tossing her hair in exaggerated hubris. "I can't believe I resisted this for so long. It's very therapeutic."

"Especially when you only knit when drinking wine," Adele replied, pouring the new arrival into fresh glasses.

Shane lifted her shiraz, made a toasting gesture and said, "Wine helps," before taking a measured sip.

Anne looked at the deep, ruby-red vintage with abject skepticism. Wine might help make knitting more palatable to Shane, but it had, so far, done very little to dull Anne's heartache.

Hashing out the implosion of her burgeoning relationship with Michael had been done—and then some. Shortly after he'd left, she'd put emergency calls in to both Shane and Adele, who responded instantly. They cancelled their plans, descended immediately onto her apartment with the DVD of *Kill Bill, Volume 2,* a two-pound box of Whitman's chocolate, and a cheap bottle of wine, all courtesy of the businesses on Lark Street.

In four hours, Anne had not only relived the keen disappointment of Michael backing off from their relationship, but also every indignity, disappointment, or heartbreak she'd endured since puberty. She was sure Michael had no idea how he'd struck her in such a vulnerable spot—but he had, and to date, she had not found the right balm to soothe the pain.

"How are you doing?" Adele asked.

The sympathetic melody in her voice scraped against the edges of Anne's spine, but she forced another smile. She hadn't minded revealing the depth of her depression right after she'd tossed Michael out, but she didn't really want them to know how little she'd recovered since. Yes, barely seven days had gone by, but she and Michael had only been seeing each other for a very short time—too short a time for her to fall in love with him. So how much despair time should she be allotted?

"Have you heard from Samir?"

Adele's question brought Shane bolt upright. "Samir? Who is this Samir you speak of?"

"Just a hot Egyptian man who couldn't keep his eyes off Anne the whole time we were on the cruise on the Nile."

Shane tossed down her knitting needles with a clatter. "Now just wait one minute. I've been at your apartment nearly every night since you got back and you never once mentioned anyone named Samir."

"That's because there's nothing to mention," Anne said, though now that Adele had brought it up, thinking about how shamelessly the man had flirted with her did beef up her confidence a little bit.

Which, undoubtedly, was why she'd brought it up.

"Besides, he had no way of contacting me," she concluded.

"Yes, he does," Adele said. "I gave him your e-mail."

"My work e-mail?"

"Your personal e-mail, you dweeb. I'm not entirely mindless."

"He's not going to contact me," Anne said. "He was getting married, remember?"

"To his cousin," Adele retorted.

Anne took another sip of her wine. Her friend did not understand the nuances of arranged marriages and she wasn't in the proper state of mind to explain. Whether or not Samir would e-mail her wasn't the issue. She had no intention of emailing him back.

His attention during her vacation had been very nice. He'd pointed her and Adele in the direction of several interesting Egyptian locations. And his transparent flirting—which they both had known would come to nothing—reminded her that while Michael might no longer be interested in her, that didn't make her any less interesting.

"So you met this guy on your trip?" Shane asked, her expression ravenous for gossip.

"Yes, but it doesn't matter," Anne insisted.

"Because he's getting married or because you're still hung up on Michael?"

She glared at her friend. Most times, she loved Shane for her ability to cut to the chase of any given situation, but Anne was done boo-hooing. At least, publicly.

"Samir is undoubtedly happily wed by now and of course I'm still hung up on Michael. It's only been a week. I still need more time than that to sort out how I feel about it all," she said. "If it can be sorted."

Shane tapped her knitting needles menacingly on the top of the table. "The whole thing makes absolutely no sense. I mean, I suppose he just got scared because you're so wonderful and he didn't think he deserved you."

"That's the only thing that would make sense," Adele piped in. "You overwhelmed him with your awesomeness."

Even as Anne pretended to make gagging noises, she smiled. She wasn't any happier about Michael's choices, but at least for the moment, she didn't feel quite so crappy about them.

"I love you guys."

"And well you should." Shane lifted her glass in a toast.

They knitted, drank, and chatted for another hour until Adele coiled her half-finished scarf into her bag and insisted she head home before her stitches got too sloppy. They made tentative plans to hook up again next week, and then Anne and Shane headed back home on foot while Adele drove off in the other direction.

"So, did you kiss him?" Shane asked, after they'd walked in silence for one city block.

"Who?" she asked. "Michael? Yeah, I kissed him right before I threw him out of my place, just so he'd know what he was missing."

"You did?"

Somehow, she didn't like how shocked Shane sounded.
"No."

"I wasn't asking about him anyway," Shane responded, waving her hand. "You should have kicked Michael, not kissed him. I meant this Samir guy. He sounds fascinating."

"Married," Anne said, holding up her ring finger, which proved nothing since hers was bare and at this rate, might remain so for the rest of her life. "And no, I didn't kiss him. I wanted Michael. I still do."

Surprisingly, Shane didn't argue and for this, Anne was grateful. Despite most outward signs, she wasn't as angry with Michael as she was disappointed. She knew in her soul that they'd connected. Her heart still clung to the bits of his essence that he'd revealed to her. His humor. His intelligence. His strong sense of justice, which balanced against an equally powerful sense of fun.

But after three weeks overseas and their nearly instantaneous breakup upon her return home, Anne knew she had to become accustomed to missing him. The ache might haunt her, but the pain would dull. She'd already thrown herself into the process by keeping busy, volunteering to take the night desk upon her return when the regular guy unexpectedly quit. Except for tonight, the four in the afternoon until midnight shift kept her out of the building during the hours Michael would likely have been home or out walking Sirus or visiting the neighbors she'd introduced him to. So far, she'd avoided running into him in the hallway or being trapped with him in the elevator, but eventually, they'd meet up and she'd have to find a way to act as if his decision to try and rewind their relationship hadn't shattered her soul.

With traffic darting past at surprising levels for the hour, she and Shane waited for the light to change at the intersection. "David and Carina are having a party Saturday night."

"David and who?"

"Carina? Oh, I forgot, you probably haven't met them. They moved in to 8-D while you were in Egypt. Great couple. He's an adjunct professor at Siena. I think she's a chef. I'm not sure. I just met them last week myself, but they are right down the hall from me, so they invited me over for a housewarming and they said I should bring friends from the building."

Anne frowned. She wasn't in the mood for a party. She was still dealing with jet lag, an unexpected breakup, and the night desk. She'd been looking forward to Saturday because she fully intended to remain in her pajamas until Sunday.

"I don't think so. I need to catch up on a few things."

"Like sleep?"

"Exactly like sleep," Anne said.

Shane mulled this over while they crossed the street. In the distance, Anne could see both their building and the streetlamp-lit park further down the block. She couldn't stop herself from scanning the landscape for any sign of Michael, who at this time of night, might be out with Sirus for her final walk of the evening.

She didn't see him.

It was just as well. If she saw him, she'd have to pretend she didn't and she had no desire to be childish about their situation. In fact, in her estimation, it was her insistence that they act like adults that was keeping them apart.

"The fact that Michael might go has nothing to do with it?" Shane asked.

Anne groaned. "I hadn't thought about that, actually, but now that you mention it, I'm definitely not going."

"You can't let him ruin your social life, sweetie."

At this, Anne snorted. She wasn't entirely sure she wanted a social life again any time soon. Not the kind that included men.

Fourteen

MIKE RAISED HIS FIST AND POUNDED again on Anne's door. He'd had enough. She was going to open up or he was going to break in. Wasn't like he didn't know how, thanks to her.

Luckily, his second barrage did the trick. She swung the door open, fury dancing in her sleepy-lidded eyes.

"What?" she snapped.

"Were you sleeping?"

It was only eight o'clock and yet she was wearing what might pass for pajamas—baggy flannel pants and an oversize Syracuse sweatshirt that had faded from crisp navy to soft cadet blue. Her normally vibrant skin struck him as pale and her irises, though flashing with annoyance, betrayed lack of rest.

"Is there a law against it?" she snapped.

He opened his mouth, but decided that any attempt he might make at humor would not be well received. He opted to cut to the chase.

"Sorry," he said. "I didn't mean to wake you up, but I had to see you."

Her mouth quivered. Her luscious lips pursed, sparking an ache deep in his gut. Her hair was mussed. She had circles under her eyes.

And yet, his need for her spiked so high, he felt dizzy.

He missed her. He missed seeing her. He missed touching her. Hearing her voice stirred him up as if she'd spoken with provocative innuendo instead of strained aggravation. A week away from her had done nothing to counteract their powerful attraction. In fact, the longer he went without her—so keenly aware that she was just a floor above him that he imagined hearing her footsteps—the more he realized how wrong he'd been.

He couldn't analyze his way out of the inevitable. He wanted Anne Miller in his life—and in his bed. Even with sloppy clothes and a bone-tired expression, she was the most beautiful woman he'd ever seen. She understood him. Connected with him. How could he throw that all away just because he might fall in love with her sooner rather than later?

"I brought you something," he said, responding to her impatient huff. "You said you liked Mexican food and *salsa verde*. I made enchiladas for that party up on eight and thought maybe you'd like to try some. Before I go up. Unless you're going, too?"

To help his case, he unfolded the aluminum foil. The smell was bright with cilantro and smoky with cumin. He'd tossed a generous helping of fresh *pico de gallo* over the top and the combination of scents and colors seemed to soften her expression.

"Smells good," she said. "I'm sure everyone will love it."

"I wasn't concerned with everyone," he said, presenting the plate. "This is for you."

She quirked an eyebrow. "Peace offering?"

"I hope so."

She shook her head and started to close the door. "I'm not playing this game, Michael."

"It's not a game," he insisted, blocking the door and thrusting the plate into her hands. "It's a gift. Really. No strings."

She hesitated, but then gripped the plate so that he could safely let go. Her expression, however, remained resolute.

"I'll take the enchiladas because they look delicious and I'm starving and because you made them. But I think I was pretty clear last week—"

"Crystal clear," he assured her. "Now it's my turn to be just as transparent. Anne, I was wrong. Painfully wrong. I haven't stopped thinking about you all week. And I hoped that if you liked the enchiladas—and even if you didn't—that you would give us another chance."

Her mouth quivered and though it might have been a result of her obvious exhaustion, her eyes glossed, heightening the richness of her deep brown eyes.

"Seriously?" she asked.

"In every sense of the word. I'm sorry, Anne. I miss you. I miss you like crazy."

She set the plate down on a table just inside the apartment. Before he could take a single step forward on his own steam, she grabbed his shirt at the chest, balled the material in her hands and launched her lips against his.

The explosion of sensations rocked him harder than any music, filled him fuller than any food. He could not get enough of her and was only vaguely aware of leaving the hallway. One of them shut the door, probably with a foot since both arms and hands were engaged in the finest make-up kiss ever shared between a guy who'd temporarily lost his mind and the woman who had the amazing capacity to forgive.

By the time they came up for breath, Mike had to lean on the back of her couch to regain his balance.

"I can't believe you're giving me a second chance," he said.

"Who said I am?" she replied, coyly toying with the top button of his Oxford shirt. "I still haven't tasted those enchiladas. Maybe my forgiveness will depend on your ratio of cilantro to tomato in the salsa."

He'd missed her sense of humor—her ability to tease and taunt him about one thing while his mind overloaded with images of something so much more important than food. But before any taste testing commenced, Mike took her hands and reeled her in, pressing full against her, knowing his body was hard and primed and wanting her to know it, too.

"I'd rather taste you." He dipped his head to nibble on her neck, savoring the flavors of her flesh and the feel of her pulse on his lips.

"I'm a mess," she said, though her conviction was weakened by the pleasured noises emanating from the back of her throat.

"No," he insisted, kissing a path from her throat to her earlobe. "You're delicious."

She chuckled and the vibration beneath his mouth drove him past caring about anything but savoring the sensation of his mouth on her skin and his hands on her body. Against him, she writhed in maddening rhythms that reminded him of cool jazz. Slow, cadenced, and quivering with barely contained sensuality.

He'd never wanted a woman this intensely. He'd never allowed himself to fall so hard, so fast. Making love to Anne wouldn't be the next step in a rising flowchart of cause and effect, but an unexpected explosion of irresistible forces.

She untucked his shirt and explored beneath the fabric, sending lightning strikes of sensation through his system as her hands ran up his back and down his obliques. He broke the kiss only long enough to whip off her sweatshirt, only briefly registering the glossy silk of her lingerie before closing his eyes and losing himself in the utter ecstasy of her kiss.

Their tongues clashed, battled and pleasured. Their hands roamed and explored. Though he was mildly aware of television voices chattering in the background, in his mind, the music shifted from jazz to rock 'n' roll. Hard-driving, guitar-heavy, drum-pounding beats surging from deep within his soul.

Wrangling every ounce of his self-control, he broke away from her. He needed her the same way he needed air, but he had to give her a chance to backdown or at the very least, slow things up.

"The enchiladas are getting cold," he said, panting.

"What enchiladas?"

Her sassy comeback stoked him to a burning point. When she took his hand and led him to her bedroom, he hardly registered the mounds of clothes on her bed. She swept them onto the floor, clearing the path for their bodies.

Out of sight, out of mind.

The mattress bounced beneath them, making them both laugh. Her drawstring pants proved easy to peel away, but his jeans resisted, giving her time to find a condom in her bedside table while he undressed.

"That's handy," he said.

"You're complaining?" she asked, incredulous.

"Not in the least," Mike said. He should have thought about protection, but he'd never dreamed he'd end up in bed with her when his first concern was securing her forgiveness.

"Then shut up and kiss me," she replied.

In his whole life, he couldn't remember wanting to follow a woman's command more. She was his to have. His to command. He'd follow her to the ends of the earth if she told him to, so long as she didn't stop touching him.

Beneath Michael's clash of a kiss, Anne squealed with happiness. Was this all a dream? For a full week, she tried to get over

Michael, but the task proved impossible. Every time she closed her eyes at night, she fantasized about precisely this moment, when he unhooked her bra and chucked it away, then gazed at her breasts with undeniable hunger. She'd tortured herself with imagined sensations of his hands cupping her, his thumbs taunting her nipples, his mouth descending until she spiraled out of control with the sensations of his tongue and teeth against her sensitized skin.

And now she was living the dream.

She scrambled her fingers into his hair, loving the lush, thick feel against her fingers. With each nipple and bite, however, she found herself wanting to explore all of him. She raked her hands down his back and traced his spine even as his own hands roamed and explored, finding the sweet erogenous zones she'd wanted him to discover so badly and for so long.

The rumble of Mike's desire as he slid her panties down her body was uncomplicated. Honest. He wanted her. She wanted him.

God, how she wanted him.

By the time they'd stripped down to nothing, his kisses left her lips pleasurably bruised. He dusted them with sweet brushes of his mouth over hers while he took care of protection and moved atop of her so their bodies melded and blended into one glorious amalgamation of man and woman.

"Michael." Hot pricks of emotion fired behind her eyes, the sharpness smoothed by the sweet rhythm of his body sliding into hers.

"I know," he said. "We're perfect. You're perfect."

Their trip to the bedroom might have been hurried, but once inside her, Michael took his time. He kissed her and caressed her, sliding her arms over her head so that he could have access to her breasts and control of the pace. Even when she hooked her ankles behind his and matched his languorous thrusts, he chuckled and slowed her down with a distraction like a hand on her hip or a mind-boggling exploration of her earlobes, throat, and neck. By the time she thought she might go mad, she could see his control slipping.

She ran her hands over his chest, tweaking his nipples as he had hers, arching up to soothe the pleasurable pain with kisses of her own. In the space of a heartbeat, his pace increased and she couldn't resist collapsing into the softness all around her, even as she touched him, kissed him, coaxed him to take what she knew he desperately wanted since she wanted all of the same—and more.

The sensations swept over her in a wild wave, and at the last possible moment before she crested, he took her hands in his so they could ride the surge together.

In the last second before the delirium of her climax overtook her, she turned her head and spied the empty bedside table.

Only now, nothing about her was empty. Absolutely nothing at all.

Mike kissed Anne lazily. Her mouth had no expression beyond exhaustion, but her eyes lit with a smile.

A smile he'd put there.

"Hungry?"

"Not particularly," she said, sounding entirely sated.

"Not even for Mexican food?"

She laughed, so he rolled out of bed, shrugged into his jeans, and strolled to the kitchen. He retrieved the enchiladas from the table by the door and popped them in microwave until the cheese bubbled. He snatched two forks from the drawer, found a dishtowel they could use for a table cloth, and brought the feast to Anne's bed. As he moved into the room, he watched her sit up against the pillows and headboard, wrapping herself in her comforter until she looked even more tasty than the Mexican staple he'd made for the party.

Although now, the only person he wanted to sate with his cooking was Anne.

Scooting in beside her, he cut into the soft corn tortilla, scooped up a balanced serving of *salsa verde* and *pico de gallo,* and fed her. Her cheeks flushed and her lips bruised from his kisses, she made his mouth water, reinvigorating his hunger for something so much more than food. When she closed her eyes and made a happy noise from the back of her throat, he nearly lost his mind.

"These are amazing," she said.

"Not nearly as amazing as you," he said, surrendering to his need to nibble a bit more on her neck.

She squealed, but didn't fight him. "I meant the food!"

He supposed he did have to be a little less insatiable. It had been, after all, their first time. "Want more?"

"Yes, please."

He had no idea if she meant enchiladas or sex, so he gave her a little of both. He fed her a bite, then kissed her temple. He fed her another bite, then shifted the comforter so that he had access to her bare shoulder. After a little while, the sting of the jalapeno became unbearable, so he returned to the kitchen, retrieved two cold bottled waters and a small carton of sour cream.

Anne swirled her fork around the last of the enchiladas, then balanced a serving on her fork and held it to his lips. He took the bite, more entranced by how she fed him than the actual food itself.

"So, you've taught me a valuable lesson about myself," she

confessed. "Evidently, enchiladas are the way back into my good graces. Very clever of you to figure that out."

He chuckled. He'd had no idea just how far into her good graces he'd get when he'd been cooking or he would have whipped up an entire meal from tortilla soup to cinnamon-dusted sopapillas.

"I didn't think you were going to open the door unless I came bearing gifts."

"I wasn't that angry," she argued.

He stared at her intently. "Yes, you were," he said. "And you should have been. I was furious at myself, once I finally realized how I'd hurt you. How I'd hurt us."

"Care to share why you did that?"

He shook his head, still so high on the endorphins of their lovemaking, he could barely tap into the guy he'd been less than an hour before, much less the moron who had invaded his body when Anne left for Egypt. How could he possibly have thought that letting Anne go was the right thing to do?

And yet, there was no denying that he'd believed he and Anne needed to re-examine the nature of their relationship before moving forward. Become friends first and lovers second had been his *modus operandi* since he'd started dating. He realized now that he tested the women in his life in a series of scenarios, ensuring his safety from hurt before he risked his heart.

But now that he and Anne had dove into the risk-infested waters of true romance, he couldn't imagine living or loving any other way.

"Trust," he said simply.

She nodded, as if she knew. As if she understood. He didn't know if she really did or not, but there would be plenty of time to figure that out.

"So what changed your mind?" she asked.

"I realized that if I didn't rethink my stance, I was going to lose you. And that outcome wasn't acceptable."

"So, in other words, I was right and you were wrong," she said.

Her grin was pure, unadulterated evil—and he loved it so thoroughly, he couldn't help pressing his lips to hers. Somewhere deep inside, he wanted to disagree with her, but only because he wasn't used to losing an argument. Instead, he decided to kiss a path from her shoulder to her ankle, skillfully weaving his hands into the folds of her comforter until he could touch her bare skin.

"I've never felt so strongly for any woman before," he confessed between kisses. "From that first night we met at the concert, I was snagged."

Her eyes widened in surprise. "At the concert? You certainly didn't show it!"

"Hey, I hugged you before I left. We'd only known each other for fifteen minutes. That's a pretty strong signal," he insisted.

She harrumphed and tucked the comforter tight around her body. He settled for massaging her feet, surprised to find that her toes sparkled with a pale, pink polish that nearly matched her skin tone.

"You didn't even ask for my number," she complained.

"That was the allergy meds," he explained. "Or maybe it was just me, afraid of feeling something so strong for someone I'd just met."

"And after that?"

She made a show of batting her eyelashes, clearly enjoying his groveling.

He lifted her adorable foot and kissed the sweet curve of her arch. "Do you want me to waste time listing all my lame excuses or would you rather go to a party?"

She eased into the cushy mattress, humming in enjoyment of his attention. "I'm not dressed for a party and you're out of enchiladas."

"I have another tray upstairs and as much as it pains me to say this, you could get dressed."

"Is that what you really want?" She allowed the comforter to fall away just enough to reveal a very luscious swath of skin.

"Just because we go to the party doesn't mean we have to stay there all night."

Fifteen

ANNE TYPED THE WORDS "PERU," "travel," and "deals" into the search engine and pressed enter. In seconds, her screen was awash in choices. She started to click on the first when Michael scooted beside her on the couch and set a steaming cup of coffee on the table.

Just a week ago, Michael had surprised her with their first trip—a weekend in the Catskills for a music festival, a one-night romantic stay at a charming bed-and-breakfast followed by a second day camping. A consummate planner, Michael left no detail ignored. And yet, when things didn't quite go their way—like the sudden downpour of rain that flooded their campsite, he proved adaptable and easygoing, setting up a nest for them in the back of his car.

He was, she decided, not only the perfect lover, but the ultimate travel companion.

Of course, a weekend excursion was nothing compared to the vacation they were now planning to South America. On the way back from the festival, they'd talked about all the places she'd visited around the world and he'd explained how part of his obsession with Phish had been not just in the music, but in the travels. They discussed dream destinations for future vacations and Anne learned that like her, Michael had always wanted to go to Peru.

Since the one hiccup, Michael had stopped trying to derail the bullet-train ride that was their relationship. Instead, he'd started looking up tours to Machu Picchu.

"What's on the itinerary so far?" he asked.

She tiled the browser windows she'd opened so that he could see the puzzle of choices. "There's a lot of ways to get there," she said, clicking through some of the main tourist sites to get an overview of the available activities. "The hike to the summit won't be a cakewalk."

"We can handle it," he said, dragging his own laptop from the coffee table and activating the Internet. "Peru is right on the Andes. What about a rafting tour? Do you like rafting?"

His question, so considerate despite the afterthought, made her laugh. They were lovers now, an exclusive couple who, work hours notwithstanding, spent more time together than they did apart. And yet, they still had so much to learn about each other. She didn't even know if an entire lifetime would be enough.

"Sure," she said. "I've never rafted in Peru, but it sounds like fun. Where's the tour?"

They coordinated their web searches, finding and bookmarking several sights before Anne broached the topic that neither of them had discussed in much detail. "Are you going to be able to get that much time off work?"

Mike nodded. "Oh, yeah. I haven't taken a day off since I started. I get two weeks a year. If we schedule this for December, we'll be cool. What about you?"

Anne grimaced. The thought of asking Pamela for time off— even for hours she'd accumulated as part of her vacation package—turned her stomach. Just getting permission to light out early on Friday for their festival trip, despite the fact that she'd filed every single story she'd been assigned early, had been a major production. And as she'd gone to Israel and Egypt, she wasn't sure she could finagle more time off.

Because of her employment start date, the trip to the Middle East technically counted as her vacation time from the previous year. By December, she'd be able to use up the next year's allotment. But following the letter of the law when it came to employee's time off wasn't Pamela's style. She preferred to keep her staff on a very short leash.

More and more, Anne had found herself with really sucky hours in an increasingly hostile work environment. She'd covered more weekends than any of her colleagues and since no one had taken the initiative to replace the night-desk guy, she'd filled that spot more than anyone else on the crime beat. Under any other administrator, Anne would have been able to use this as leverage to negotiate the time off in December, but with Pamela, there was just no telling.

"I can try," she said, her fingers hovering over her keyboard as amazing pictures of the rain forest scrolled across her screen.

The next morning, after a particularly long staff meeting where everyone seemed to yet again ignore the serious need for a new night-desk reporter, Anne asked Pamela if she could meet with her for a few minutes.

The woman grunted in response, then charged off to her office. Once inside, Anne shut the door.

"Actually, I'm glad you came in," Pamela said, tossing a stack of old papers off of her chair before logging in to her computer. Her frown emphasized the wrinkles on her chin. If this was her version of *glad*, Anne wondered if she understood the meaning of the word.

"Really?" Anne asked, skeptical. "Why?"

"You've been doing a good job on the night desk."

Anne nearly lost her footing. A compliment? From Pamela?

She narrowed her eyes and then crossed her arms. With any other editor, opening with a compliment would have boded well. Not with Pamela.

Never with Pamela.

"I do a good job whatever shift I'm on," Anne insisted.

Her confident reply caused Pamela's right eyebrow to arch as if challenging this claim, but instead, the editor smiled in a way that made the skin on Anne's neck crawl. "So good that you've become our most versatile reporter. The powers that be have decided to put you on the night desk permanently."

"What?"

This was what she got for venturing into Pamela's lair willingly. The night desk, with its four o'clock to midnight shift, was bad enough as a temporary fill-in, but on a weekly basis? Every weekday? She might as well slice her wrists open because she'd have no life anyway.

"And by powers that be, you mean you?" Anne asked, unable and unwilling to restrain the rancor in her voice.

Pamela chuckled. "For the most part, yeah. You always show up. You always file competent stories. What more can I ask for?"

She let the *competent* insult slide.

"Oh, I don't know," Anne snapped. "How about someone who actually wants that job?"

The glint of sick humor dancing in Pamela's keen blue eyes narrowed into a deadly stare. "But can I assume that you do, at least, want *a* job?"

Anne's heart seized. She'd never seen Pamela resort to blackmail before, but there was a first time for everything.

"Of course I want a job," Anne said, her brain working to find another option, even though she knew there wasn't one. Pamela wouldn't be taking such sadistic pleasure from this tête-à-tête unless Anne was going to walk out the door miserable.

"Then this is it," Pamela said. "Take it or leave it."

Anne concentrated on keeping her jaw shut while her brain processed this cruel turn. The *Daily Journal* had, from the beginning, been her stepping stone to the bigger publications. The newspaper was, current management notwithstanding, highly respected. And it was also pretty much the only game in town.

Although she had every intention of living in one of the five boroughs of New York City sometime in the near future, she loved her life in Albany. She had a new man in her life—one who wanted to sweep her off on a grand adventure in another hemisphere. But even beyond Michael, she had friends and an apartment she loved. Even Sirus was getting used to sharing Michael with her for more than an hour at a time.

She loved being a journalist, but if she left the *Daily Journal*, she'd have to move to another market. She couldn't make such an important decision based on her fury at Pamela. Her editor had placed her in a no-win situation—which doubly sucked because she was enjoying it.

"I want two weeks off in December," Anne said.

"You just had three weeks off," Pamela argued, waving her hand dismissively.

"I have two weeks coming to me after November, because that's my anniversary date. If you're going to stick me with the night shift, I want two weeks off. Paid."

Pamela leaned on her hand, stroking her chin like some sort of maniacal villain out of a bad B movie. "You'll have to do some weekends, too, then."

"No way," Anne shot back. She may need this job bad enough to take one untenable work situation, but not two. "You've got me nights. That's more than enough torture."

With a curt nod of acknowledgment, Pamela turned to her computer and grunted. Anne took this as agreement—though she would get it in writing the minute she returned to her desk.

She resisted the urge to slam Pamela's door on her way out. She'd gotten her time off, but the price had been exorbitant. What good was a vacation with the man you loved if chances were you'd be broken up before the plane tickets arrived in the mail?

Sixteen

SOMEHOW, ANNE MANAGED TO remain focused on her work for the rest of the day. After filing the vacation request and ensuring that Pamela signed it, she skipped lunch in lieu of punching through her last two articles and cutting out an hour early. Pamela, oddly enough, had the sense not to complain. She'd already wrecked Anne's life. Yelling at her for taking off when all her articles were ready for print would only have been salt in the wound. Apparently, even her editor had limits to her taste for torture.

She avoided the concerned stares from Billy, the intern, and the gossipy whispers of her colleagues, grabbed her stuff, and headed down to her car. Without petty crimes and contentious trials to keep her mind occupied, she could think about nothing but Michael.

His excitement over their trip to Peru had been palpable. All day, she'd been ignoring e-mails dropping into her inbox with subject lines like *Machu Picchu with You* and *Lima is Prima*. He'd even hinted that he'd been scouring the Victoria's Secret website with the expressed purpose of selecting a sexy swimsuit for her to wear that bore remarkable resemblance to the tropical print lingerie she'd worn last weekend in the Catskills.

Desperately, she wanted to fill her mind with fantasies about making love in the raw Peruvian jungle, but she and Michael couldn't keep up a relationship with her new schedule. He worked the traditional eight a.m. until five p.m. He enjoyed rising early on Saturdays so they could hike until late afternoon or spend hours in a park with Sirus before heading home, showering and hitting a cool café for dinner or cooking an elaborate meal at home so they could enjoy the privacy of his bedroom instead of dessert.

They'd already fallen into this intimate routine and Anne cherished every minute. After hitting the momentary bump in the road after her trip to the Middle East, they'd finally reached the point where spending time together wasn't something they asked for, but simply assumed they'd do whenever possible.

Now, it would be impossible.

On the night desk, she'd leave for work an hour before he got home. She wouldn't wake up until after he'd left for the office. She'd need her Saturday mornings to catch up on sleep while he explored the New York state hiking trails alone. She wasn't a night-shift virgin—she knew the toll this job would take.

In the parking lot, she loaded her bag into her car, climbed into the front seat, and after turning the key and fiddling with the radio settings, she stopped, unable to move. Automatic action couldn't withstand the welling of her emotions. Fear. Anger. Regret. Utter and complete sadness. She'd worked hard. Her reliability and talent should have been rewarded by her employer— not punished. The indignity and injustice were just too much and in seconds, tears splashed down her face while her chest heaved and her lungs burned.

She didn't know how long she cried, unaware of anything until her cell phone rang. She scavenged for a tissue and then glanced at the caller ID.

Michael.

She let the call go into voice-mail, but before she could shove her car into drive and try to make her way home through clouded eyes, he called again. She shut the engine and answered the phone.

"What's wrong?" he asked immediately.

"You don't want to know," she said.

"Did someone die?"

Her chest ached when she forced a laugh. "No, but our relationship just received a death sentence with no chance for reprieve."

"What are you talking about? Where are you?"

"In the parking lot. At work." In between each phrase, she sniffled loudly.

"I'll be there in ten minutes," he said and before she could beg him not to come, he'd disconnected the call.

She scrambled to put herself back together. She didn't want him to see her this way. She didn't want anyone to see her this way. She found a pile of napkins from the bakery in the console and tried to remove all evidence of her breakdown. She dug into her purse for makeup and was just swiping lip balm across her mouth when Michael pulled up behind her. She took a deep breath and blinked rapidly to dry the last of her tears from her eyes.

He rapped on her window. "Open the door."

She did as he ordered and immediately fell into his waiting arms. Unbidden, her tears renewed, and though his muscles tensed around her, he didn't let her go. He smoothed his hand up and down her back and kissed her hair, attempting to soothe her misery with words she couldn't entirely process.

"Damn it, Anne. You're scaring the hell out of me. Whatever is wrong, we'll fix it."

She tugged out of his embrace. God, she couldn't believe she'd broken down like this in front of him! No one had died. The world hadn't ended. There were so many more worthy things to be blubbering about than her stupid job. She recriminated herself until she was able to switch off the waterworks.

"I'm sorry," Anne said. "Ignore me. I just had a bad day."

"A bad day?" he asked. "Whatever happened had to be more than a generic bad day to rip you apart like this. Tell me what's wrong."

He had every right to know, but she needed time to regain her calm before she opened up. "Not here."

She scowled toward the building.

He didn't argue. "Want to go home?"

"Yeah," she said. "I think I could use some snuggling on the couch."

"I'm sure Sirus would be happy to oblige," he joked.

She couldn't help but smile. She brushed a kiss over his cheek, loving how the rough texture along his jaw ignited the sensitive skin of her tear-stained lips. The thought of losing him on account of her career tore at her insides.

"You're okay to drive?" he asked.

"I'll be fine. I just had a moment. I don't have them often."

Her attempt at humor failed. His brow was knit tight and for the first time in a while, she noticed the twitch in his neck and eye.

"Seriously," she said, not wanting to make his Tourette's worse by adding to his stress. "Once we're home and I'm in your arms, I'll be fine."

Mildly satisfied, Michael headed back to his car. Anne had absolutely no doubt that once she spilled the whole disastrous day to him, he'd reassure her that they'd adjust. What else could he possibly say? That he wouldn't stand for not coming first in her life and that she had to either pick him or pick her job? She'd met more than a few guys who would make that demand, but not Michael.

No, she wasn't afraid he was going to dump her outright, even if that might be the less cruel way to go in the long run. Her job would kill their relationship slowly and quietly, like poison gas rather than a flash explosion. And there was nothing she could do. She couldn't quit. She wouldn't. Outrage at Pamela's treatment of her was one thing—her ambitions were quite another.

The trouble was, as much as she wanted a long career as a journalist, she also wanted Michael. And for the first time, she simply couldn't see how the two needs could coexist.

"How many days?"

At Anne's question, Mike thumbed through his calendar and checked the tally he kept in the corner of each successive day. He wished they'd reached the double-digits, but three numbers stared at him today just as they had yesterday. He hesitated before answering, then decided that they were going to have this conversation anyway, no matter how much time was left until they left for Peru.

"One hundred and eleven," he answered.

She collapsed against his shoulder, groaned, and made whimpering noises. Except for times like this when they met for lunch (her breakfast) in the park, ate sandwiches out of their laps, and watched Sirus scamper around on the long leash Mike had tethered to the bench, they rarely saw each other anymore. They had a standing Saturday-night date that lasted well into Sunday, but even that was being disrupted more often as Mike's responsibilities to the Quality Education Initiative had started to include weekend events. The only thing keeping him going was knowing that with every twenty-four hours that passed, he was one day closer to the vacation of a lifetime—with the woman of his dreams.

But the hardship on him was nothing compared to the torture she was going through. The shadows beneath her eyes had darkened to the point where she'd started wearing heavier makeup everyday rather than just on special occasions. He'd also noticed that her jeans looked a little snugger around her backside, her face was fuller and her arms thicker.

But there was no way in hell he was going to mention it.

He knew she'd let her yoga and spinning classes go by the wayside. Their time together was already restrained to a few hours a week—he certainly didn't want to put it in her head that he'd prefer her to spend that time in the gym rather than in his bed. However, with her mental health so beaten down, did he really want her physical health to suffer, too?

Mike kept hoping that Anne would, eventually, find her own way to adjust to this freakish schedule without any input from him. He was a fixer. He could think of a half-dozen more effective means for her to reorganize her life, but Anne did not like to be fixed. Any repairs had to be done on her terms . . . and in her own time.

"Four months sounds better than one hundred and eleven days," he pointed out, not wanting to ruin the brief time they had together with yet another conversation about how much she hated her job. Instead, he dipped into his own expertise and created a positive spin. "So let's say four months, which I should point out, is much shorter than five months."

Unfortunately, Anne's dour mood would not be deterred.

"I should quit," she said.

"You could quit," he repeated, emphasizing the second word without really meaning to.

"The *Daily Journal* was supposed to be my stepping stone. Maybe I should start looking for something else."

"That's not a bad idea," he said.

"But newspapers are hurting right now. Jobs are harder to come by. I'd have to move and I don't want to move."

"I'm very glad to hear that," he said, giving her a squeeze.

She snuggled closer. "Maybe I should try something different. But what?"

He didn't answer. She didn't expect him to answer. The first time he'd attempted to list a number of jobs she'd be incredibly suited for with her top-notch talent at research and mad skills with the written word, she'd jumped down his throat. He didn't need more than one press to learn a woman's hot buttons.

"What could you do?" he asked, keeping his voice even and calm, posing the question without any hint that he might have an answer on the tip of his tongue.

"I could go back to school," she said. "Get my masters degree."

"Yes, you could," he agreed.

"But that takes money," she lamented.

"Yes, it does."

She crumbled the napkin she'd laid across her lap and together with the sandwich wrapper from the deli, she formed a ball and tossed it, free-throw style, into the nearest trash can.

"Maybe the Knicks are looking for someone," he suggested, risking a joke.

The pay off was a rare, but genuine, smile.

"You're getting tired of listening to this, aren't you?" she asked.

He shifted so that her torso slipped across his lap and he could gaze unhampered into her fathomless brown eyes. Deep inside those mesmerizing irises, he caught a glimpse of the light that used to shine there so brightly. She wasn't entirely beat down by her new hours and her isolation from him and her friends, but she was getting close. Too close.

"No," he said. "I'm not getting sick of hearing any of this. What I am worried about is you. No one should be this unhappy."

She allowed him to kiss her for a second, but before he could get his groove on, she was twisting out of his reach. "Did you read my piece on the boy who draws comic books to help him deal with cancer?"

"With my morning coffee," he said, not surprised by her sudden change of subject, but not happy about it, either. "Some of your best work."

"I wouldn't have had the time and concentration to do that type of lifestyle story if I wasn't working the night shift."

Mike didn't think this was necessarily true, but if following this thought process helped her deal with the upheaval, then he was willing to go along with it. He'd do anything to bring some carefree joy to the woman he was falling in love with, but short of winning the lottery and buying the newspaper so he could fire her tyrant of an editor and get her back on her regular schedule, he couldn't think of any way to ease her pain.

"What are you working on this week?"

For her normal duties, she mostly had to listen to the police scanner and pick up information about breaking stories. She fed facts to reporters in the field or went out herself to interview neighbors outside a fresh crime scene or wait for the fire chief to give an initial report about a three-alarm blaze.

But in the quiet hours after the late edition had been put to bed, she worked on human interest stories. Talking about them, even when they were usually fraught with tragedy, seemed to lighten her mood.

"It's so sad," she said. "This class at the high school was working on a production of *Little Shop of Horrors* and their lead died
in a car crash. They're devastated. I saw the kid on YouTube. What
an amazing talent. They're trying to work out how to put on the
show and do something in his honor. I'm going to see their
rehearsal tomorrow night. Keeping myself objective during this
one is going to be tough."

"Want me to go with you?"

She jumped up from the bench with more energy than he'd
seen in her for a while. "Really?"

"Of course, really."

"I'll be working," she warned him.

He nodded. They'd had this conversation before, too. "I'll meet
you at the rehearsal and then you can go right back to the paper. I
won't even entice you to stop on the way back for a cup of coffee."

He untied Sirus and took Anne's hand, loving how she suddenly had a skip in her step.

"Well," she said, leaning her head against his shoulder again. "I
don't think a cup of coffee will stop the cogs of the *Daily
Journal*."

He bit back a comment about how those cogs were crushing
her hopes and dreams and instead kissed her. He missed her like
crazy, but if he didn't let her work this out on her own, they
wouldn't survive. He could only hope that by the time they
reached Peru, the misery at her job would be long behind them—
with only their glowing future on the horizon.

Seventeen

FROM THE MOMENT THEIR PLANE LIFTED OFF from Kennedy airport, Michael watched Anne for any sign that would indicate she'd left her troubles behind her. He had a very long wait. A seasoned traveler, Anne was impervious to the stress of flying and yet, for most of the nine hour flight, she'd glanced out of the tiny round window more times than generally necessary—not to make sure they were still in the air, but according to her, to reassure herself that they really were leaving the United States.

She read through her guidebooks and chitchatted with him about restaurants she wanted to go to and sights she wanted to make sure they didn't miss, was friendly to the flight crew, and even struck up a conversation with the woman across the aisle from them, but he hadn't been fooled. Her anxiety remained at peak levels until they completed their connecting flight from Lima to Cusco and she set her bags down inside the hotel.

Compared to the bed-and-breakfast where they'd stayed in the Catskills, this place was a hovel. And yet, as she leaned halfway out the open window and inhaled the mountain-scented air, he watched the miasma of her work frustrations sizzle off her body. Her shoulders dropped. Her neck curved and even her hands, as she reached out toward the plaza outside, possessed a peaceful grace.

"We made it," she said, twisting her arms until she was hugging herself. She threw a glance over her shoulder that was part coy invitation and part surprise.

"You doubted we would?" he asked.

"Well," she said, turning back toward the window and giving the breeze one last, long inhale. "The turbulence on the flight here was kind of scary."

Michael sidled up behind her and layered his arms over hers. She molded her body to his and he tightened his squeeze, just in case her sudden onset of bliss made her unsteady.

"I'm not talking about the plane," he clarified. "You didn't think *we*'d make it. As in, you and me."

She leaned back so that he caught the doubtful look in her soulful brown eyes. "Like you were confident the whole time?"

"Good point."

He didn't want to rehash the past six months or relive the moments when he'd been alone in his bed, sending her instant messages from his laptop and wondering how much longer he could stand having a woman in his life whom he never actually saw in person. Needing Anne hadn't come as a complete surprise to him—the week after she'd returned from her vacation in Egypt had taught him how deeply they were connected. What had shocked him was how irritable he could become when the woman he adored was dangled in front of him through voice mails, short phone conversations, and notes left on each other's doors. His inner selfish bastard had made his presence known on more than one occasion, and in truth, he suspected she might dump him long before they boarded the plane for Lima.

But now they were here. For the next two weeks, they'd be together twenty-four/seven, with no interruptions from work or family or even a dog that needed walking. Traveling to a cradle of civilization put them into a world that could easily have existed in an alternate universe. He intended to make sure they milked every single minute of joy from every flavor, every terrain, every sight, sound and smell of Peru.

But first, he intended to find that same bliss exploring the spot just beneath Anne's ear with his tongue. He slipped his hands beneath her T-shirt and worked the top button of her jeans so that he could slide his palms over her hips and imprint her curves back into his memory.

She chuckled throatily, but then twisted around to face him.

"We don't have that much time in Cusco," she said, stretching her arms behind her so she could run her fingers through his hair. "We should use our time to explore."

"I am exploring," he assured her, divesting her of her jeans.

"I meant the sights," she clarified.

He leaned forward, pulled the window in at an angle that blocked any view of them from the street, but still allowed the fresh breeze to flutter the gauzy curtains. He then went to work on the buttons and ties on her blouse. "I like what I'm seeing right now."

He peeled away the material, revealing that one lacy white bra of hers he loved. The one with the tiny red heart in the center between her amazingly lush breasts. He turned her around and backed them up to the bed.

"But we don't have a lot of time here," she said, tugging his shirt over his head.

"Sex doesn't always have to be a leisurely activity," he reminded her.

He hadn't realized how hot he was for her until they were naked and kissing and rediscovering each other after so many months apart. The casting off of their mundane worries tore open a heavy curtain that had hung between them for months.

For the first time in forever, they saw each other—and felt each other—with searing clarity.

Making love with Anne, unencumbered and on the spur of the moment, heightened his senses so that the colors around him seemed extra vibrant and the smells stronger and more enticing. The muscles in his neck and shoulder that so often succumbed to the whims of his disorder obeyed his every command. For a whimsical moment, he imagined taking Anne's hand and floating to Machu Picchu. Instead, he simply made sure they both climaxed in a wild spin of color, texture, and taste.

Once dressed, they strolled through the city like the tourists they were. Cusco was the ancient capital of Peru, a main site for the Incas and the center of their sun worship. He and Anne wandered through amazing markets, explored several colonial Spanish churches, and shared dinner in the central square while the locals tried to sell them finger puppets or entertained the crowds with native dance and music.

By the time they returned to the hotel, their only comfortable stop on what would be a rustic vacation in the mountains, they were bone weary and feeling the effects of the altitude. Mike was glad he'd seduced Anne when they first arrived because by the time they'd both crawled into bed, they were too tired to do much more than exchange a quick kiss good night.

By morning, Anne hadn't recovered her physical strength, but her emotional well-being soared. She downed two bottles of water, which revived her well enough to meet with the tour guides and embark on a rafting tour on the Urubamba River. They napped upon their return, then took advantage of the Cusco nightlife and danced until midnight.

In the morning, Michael rolled over to find Anne curled into a ball, her face pale.

"Hey, babe. What's wrong?"

She shut her eyes tight, which emphasized a slightly pale line around her lips. "Too much *chicha* last night, I guess."

Mike smirked. They'd both had a small glass of the fermented corn drink, but neither had drunk enough to cause anything resembling a hangover. "Let me get you some water."

He threw on his pants and a shirt and jogged to the lobby for cold bottled waters. When he got back, she hadn't moved. He helped her sit up, then smoothed his hand up and down her back while he supervised her sipping. After a little while, her color returned and she perked up.

"Dehydration?" she asked, recognizing the signs.

"Probably on account of the altitude," he said. "We need to make sure to pack extra water today. Unless you want to cancel?"

From her scandalized expression, Mike knew that waylaying the hike to Machu Picchu was out of the question. Anne took a little longer getting herself together, but he took charge of packing so that by the time they checked out of the hotel, they weren't behind schedule. They met the guides at the prearranged location, met the other people on the tour, checked their packs to ensure they had everything they needed, and then headed off.

Mike kept a close eye on Anne. She wasn't one-hundred percent, but if he attempted to coddle her, the results wouldn't be pretty. While the tour had porters who carried the heavy items such as the food and tents, their packs were laden with water, snacks, changes of clothes, and basic toiletries—enough to put a strain on someone who wasn't feeling well. Luckily, the tour guides didn't seem to be in any hurry, allowed for a lot of breaks, and even carried oxygen tanks for anyone who started losing the battle with the lower atmosphere.

In the meantime, the porters sprinted ahead of them so that by the time they reached the halfway point of the day's hike, they'd set up tents and campfires and had prepared lunch. Anne nibbled at cheese and fruit, but drank deeply enough from her canteen for Mike to keep his opinions about her food intake to himself.

Still, as she repacked her rucksack so she could reach the extra batteries she'd tucked in the bottom for her camera, he sat beside her on the rock and brushed her hair away from her face.

"Feeling okay?"

She shrugged. "I'll live."

When she stood and stretched, he took the opportunity to grab her bag and sling it over his shoulder. Surprisingly, she didn't object, but instead pressed her head against his shoulder and laced her hand in his. The spring-powered walking sticks they'd purchased in Cusco came in very handy during the climb, but by the time they reached their last stop for the night, Anne tumbled into their tent and did not emerge during the entire dinner.

Mike took her a plate and a canteen filled with creek water fed by the melting snow on the nearest mountain peak.

"You're babying me," she said, her tone only half accusatory.

"Is that a capital offense? Under the circumstances?"

She forced a grin. "No, but I'm not very good at being taken care of."

Mike laughed. "I noticed, but I've also noticed that the sky is blue, the mountains are tall, and the plants in the rain forest are very green."

"Always the comedian," she said, then groaned and collapsed onto her sleeping bag.

Since Mike knew she was being dramatic to enhance his worry more than actually fainting, he grabbed her plate and decided to feed her like he had all those months ago—right after the first time they'd made love. Moments like these filled him with wonder. How had he found such a perfect woman? Who had decided he deserved to be the luckiest man on earth?

When he first held a forkful of roasted meat toward her, she eyed him skeptically, but without a word, he convinced her that he wasn't going to give up until she'd filled her belly with some fortifying protein. Every time she took an obedient bite, he skewered another until the plate was clean. She finished off the water, took a trip out to the latrine, and when she returned, closed her eyes and relaxed against her rucksack.

"I'm stuffed," she said.

"You're going to need the energy."

She opened one eye. "Why? The mountain air isn't making you feel randy, is it?"

"As a matter of fact," he said, sliding down beside her.

The tents in the encampment were very close together, so while Mike had no intention of making love with Anne while so many people were in earshot and she was still feeling so weak, he did enjoy the feel of her body pressed against his. Despite the occasional arm twitch or neck spasm, he held her, smoothing his hand across her shoulder or across her waist. The Tourette's had not stolen this pleasure from him. He wouldn't let it.

And neither would Anne. She scooted closer so that their bodies touched in all the places that mattered. Her kiss was long and deep and full of desire. Surprised, he pulled back to stare into her eyes, which sparked with what he recognized as undeniable lust.

"Now who's the one feeling randy?"

"I confess," she said, nipping at his chin. "I never realized how arousing it is when you take care of me."

"This would not be a surprise if you let me do it a little more often," he chided.

She hummed, her lips vibrating against his throat in a way that ignited his bloodstream and had him rethinking the assessment that the tents were too close together. After all, most if not all the people on the tour were still sitting around the campfire, finishing up dinner under the stars.

If he and Anne decided to turn in early, he doubted anyone would notice.

Anne woke feeling as if she'd slept for a week rather than one night. The grogginess she'd battled for the past couple of days had lifted. Maybe her body had finally adjusted to the elevated altitude. Maybe it was Michael's tender, loving care—not to mention his mad skills with making love to her in total, complete, yet intensely thorough, silence. Her body still ached pleasantly from all the places he'd touched, caressed, and pleasured. He was dead to the world. Before she grabbed fresh clothes and her toothbrush, she placed a soft kiss on his cheek, which caused his eyes to flutter open.

"What time is it?" he asked.

Sunlight glowed along the edges of the horizon, but not with enough brilliance for her to read her watch. "Early," she answered. "Go back to sleep."

"How are you feeling?"

"Like a new woman," she assured him, then slipped out of the tent.

For the first time since they'd landed in Cusco, she truly appreciated the majesty of the landscape around them. The birds cawing and whistling in the treetops fluttered in and out of the sky, grabbing breakfast and darting back to their nests. Just on the edge of camp, a creek rushed across the rocks. The frigid water she splashed on her face knocked any last vestiges of sleepiness right out of her system.

She was in paradise. A rustic paradise, to be sure, but despite the fact that tourists trekked through the area on a daily basis, this portion of the Incan empire, undiscovered by their Spanish conquerors, remained as close to untouched as possible after centuries. Even after she'd finished getting ready for the day, she sat on a boulder beside the creek and watched the sunrise.

"There you are," Michael said, moving toward her with two cups of coffee. "Still feeling on top of the world?"

"You bet," she said, squeezing her arms into the space between his laden hands. "When are we breaking camp?"

"Twenty minutes. Ready to go?"

"I'll follow you anywhere." She took the coffee and then extended her fist so they could bump.

The brief connection of their knuckles made them both laugh. She wasn't sure what had inspired the ultra-hip gesture, but in so many ways, it represented all she and Mike had become. Casual. Comfortable. Fun. Despite her love of travel, she was pretty sure no other guy could have convinced her to climb a mountain. And she was entirely sure that she wouldn't have enjoyed the experience with anyone but him.

Eighteen

FOR THE NEXT TWO DAYS, living at the top of the world wasn't just a metaphor for spending time with Michael. They hiked treacherous trails, including one called Dead Woman's Pass that Anne thought had earned its name. Passing out at the top had been a distinct possibility.

Once they reached the summit, their guide passed around capfuls of an unnamed liquor to celebrate. The porters set up camp and they ate dinner among the stars, slept in the clouds, and in the morning took photographs of the mossy rocks while learning improved techniques for breathing to deal with both the exertion of the trail and the ever-increasing altitude. By the time they reached Machu Picchu and spent the day exploring the amazingly untouched city, Anne decided that no other trip she'd taken equalled this one. Mostly because of Michael.

The pervasive silence of the ruins intensified the intimacy between them every time he held her hand, touched her shoulder, or whispered some obscure fact about the Incas in her ear. Despite his claim that his Tourette's had made school difficult for him, he'd researched enough so that he knew just as much as the guides, if not more. In whispers, he shared a few facts about the

Incas ideas about eroticism that she definitely hadn't read about in any of her guidebooks.

They ended their adventure in Aguas Calientes, a pueblo that was not only the end of the road for hikers and provided train service back to Cusco, but also catered to tourists who wished to experience Machu Picchu without the arduous climb. They found a very nice public shower just outside the famous hot springs that had lent the village its name, then soaked in a heated pool for over an hour. Each moment washed away not only the grit and sweat from the climb, but also eased their sore muscles and battered feet.

Just underneath a bridge that shaded them from the sun and the prying eyes of too many fellow visitors, they found a semi-private corner of a pool where they could be alone. They imbibed a few exotic drinks, soaked, and talked about what they would do once they returned to Lima, all while kissing and cuddling and making up for the past few days when their concentration had been on not falling off the mountain.

After sundown, the other tourists headed back to town either for dinner or to the ramshackle train station that would take them back to Cusco. Michael and Anne remained behind and as night descended, they were entirely alone, except for a few employees mopping up the water around the springs and cleaning up the bar area. Mike ordered one last round of pisco sours, made with a Peruvian liquor distilled from grapes. When the iced cup met Anne's hand, the chill chased straight through her body.

"Last one," she said. "I don't know if I'm tipsy from the drinks or the heat. But this is heaven. Pure heaven."

The heated water was a steaming stew of natural minerals that seemed to open her pores to the crisp night air and her mind to endless possibilities. She closed her eyes and basked in the quiet swirl of the water against her flesh and the heat inside her skin.

When the current eddied against her, she knew Michael had finished his lap around the pool.

"We're all alone," he murmured.

Anticipation lit through her body like fireworks. She opened one eye first, then the other, to scan the area. "Well, look at that," she said.

"Whatever should we do with all this privacy?"

Michael's question, fraught with suggestion, sparked the nerve endings in her fingertips so that she simply had to touch him. She smoothed her hands over his shoulders, chest, and arms, suddenly jealous that as a man, he could go topless without drawing a single stare. Her breasts, heavy with need, strained against her swimsuit. She knew exactly what she wanted to do now that they were entirely alone, but did she dare?

They were out in the open, even if they were hidden by the darkness.

But they were on vacation—one they'd worked hard for, both emotionally and physically. What was the worst that could happen?

And how could she think about the bad when the best was right in front of her?

"You could start by kissing me," she suggested.

In a heartbeat, his lips were on hers. He tasted of fruit juices and liquor, his tongue chilled from the icy drink he'd set down on the side of the pool beside her head. Submerged to her shoulders, she opened her knees so that Michael could slide in close. He braced his hands on either side of her neck and as if he'd read her mind, surreptitiously undid the top of her suit.

His boldness was not only invigorating, it was contagious. She slid her fingers around his backside and moved his trunks so that she could hold him, stroke him, and then, when she could take no more of his long, languorous kisses that seemed to milk every ounce of sensual pleasure from her body, she guided him inside. He leaned back so that a swath of light from somewhere above streaked across his face and illuminated nothing but his eyes. The blue, so powerful and intense with passion, penetrated straight to her soul. She surrendered to the sensations around her and inside her until their climaxes peaked.

Soon, the sounds muted moments ago by their mutual desire registered in their brains. Voices. Someone was coming. Mike unobtrusively retied her swimsuit and readjusted his shorts. In the space of an instant, they were relaxing in the pool again as if nothing had happened.

But so much had happened—beyond the lovemaking, though as her passion receded, Anne couldn't believe they'd done something so intimate in such a public place. Whenever Mike released his inner wild child, the results always exceeded her expectations.

He surprised her. Even after being together long enough to fall into routines, he managed to find ways to inject new life and laughter into their relationship. She had every confidence that he cared about her deeply. Maybe even loved her. He'd definitely shown he had, even if he hadn't said the words.

But then again, neither had she.

As liberated and nontraditional as she was, there were just some things a woman didn't say or do first. Just like their first official date, their first kiss, their first trip together—Mike had made the first move. Until he was ready to say it out loud, she'd simply have to keep her overwhelming emotions to herself.

Mike retrieved their drinks. The ice had melted, but the liquid was still cool, particularly against the heat steaming up from the spring—not to mention what they'd just done.

"That was close," she said, sipping the potent concoction.

He waggled his eyebrows, unashamed. "That's what made it so fun."

".That's the only thing?" she questioned.

He pulled her to him, wrapping his free hand around her waist. "Not by a long shot."

Up until the moment they reached Arequipa, the trip to Peru had exceeded all of Mike's expectations. Aside from the brief and mildly annoying bout of altitude sickness Anne had experienced during the ascent to Machu Picchu, Mike figured he'd remember this trip mostly for the breathtaking vistas, the triumph of mastering the physical challenge of the actual mountain climb, and, of course, making illicit love with Anne in a secluded yet entirely public place.

Unfortunately, the trip highlights would not be what he would remember most.

They'd had dinner in town. The restaurant, tucked into an old, light-pink Spanish colonial structure carved with volcanic rock, featured a lovely courtyard surrounded by tall palms that had swayed in the dry night breeze. They'd enjoyed a delicious ceviche, one of Peru's national dishes and one of Mike's favorite foods. Then, about an hour after they reached the hotel, Michael wasn't so fond of the seafood dish anymore. The way down had definitely been more enjoyable than the way back up.

There wasn't much he wanted to forget about Peru, but food poisoning was at the top of his list.

Sluggish and fighting cramps in his lower abdomen, Mike was only vaguely aware of Anne leaving the room an hour or so after he got sick. He unloaded the last of his dinner in two separate trips to the toilet bowl, glad that the woman he cared about was not around to hear him heaving in porcelain stereo. He'd just climbed back into bed when he heard the door open and she slid back into the room holding a couple of green bottles that clinked against each other as she locked the door.

"Hey," she said, her voice a reverential whisper. "I got you some ginger ale."

She used the bottom of her T-shirt to protect her hand while she twisted open the top. She dug into her pocket and retrieved a paper-covered straw, which she inserted into the bottle. She dropped to her knees beside the bed and smoothed the hair away from his sweaty forehead.

"Think you can take a sip?"

For her, he'd do anything.

The liquid enhanced the dry, cracked feeling of his throat, but even without her saying so, he knew the ginger would help settle his stomach. How many times in his childhood had his mother prescribed the same? That Anne knew this home remedy surprised him a little. She was a strong woman, capable and independent and well-traveled and beautiful. But he'd never pegged her for nurturing, too.

He managed a few sips before his lids, which he'd strained to keep open, fell tight over his eyes. He needed sleep. In all of their hikes up and down the Andes trails, he'd never experienced exhaustion like this. And yet, he doubted he'd sleep a wink until whatever microorganism he'd taken into his body at dinner had completely left his system.

Hot and sweaty, he tore away the covers and tried to concentrate on the nearly imperceptible breeze floating down from the lazy ceiling fan twirling above the bed. His eyes flew open when he felt a soft, cool sensation on his forehead.

"Sh," Anne said. "You're burning up. This will cool you down. Just relax."

In a haze, he surrendered, relaxing as she ran the damp cloth over his face, down his neck and throat, then across his chest and arms.

"You should sleep," he said, his voice raspy.

The only light in the room came from the tiny bathroom. The golden glow spilled across Anne's unbrushed hair and oversize nightshirt, illuminating her as if she were an angel straight out of Botticelli. She was ringing out the towel inside the ice bucket, which she'd filled with cool, clean water.

"I'll sleep once you're comfortable," she replied.

"I'll be fine."

"Yes, you will," she agreed, then placed the folded towel across his forehead and forced his eyelids shut with a gentle sweep of her hand.

Mike slept on and off, waking once to empty the last of his stomach contents. During other hazy, yet wakeful moments, he sipped more ginger ale at Anne's insistence or felt the cool compress she wiped across his skin. At daybreak, she showered and then disappeared out the door. By the time the sun had completely risen in the sky, she was back with the announcement that a driver was waiting for them downstairs and she had the address of a medical clinic.

Mike didn't have the strength to argue. Anne took complete control from directing the cab to the correct location, filling the doctors in on his condition in surprisingly clear Spanish, and remaining at his side while the nurse hooked him up to an intravenous drip to replenish the fluids he'd lost.

By midafternoon, his strength had returned enough for him to leave. They returned to the hotel and after a brief nap, he woke up, showered, and brushed his teeth, but decided that shaving while he was still so unsteady on his feet was not a good idea. Anne stripped the sheets off the bed and was tucking the last corner of a fresh set beneath the mattress when he returned. He leaned against the wall for support while he waited, watching her move with quick efficiency. Once she'd floated the bedspread across the top, she motioned him back into bed.

"You catch up on some sleep, too," he said. "I'm done hurling now. Join me?" He moved the sheets aside to make room.

"Eat some crackers first," she insisted. "The doctor said you needed to fill your stomach with something to stave off the excess acid."

He shook his head, unable to process the thought of putting food—even the blandest food possible—into his digestive system.

"No, I'm fine."

"Just nibble on one. The salt helps, too, though I have no idea why. Just do it, okay? Please? For me?"

Even at his strongest, he doubted he could deny anything Anne requested, wanted, or wished for. After he bit half a cracker, chewed, swallowed, and washed it down with semiflat ginger ale, she smiled.

God, he'd do anything for that smile. Anything at all.

The most he could do right now, however, was obey her commands. Until he had more strength. After that, all bets were off.

Nineteen

BY THE NEXT DAY, MIKE FELT NINETY-PERCENT BETTER. He celebrated by suggesting they get out of the hotel room and explore the city for an hour or two, or until he had a relapse. He had not traveled to a different hemisphere to spend his time in bed—well, not unless he was making love to Anne, and he wasn't quite ready for that type of physical exertion just yet.

Arequipa overflowed with stunning architecture. Five distinct influences, each introduced to the landscape after a huge earthquake hit the region, that created a magical maze of buildings. Anne read aloud from a travel brochure and they wandered around for hours, keeping their pace slow. Moving at a relaxed tempo not only reserved his strength, it gave them more time to hold hands and kiss under impressive archways.

They returned to Lima the next day. Before they'd even left New York, Anne had made reservations for them at a restaurant she'd heard about that overlooked the Pacific. For the occasion, Mike bought her a dress, a pretty pair of beaded sandals, and a handmade shawl from a local market. He'd even sprung for a new cotton shirt for himself, which he wore untucked with a pair of khakis and his favorite sandals. They weren't the dressiest pair waiting for a cab outside their downtown hotel, but if Mike wasn't wrong, they were the happiest.

Before walking across the long pier to the glittering restaurant that dominated the entire space with a rich, Wedgwood-blue roof and intricately patterned, crisp-white gingerbread latticework, they strolled along the rocky shore. The salty breeze tousled Anne's hair so that she tied it back from her face with a ribbon, which gave Mike easy access to her neck once they'd settled onto a rock, their feet dangling above the misting ocean.

"Thank you for taking care of me when I was sick," he said.

She looked at him like he'd sprouted another head. "You keep saying that. What did you expect me to do when you were puking your guts out?"

He sat back, struck by her question. He certainly hadn't thought she'd abandon him in his hour of need, any more than he would have deserted her. And yet, he couldn't lie and say that he'd assumed she'd pamper him the way she had.

"I don't know," he replied.

She rolled her eyes heavenward. "I can be very considerate when I need to be."

"You were more than considerate," he assured her. "Don't take this the wrong way, but you reminded me of my mother."

She snorted. "How can I not take that the wrong way?"

"You haven't met my mother," he reminded her. "She's totally cool. Very nurturing and a fabulous cook, but she's just as strong and independent as you are. I want her to meet you. I want you to meet her. And my father. And my sisters. The holidays are coming up, right? Come with me to Syracuse."

Mike's heart skipped a beat for the split second it took for Anne to smile. They both lived close to their families and took time away from each other occasionally to go home and visit. But they'd yet to do the "introduction to the family" bit on either side that would take their relationship to yet another level.

Even though they were in South America after experiencing a trip full of mind-boggling highs and literally gut-wrenching lows, he could think of nothing more terrifying than bringing Anne with him to his aunt's house on Christmas Eve where his entire family would catch their first glimpse of the woman who'd turned his life upside down in the most spectacular way.

"Really? At Christmas?" she asked. "Won't your entire family be there?"

He smiled. "Every aunt, uncle, cousin, sibling, niece, nephew, and parent will be there," he confirmed. "But you have nothing to worry about because they're all going to love you."

"And how could you possibly know that?" she asked.

He almost said, *because I love you,* but the words caught in his throat.

"What's not to love?"

He slipped his arm around her, and with her head on his shoulder, they watched the sunset prism of oranges, golds, and pinks streak across the horizon. The crash of the ocean against the rocks echoed in Mike's ears, but even the raucous sound couldn't block out what he'd nearly said aloud.

He loved her.

After a moment's consideration, he realized that the fact that he'd fallen in love with Anne did not surprise him in the least. What took him off guard was the fact that he'd stopped himself from saying it out loud.

In his life, he'd only told one woman that he loved her, and back then, when he was so young and inexperienced, the words hadn't had the power to change anything about their relationship. Love or no love, they'd still hang out, listen to music, and have fun with their friends. With Anne, however, it would be different.

He was different.

Loving Anne meant changing his life. Loving Anne meant looking farther into his future than he ever had before. He loved his life as is. He had a great job, a fabulous dog, an amazing apartment in a neighborhood that rocked. But things couldn't remain the same. And he didn't want them to. Without change, there would have been no Anne at all. Her job situation notwithstanding, they'd worked through their rough patches with humor and patience. She understood about his disorder, his ambitions, and his passions. He'd come to trust her in ways he never thought possible.

And then there was the sex.

God, the sex.

Anne cherished intimacy, and with him, she didn't shy away from anything. She was bold and adventurous and sexy. And trusting. Strong, independent-thinking Anne Miller counted on him as much as he did on her.

Yes, he loved her, but was he ready to make that bold confession? Was she?

He decided to keep silent. He wanted to enjoy the secret for a little while, mull it over, make sure that when he said the words aloud, both he and Anne would be ready to take their relationship to the inevitable next step.

"Ready for dinner?" he asked.

She snuggled closer to him. "I could sit here with you for the rest of my life and be perfectly content," she said, sighing as the last arc of the sun kissed the water's edge.

He laughed with a bit more nervousness than was warranted, then stood, tugged her to her feet, and kissed her with a kind of passion he hadn't known existed until right that moment.

This passion scraped his insides and left him raw. This passion couldn't be doused by bad work hours, illness, or any other curve-ball. This passion might just last a lifetime.

And that changed everything.

Christmas at Mike's house was always a wild and exciting affair. And as it was the first time Anne would meet his family, Mike's anticipation was a mixture of tension, happiness, and fear. He loved his family. They were loud and boisterous, particularly his father's Italian-Catholic side, with whom they spent every Christmas Eve. His own Jewish mother had never had trouble fitting in—and not surprisingly, Anne did not either.

Their relationship had changed since Peru. Mike hadn't believed they could get any closer, but after she'd seen him at his absolute worst, she seemed to rely on him a little more than she had before. Now when they talked about her unhappiness at work, she didn't shut him down. When he made suggestions of how she might take a new perspective on her future in journalism, she listened. When she wanted to brainstorm about the possibility of going to graduate school or moving to the city or even working for a rival newspaper, she chose him to talk to.

He still had the sense not to tell her what to do, mainly because he knew that no one could figure out the answer better than Anne herself. She'd find her own way. She'd discover the best solution. And when she did, the first person she'd share that milestone with would be him. Of this, he had no doubt.

Before, during, and after the traditional Italian Christmas Eve, Anne hung out with his mother, shared funny stories about him with his sisters, and endured his father's tales of raising three children in two faiths. Amid all the conversations, they ate. His cousin, Erin, had once again outdone herself by making pounds and pounds

of more than twenty varieties of cookies using every family recipe
their aunts and grandmothers had ever created. They feasted on
homemade pasta, meatballs, and seafood dishes that his aunt,
cousins, and their daughters had been cooking for more than a week.

As the night progressed, more than fifty relatives and friends
came in and out of the house. With each round of greetings and
introductions, Anne's eyes widened in surprise, then excitement.
She loved meeting new people. She loved sampling all the wonderful cooking, playing with the kids running up and down from
the basement playroom, and helping out in the kitchen whenever
she could coax someone into allowing her to.

Mike was so head over heels in love, he could barely stand it.
And yet, he still hadn't said the words.

They'd been on the tip of his tongue since that night in Lima.
He'd had to get used to the idea, accept the fact that his bachelor
days were long gone—right along with the key to his heart. Anne
had that in her possession, whether she knew it or not.

Now that he knew how seamlessly she folded into his family, he
could hardly contain the declaration. But first, he had to get her
alone. He'didn't know when or where, but before the night was
over, he'd hit her with his big confession and hope she felt the
same way.

By the time the festivities ended, they were both exhausted.
They drove back to his father's house, where Anne would sleep in
his sister's old room. When he volunteered to take Sirus and his
father's two Weimaraners, Lucy and Morgan, for a walk, Anne
asked to come along. He considered reminding her of how the
temperature had dipped to freezing and snow had been dusting
down from the sky for over an hour, but he wanted her all to himself, even if they were too bundled to do anything more than hold
hands through fur-lined mittens.

The dogs wasted no time doing their business, but after a twenty-minute walk around the block, Mike let them scamper around the snow-covered yard while he and Anne watched from the driveway. She cuddled into his arms—or as close to his arms as she could get with so many layers of clothing between them. While he appreciated his father's old-fashioned insistence that they not share a room since they were neither married nor engaged, he also wanted to wake up with Anne. Not just on Christmas morning, but on the ordinary days, too.

"I told you my family would love you," he said, knowing the time had come. He wanted to remember this moment. He wanted her to remember it. He wanted the whole world in on his secret, but first, he had to tell her.

"I loved them, too," Anne said. "But like you said, what's not to love? Of course, I'm going to gain back all that weight I lost before Peru. Your cousin's cookies are too delicious to be believed. And I am a connoisseur of cookies."

"Is that why you're so sweet?" he asked, kissing her.

She slapped him on the arm, but with all the padding of their clothes, he didn't feel anything but the iciness of her lips and then the comforting warmth of her tongue.

"Not the most original compliment that's ever come out of your mouth, Mike Davoli."

"Sometimes, the old standbys can't be beat. Like, I can't help but wonder what I ever did to deserve you."

Cliché or not, he delivered the line straight from the soul. He stared into Anne's eyes, brushing away the feathery snowflakes that had fluttered across her lashes.

"Right back at you," she said.

"I'm serious," he insisted.

The wattage of her smile dimmed, but not the power. He'd

somehow tethered her happiness to the innermost chamber of his heart and knew he'd move heaven and earth to keep that smile shining for the rest of his life.

"You are, aren't you?" she asked. "And you're rarely this serious. What's up?"

"Anne, I love you."

The words exploded as if shot from a cannon embedded in his chest. For the first time in a month, he'd done nothing to stop them and the result was both terrifying and liberating. "Michael?" she questioned.

"I love you, Anne. I truly, deeply, and desperately love you."

"Oh my God," she said with a gasp. "I love you, too."

He thought he heard relief in her voice, but he didn't have time to sort out anything more than the feel of her mouth, her arms around his shoulders, and her body pressed against his. A long moment elapsed before he understood that he was not only making out with Anne in the driveway of his parent's home, but he was kissing the woman he loved in the same spot where he'd once played one-on-one with his dad, where he'd scraped his knees riding his skateboard, and where he'd first learned to park a car.

In the cradle of his childhood, he held Anne close and kissed her even deeper.

"I can't believe I waited this long to say it," he said once they finally broke apart.

"I can't either," she said, and this time, he couldn't miss a hint of impatience, as if she'd been waiting for him to break this barrier for quite some time. "How long have you known?"

"If I said the minute you agreed to watch Sirus for me while I moved into my new apartment, would you believe me?" he asked.

"No," she said.

"How about the night you broke into my apartment with my credit card?"

"Try again."

"Okay." He slid his arms around her waist and tugging her so close that their down jackets squeaked together. "How about when you threw me out of your apartment because you weren't going to settle for anything less than a full, committed relationship?"

"That's believable," she said, kissing the frozen tip of his nose. "I knew I was falling in love with you then, too. I just didn't want to be the only one."

"You'll never be the only one ever again."

After falling asleep in Peru while listening to her breathe and then dealing with their separate apartments the moment they returned to New York, he wondered how he'd survive staying in different rooms in his father's house. He didn't want to spend another night without her. Not ever.

He swallowed deeply, clutched her just above her down-padded elbows, and said, "Move in with me."

Twenty

HER MIND ALREADY REELING from his unexpected declaration of love, Anne had trouble comprehending what he'd just suggested.

Move in together? Mix her predilection for messy comfort with his insistence on precise order? Share the rare quiet moments with not only her man, but his dog? Was she ready for such a huge step?

"Look, I've been thinking about this," he said. "With your hours, we hardly see each other. If we lived in the same apartment, we'd be together more often. It seems silly for us to be running up and down between apartments and paying rent twice. If the only time I get to sleep with you is between one and six o'clock in the morning when I get up for work, then so be it. I'll take what I can get."

Even blindsided by this suggestion, Anne couldn't deny his logic. Lying side by side in the tiny tent on the side of a mountain in the Andes had been preferable to what they were doing now. One floor away—or one room away, like here at his dad's—felt like the whole of the South American continent.

But she loved her apartment. She'd lovingly picked out every mismatched piece of furniture and she adored being able to drop her clothes in a trail from her front door to her bathroom on her way to the shower without worrying about it annoying anyone.

And it would annoy Michael. He hadn't said anything out loud, but as he'd picked up after her in their hotel room in Lima on the last night before they'd left, he'd huffed and puffed a little louder than was necessary. On the high of finding out that the deep feelings she held for him were not one-sided, she didn't want to ruin it with talk of their Felix and Oscar tendencies.

"I don't know, Michael. My job is so weird right now. Can we talk about it again after I get back on a regular schedule? I'm not saying no—"

In typical Michael fashion, he waylaid any conflict by kissing her soundly. Only after Sirus pushed her way through Michael's legs to alert them both that she'd had enough of the cold white stuff did they break apart.

His father had brewed a pot of decaf before going to bed. She poured a mug for each of them while he dried off the dogs with towels from the laundry room. They drank, quietly holding hands across the kitchen table, and chatted about Christmas Eve, reviewing the string of relatives she'd met and matching them to their respective offspring.

Thankfully, Mike dropped the subject of them living together. She needed time to mull the idea over at her own pace, and as usual, he seemed to know this without her saying a word. He filled the quiet kitchen with reminders about the fabulous gourmet breakfast his mother and sisters would prepare, after which they'd retire to the Christmas tree for a gift exchange and then work off their meal with a long walk and a marathon viewing of all three *Godfather* movies.

While he ran down the list of activities, her mind snapped back to that moment in the driveway. Michael loved her. And not only had he confessed his deepest feelings, but he also wanted to live with her. He wanted her perennial mess in his pin-neat space. He wanted to share a bed with her each and every night, even though she knew how much he worried about how his Tourette's might cause him to hurt her while they slept. On the nights she stayed at his place or he at hers, she'd sensed his reluctance to hold her as they fell asleep.

And now, he was willing to face that anxiety every night? Why?

Because he loved her, that's why.

"Then around five o'clock," he explained, holding out his hand and bringing her back into the present. "The cousins will descend again for another seafood feast, this time courtesy of my mother. She may be Jewish, but she's embraced the whole Italian experience."

Anne laughed. She'd worry about living arrangements later. Right now, she just wanted to revel in the happiness of the holiday. Every last bit. Even the calories.

"I'm going to need serious gym time to work off this weekend," she said.

He pulled her close. "Or, we could work it off at home, if you know what I mean."

If she hadn't caught his innuendo in the kitchen, she understood it completely when he walked her upstairs and kissed her good night. His lips and tongue made promises that set her body on fire. He slid his hands into her hair, bracing her cheeks in that intimate way that always made her mad with wanting. She couldn't resist smoothing her hands over his backside and pressing him close so she could feel him harden against her.

"You're killing me," he said with a groan.

"It's murder-suicide, trust me," she replied. "I love you, Michael, but if you don't get out of here soon, I may tug you into your sister's room and force you to make love to me."

"Don't tempt me," he chided.

After one last long, languorous kiss in the hallway and another "I love you," Michael disappeared into his childhood bedroom with Sirus. Somewhat in a daze, Anne closed the door in his sister's old room. She changed into her pajamas and climbed under the flowered bedspread and turned out the lights. In the combination of moonlight and streetlamp through the lacy curtains, she could see the vintage teddy bears and dolls staring down at her with their button eyes and painted lips, so incongruous next to the MTV poster of some teen heartthrob Anne only vaguely recognized.

Then she couldn't help giggling like she was ten again. Of all the places she'd expected to spend the night after the man she loved finally admitted his feelings for her, this certainly wasn't it. Her entire body yearned to share his bed all night long, putting into action the words they'd just exchanged.

Instead, the space she wanted to occupy was being filled by a dog.

She laughed even harder. During the nights she slept over at Mike's place, she and Sirus already fought for the space closest to him. If she moved in, the territorial showdowns were going to make things interesting. And yet, no matter how things worked out with the dog, Anne knew that living with Mike—and loving him—made her the winner.

Six months later, Anne told the management that her Albany apartment would soon be available for rental.

"I can't believe you're moving in with him," Shane said.

After nearly a year of knitting, she'd become fairly adept at the craft. She stuck to scarves and blankets, as more complicated projects would have been inhibited by the wine they drank during their outings. Still preferring bright colors, this night's afghan featured bright summer pinks and oranges that evoked memories of the blazing sun that had turned June hotter than normal. Anne, on the other hand, was working with a delicate blue and silver angora yarn that was soft and fluffy and reminded her of icy cold snowflakes.

Thanks to a pitcher of iced sangria made with the bar's house red and a generous dose of brandy, they were enjoying a cool, relaxing minimeeting of their knitting club. Adele was out of town and Kate, who'd started joining them last week, had to attend a piano recital for her teenage daughter.

"Don't you think I should move in with him?" Anne asked, surprised at Shane's reaction. None of her friends had voiced any trepidation over her and Mike's plan to cohabitate. Even her parents admitted that this was a good move.

"Of course I do," Shane said, waving her hand dismissively. "I just thought you'd cling to your independence until the day you died."

"Where I live has nothing to do with who I am," Anne insisted. "Besides, Mike gives me my space. I've never met anyone who is so open-minded and nonjudgmental. Except for my messiness. It already drives him crazy and I'm not even living with him yet."

"You going to try and straighten up?" Shane asked, wiggling her eyebrows at her incredibly bad pun.

Anne sighed. "I'm not wired to be neat. Ask my mother. Ask my college roommate! It really makes no sense. I'm so organized in every other aspect of my life. I suppose I use up all my left brain on work."

"And speaking of work—" Shane started, but Anne's groan cut her off.

"Please, let's not. Tomorrow will be my day of reckoning."

She'd managed to maneuver herself off of the night shift for a week, but only because she'd been covering a murder trial that had started as an arson investigation. On the midnight shift, she'd been the first reporter on the scene. She'd filed the first articles linking the suspicious blaze to the domestic problems of the couple who owned the charred house.

Since the situation had now turned into a trial, she'd insisted on being moved to the day shift so she could cover the court proceedings.

Unfortunately, the case was turning out to be a snoozefest of filings and objections and procedural issues. Pamela had hinted more than once that she wanted Anne back on nights.

Only Anne wasn't willing to go back.

Ever.

Shane refilled their glasses and they were toasting her showdown with her boss when Mike tapped on the window. The wine bar and bistro had seating outdoors, but in the sultry summer, they'd stayed inside. Mike had Sirus on her leash, so Anne darted to the side exit door.

"What's up?"

"Sorry to interrupt your knitting," he said, waving at Shane over her shoulder.

Sirus wriggled and whined until Anne bent and gave the dog a hearty scratch behind her ears. "Grab some needles and join us."

"I'd probably stick my eye," he said. "I just came by to bring you your cell phone. You forgot it at the apartment."

The apartment.

Not *my* apartment. Their apartment. Anne reeled, but in an excited way.

He tucked the phone into her back pocket, his hand lingering on her backside longer than was strictly necessary. She didn't mind one bit. Her entire body tingled at the knowledge that no matter what time she wandered home tonight, at some point, she was going to end up in Michael's bed.

"Sure you didn't stop by just to cop a feel?"

"I plead the fifth," he said, holding his hand to his heart.

"Pleading guilty in this case would be much more interesting," she teased.

"Well, if that's what you want," he said, pressing closer so that no question remained about what they'd be doing once she finally came home. "I'm guilty as charged. Gonna write a story about me?"

"And expose all your deep, dark secrets to the world? I'd rather keep them to myself."

Two things stopped the intense make-out session that commenced. One was Shane tapping on the glass window to remind Anne that she had a pitcher of fresh sangria waiting at their table and the other was Sirus, who'd nuzzled in between them as she often did whenever they were kissing.

One challenge they'd yet to overcome in their new living arrangements was finding a way to coexist with the dog. She loved the pup, but the competition for attention and affection was going to have to stop.

"See you later, then?" he asked, untangling his legs from the leash trap Sirus had created around his knees.

"Not too much later," Anne replied.

She returned to the table, determined not to make eye contact with Shane until she had to.

"You're whipped," Shane said.

"No, I'm in love. There's a distinct difference."

"You'd better be in love. Nothing else is going to help you survive living together."

"What do you know? You've never shacked up with anyone."

"Not for the lack of being asked," Shane countered. "But I haven't ruled it out. I just haven't met the right guy. Maybe you have. I hope you have. I'd like to think someone can still find true love in this world."

Anne stared down into her wine, suddenly struck by the import of what was happening. She and Mike had been together for over a year and while things between them hadn't always been perfect, they were definitely on a romantic road she'd never traveled with anyone else. The decision to move in with him had not been an easy one. Giving up her space came with a price.

But the potential payoff was too tempting to resist. She loved him. He loved her. The idea of sharing her world with him all the time consumed her, even if it also scared her to death.

She and Shane headed back to the apartment building around ten o'clock. She was just about to open Mike's door with her key when her cell phone buzzed in her back pocket. Glancing at the caller ID, she expected to see Michael's number and had a sultry greeting on the tip of her tongue.

She stopped up short when she saw the caller was the *Daily Journal*.

Not wanting to disturb her neighbors with what would likely be an unpleasant conversation, she went inside Mike's place before she said, "Hello?"

Sirus bounded over, twirling in a circle to celebrate Anne's arrival. She petted the dog while Pamela said something on the other end of the phone that she missed entirely.

"Excuse me?"

"We need you at the paper," the editor said tersely. "Drop whatever you're doing and get here ASAP."

"I just finished a ten-hour day. Isn't there anyone else?"

Pamela nearly growled. "If there was someone else, I wouldn't be calling you, would I? You've got fifteen minutes."

Mike came into the room and stopped short at what must have been the livid expression on her face. Never in her life had anyone spoken to her with so much disdain. Not even Pamela. She couldn't take it anymore.

She wouldn't.

Digging deep into the well of her professional soul, Anne managed to reassure her boss that she'd be there with maximum speed, then disconnected the call.

She'd go, because it was her job. She'd go, because despite how bone tired she was, she had a responsibility. But for how much longer she called the *Daily Journal* her employer was another matter entirely.

All her adult life, she'd wanted to be a reporter. She'd traveled across the country to make her dream come true, but nothing had topped finding a job in journalism in New York. She'd nearly sacrificed her relationship to keep her job. It was a testament to her bond with Michael that bickering over her hours or her unhappiness hadn't torn them apart. Protecting her relationship at the same time she protected her job had sapped her dry. She had no more energy left to build a shield for her self-esteem.

She'd had enough.

"What's up?" Mike asked.

Her eyes burned, but she blinked back tears. She was beyond crying. Beyond rage. She was numb.

"Pamela wants me back at the paper now."

"You just left!" Mike said.

Anne shrugged and headed toward the couch where she'd left her laptop.

"You're going to go?" he asked, shocked.

She nodded, but couldn't reply. If she didn't make this one last effort, Pamela might fire her—might ruin her chances for another job elsewhere. But Pamela's unreasonable request had acted like a line in the sand. Anne had to make a choice about whether or not to cross.

"Tonight, yes, but Michael, this is it. I used to love my job. I used to feel like I could take on the world as long as I had a story to follow. But I've worked too hard to be treated this way."

Mike sidled up beside her, his bright blue eyes alight with pride. He wrapped her in his arms, but didn't say a word. He didn't need to. Her body shook, but he compressed her fear and anger until she felt nothing but peace.

She should have done this months ago.

"You're going to quit?"

Against his shoulder, she nodded. "I'll go in tonight, file whatever story that's got her so desperate for me and then tender my resignation first thing in the morning. Or maybe I'll look in to that buyout thing the guys in HR were talking about a couple of months ago. I don't know anything for sure except I can't work there anymore."

She couldn't bear to look up at him. She'd intended to give Pamela an ultimatum regarding her hours tomorrow, one that the editor would have to capitulate to because Anne was a valued employee. She'd worked the night shift for longer than anyone else on the crime desk. She'd consistently turned in good work and had been reliable and diligent.

But the tone of her editor's voice and the unreasonable demand that she work another eight-hour shift in the same day had simply been the last straw. Her tolerance had reached its limit.

Her stomach rolled over, then dropped to her feet.

She was going to quit her job.

"You're doing the right thing," Mike assured her.

She managed a little nod.

Mike took her hand. "Come sit down. I'll pour you something."

"I just drank a whole pitcher of sangria," she confessed, and then her heart stopped. "Do you think that's it? I'm drunk and making rash decisions?"

"No," he said, a grin teasing the edges of his mouth that should have annoyed her, but didn't. "I think you just had a moment of extreme clarity. They tend to knock the equilibrium out of you, though, so you really should take a load off. And as for that pitcher of sangria, I'll make coffee and drive you in myself."

She allowed Mike to lead her to the couch. The cushions cradled her, and seconds later, Sirus was lying across her lap, pawing her hand so that she'd pet her, which she did. At some point, Mike placed a mug in her hand. The smell of the coffee at once repelled and lured her. She sipped, and then shook her head in utter disbelief.

"I'm going to be unemployed for the first time in . . . " Her voice trailed off. It was too taxing on her brain to think that far back. Except for college, she'd been working since she was a counselor at Camp Odyssey in her early teens.

"Good thing that you're moving in with me, then," he said.

Her entire chest seized up. "Oh! God, no. Now I can't move in with you! I don't have a salary. I can't pay my half of the rent. There's no way . . ."

Mike sat on the coffee table, his face frozen in a stoic, no-nonsense expression that was foreign, and yet, completely trustworthy. "You *will* move in with me. We'll figure it all out, but if I have to support you in the manner to which you are accustomed, which luckily for me, isn't all that extravagant," he said as an aside, his mouth softening into a deeper smile, "then that's what we'll do. I love you, Anne. I love us. We will take care of each other. It's what people in love do."

Twenty-One

"MIKE, HONEY, YOU OKAY?"

Startled, Mike looked up from the report he'd been trying to read for nearly half an hour. He blinked, trying to focus his eyes. Only when he looked up at Nikki, who was standing over him with concern etched on her pretty copper-brown face, did his vision clear.

"I'm sorry?" he asked.

"Are your allergies acting up again? You were kind of coughing, like," she said, then imitated the sound.

Mike's stomach turned. He had not been aware of any coughing and his allergies were fine. He was struggling with his eyes, which had fluttered shut. The muscles in his lids battled against the pulses sent to his brain. He couldn't remember the last time his disorder had manifested with both physical and vocal tics to this degree. In fact, he wasn't sure it had ever happened before.

"It's the Tourette's," he replied.

Nikki's eyebrows popped high on her head. As a close friend, she knew about his disorder. He wasn't shy talking about it to people he met who might be put off by his symptoms if they didn't understand why he had them. But in all the time she'd

209

known him, he'd never experienced such pronounced signs of his disorder.

She grabbed the chair beside his desk and wheeled it closer to sit down knee to knee with him. "Since when?"

He closed the cover of the report, certain he wasn't going to be able to process anything more today. "Since the new job, the new living arrangements, the new everything."

Though Mike was currently working at the Quality Education Alliance, he'd given his two weeks notice a couple of days before. He'd received an offer from the teacher's union in New York City, an opportunity he'd worked toward his entire career. His colleagues at the Alliance, supportive of educators, lauded his move to a more visible position as a lobbyist. Despite the fact that he'd have to commute to the city for his work week until Anne finished graduate school, they had decided that the move, in the end, would be a good thing.

Too bad his body did not agree.

In a split second, Nikki's expression of concern morphed into one of focused energy. He couldn't help but laugh. The woman was unstoppable. When presented with a problem, even one that wasn't hers, she set her mind on finding a solution. "Okay, call Anne. Tell her to meet us at Lark Tavern at seven o'clock."

"Lark?"

"I blame you for getting me hooked on their artichoke dip," she said with mock indignation. "But you need to relax and I'm going to see to it that you do."

Knowing better than to contradict his friend once she made an executive decision, he agreed. He was going to miss working with her. He was going to miss this job all together. But the union would give him an opportunity to work with the highest levels of state government. He'd make a difference in the educational programs he believed in.

But at what cost?

And how was he going to do his job—which was essentially, public speaking—if he couldn't form a sentence without coughing, humming or sounding like a cursed mummy from a bad B-movie?

He dialed Anne's cell, catching her as she left class.

"Hey," he said, then cleared his throat. "How was school?"

He'd made a habit of asking this question every day since she'd started her graduate studies, even though it sounded like something one would ask a child. Still, it made her laugh, so he asked it anyway.

"No offense, but I'm in desperate need of estrogen," she said.

Mike chuckled. Six months after leaving the *Daily Journal,* Anne was now a full-time graduate student working toward a Master of Science degree in Human-Computer Interaction. Which meant, she worked mostly with men. Cognizant of the rapid change in the delivery of news content from traditional paper to the Internet, Anne had decided to turn her unexpected break from gainful employment into time to pursue an advanced degree.

Mike had been one-hundred percent behind the idea, up until the moment he realized that if she was in school, she wouldn't be able to move when he accepted the job in New York City.

"Too many engineering students in your personal space today?" he asked.

"Too many engineering students in existence," she quipped. "I was going to call Shane and see if her knitting needles were sharp."

"How about a trip to Lark Tavern instead?"

"Why not both?"

They made plans to meet in an hour. Mike kept the conversation short. He had every intention of telling Anne about this new development in his Tourette's, but as her frustration level seemed to have peaked, he decided to wait until they'd both had a chance to relax.

He attempted to return to the report, but just as he'd struggled with written text so often during his life because of his disorder, he couldn't manage to focus his eyes long enough to process the content. Instead, he bugged out early, went home, changed clothes, and took Sirus for a quick walk around the block. After they returned, he sat on the couch, willing his body to calm.

Sirus jumped up beside him, so he proceeded to scratch her behind her ears until she was nearly passed out with pleasure. Some of the tension overloading his nervous system eased out through the fingers buried in her short fur, but not enough to counteract the Tourette's when it had progressed so far. In two short weeks, he wouldn't be able to just relax with Sirus on the couch after a long day. She'd be here in Albany with Anne while he lived alone in the rented room of a friend's apartment.

When he thought about living without his two constant companions, his chest hurt. But Sirus needed more space than the single bedroom and Anne had to finish school. She had just received a grant and an appointment as a research assistant. She couldn't walk away now. Not when she was so close to achieving an advanced degree that would help her find a better job—specifically, a better job in New York City.

He'd factored Anne's increased opportunities for better employment when he'd accepted the offer from the union. New York had always been the setting for their career ambitions, but he'd never anticipated, not after they'd finally settled in to a comfortable routine, that they'd be living the dream, at least initially, separately.

But if they could make it through her last few months of hell at the *Daily Journal,* then they could make it through a year of commuting. Yet again, they faced a test to their happiness. One they'd pass.

They had to, because he wasn't entirely sure if he could live without her.

They had a fabulous dinner at Lark Tavern. They feasted on the exquisite greens and beans dinner with escarole, shared a pitcher of beer, and listened to live music by a band. Shane had been unable to join them, so Nikki and Anne commiserated about everything from silly fashion trends to men while Anne showed Mike's coworker her latest knitting project.

Mike tried to enjoy the company while he had it. Several times, his shoulder jerked or his hand smacked against Anne's on the way to the artichoke dip. The more he recognized how his symptoms had escalated, the worse they got. When they'd finished dinner, he skipped coffee. The caffeine and sugar would make his situation worse.

On the walk home, he dug his hands deep into his pockets and walked a few steps ahead of Anne so she wouldn't lock her arm with his. In his state, he wasn't sure he wouldn't inadvertently hurt her. Even when she'd first moved in and he'd eschewed holding her as they fell asleep for fear an involuntary muscle spasm might injure her, he'd never been so determined to keep his distance. But once they got up to the apartment and both had showered and changed into sleepwear, he couldn't avoid her anymore.

"Are you going to talk to me?" she asked, folding her foot underneath her as she sat beside him on the couch.

Sirus lifted her head as if considering whether or not to join them, but Mike signaled her to stay in her bed. She slumped her chin back onto the cushion with a discernible canine huff.

"Nikki heard me coughing at work," he explained. "Not a sick cough. A Tourette's cough. Throat clearing, but louder. I wasn't even aware of it until she said something. Then, once I noticed, it got worse. I was already having trouble reading. Reports and memos don't come in audio books like my college textbooks did. I don't know what I'm going to do. I couldn't even hold your hand on the way home. It's never been this bad. Never."

Anne scooted closer and ran her hand softly over his shoulder. That she wasn't afraid to touch him when he didn't trust his own physical control meant the world to him, even as it increased his anxiety.

He'd cut off his limbs before he hurt her. That much he knew.

"What do you do when this happens?" she asked.

"I don't know," he said. "It's never happened like this. I've always struggled with physical tics, but the vocalizations have never been a problem. It's what surprises people most when I tell them I have Tourette's."

She continued her slow, sensual rubbing of his arm, nodding in understanding. They'd had countless discussions about the general public's belief that Tourette's sufferers were crazy lunatics who barked curse words and jerked uncontrollably up and down dark alleys. In truth, the vast majority were like him, managing their symptoms with combinations of good medical care, adequate rest, diet, and exercise.

But those things weren't helping him right now. He'd moved beyond his normal coping mechanisms into unknown territory.

"Talking about it usually helps," she reminded him. "You're under a lot of stress. Changing jobs. Moving. Leaving your girls behind."

She kneeled onto the couch beside him. With deft hands, she dug into muscles so tense, her gentle ministrations at first felt as if he were being handled by a mad masseuse named Sven.

He winced, but she persisted. "You need to relax."

"That much I know," he said. Unfortunately, with his

Tourette's, wanting to relax and actually achieving a state of calm were two different things.

As she continued to unsuccessfully work into his muscles, Anne whispered softly in his ear, coaxing him to concentrate only on the feel of her hands on his body. When he couldn't manage it, she did not give up. She took his hand and led him into the bedroom.

"Shirt off," she ordered.

"You first," he countered, defiantly, though he liked where this exercise was going.

Without a second's hesitation, she whipped off her top.

He took of his shirt and for good measure, his shoes and socks, so that he wore nothing but jeans when he splayed crossways on the bed and grabbed a pillow to buoy his chest. Anne had given him massages before—and vice versa, but never when his body was being such a pain in the ass.

While he slowly undressed, she lit candles around the room. She dug up a stick of patchouli-scented incense, lit it, and set the fragrant herbs on the side table closest to his face.

He inhaled and the smell instantly transported him to the park where he most loved to hike. The loamy smell of freshly turned earth and the piquant perfume of pine teased his nostrils and lulled his brain into memories of the outdoors. Even before Anne climbed over him, her hands warming something she'd squeezed onto her palms, he'd started to let go of some of the stress.

When her slick hands met his flesh, he groaned in pleasure.

"There we go," she coaxed. "Just concentrate on the feel of my hands."

"What is that?" he asked, his voice growing huskier with each loosening of sinew and muscle. They had massage oil in the bathroom cabinet, but nothing that heated with friction.

She shifted so that her thighs cradled his hips and her thumbs dug a little deeper into the bunched cords of his neck. The erotic rasp of lace sparked the skin on his lower back.

"Something I picked up at the lingerie store."

He attempted to turn around to see if she'd also picked up new panties, but she forced him back into the prone position.

"No peeking. This is not a visual exercise. This is strictly tactile. Close your eyes."

"You know this is a temporary fix, right?" he said, experiencing a jerk in his muscles even as he said it.

"That's not the right attitude," she chanted, characteristically upbeat. "Take what you can get. Enjoy the moment. Then you'll have something to think about when your stress levels go back up. You can imagine my hands on your body, digging into that spot right here—"

He gasped when her fingers twisted through the bunched flesh.

"And then you'll relax."

"But what if—" he asked, clearing his throat involuntarily.

She smacked him on the shoulder. "No negative thoughts."

She leaned across to the bedside table to turn up the music, which gave him a particularly impressive view of her bare breasts. He reached for her, but she maneuvered out of his way.

"Oh, no," she teased. "Until you relax, the only tactile experience you need is my hands on you. Not the other way around."

Talk about incentive. Mike squeezed his eyes shut. He heard the squelch and stream of her putting more oil in her hands and he concentrated on the anticipation of feeling the slippery, warm sensation on his skin. One kind of tension left his body as another kind—a much more pleasurable kind—increased. She worked magic with her hands, pressing hard into the constricted muscles in his neck, shoulders, and back, then working out the kinks between his shoulder blades. Then, with infinite patience, she traced down every vertebrae in his spine until he felt like the candle flickering on the window sill—slowly melting to nothing but the flame.

And every time she bent low across him so that her nipples skimmed over his skin, his mind let go of another worry, another concern. By the time she gave him permission to turn over, he could hardly remember how they'd gotten into the bedroom in the first place or what he'd done to rate such an amazing massage.

"Feel better?" she asked, her eyelids hooded and heavy.

Try as he might, he could only keep his gaze on her face for about a split second. After that, all bets were off. He managed a quick flip so that she was underneath him, her slippery hands pinned by his just above her head.

"You're one hell of a physical therapist," he said, bending to taste the delicious skin of her neck. "But I want in on the oil action. Where is it?"

She glanced at the edge of the bed, where the bottle had nearly tumbled off the comforter. He snagged it and as he tried to pour some into his palm, she moved to turn over.

"Oh no," he said, holding her in place. "I've got you right where I want you, my love. Trust me, I'll make it worth your while."

By the time he finished, they were both so slick, their bodies slid together without resistance. He banished the thought of how rare nights like this would be once he was living in New York City by memorizing every taste, every texture, every pleasure spot on her body. They wouldn't be living on opposite sides of the world. They'd only be about four hours apart. Knowing Anne would be waiting for him, missing him, wanting him, was more than enough incentive to face this crisis like every other one that had crossed their paths.

Together.

He tugged her closer to him, right up against the arm that had been jerking and twitching all day. "I'm going to go crazy living without you," he confessed.

"I won't be far away. And you are going to be living in my favorite city on the planet. It won't be hard to entice me to visit."

"You'll come meet me in Manhattan?" he asked.

She kissed him, naked and slick, and his body renewed for another round. "You just have to say the word."

Twenty-Two

"I THINK I WANT TO GO BACK TO THE HOUSE," Anne said, handing him her half-eaten pretzel with a look that said the salty baked dough slathered in mustard wasn't agreeing with her.

But they couldn't leave Camden Yards just now. Not because Mike had any particular interest in seeing his beloved Yankees massacred by the Orioles—who were already one run up and seemed to have much stronger pitching than his Bronx Bombers—but because he had a question to ask Anne that needed to be asked here.

Just not right this minute.

But soon.

Or . . . not.

His brain swam. When Anne's father, David, had called with the news that he'd secured tickets for the game, Mike had been struck by inspiration. How often did the two teams they'd followed since childhood battle each other in Baltimore, only a few hours from Anne's hometown in Salisbury, on the eve of the Jewish holidays?

Besides their trip to Peru, their excursion shortly after she'd left her job at the *Daily Journal* to Cooperstown for the Baseball Hall of Fame induction of Cal Ripken, one of Anne's all-time favorite players and Baltimore's favorite son, had been an amazing trip. She'd even freelanced a job writing a "Quick Guide to Cooperstown," for her hometown magazine.

They'd had a blast exploring the restaurants, parks, and museums she'd recommended. It was memories like that one that he clung to on the nights when their only communication was through instant messaging, telephone, or e-mails or on weekends when her school work kept their interactions limited to quick kisses in between her trips to the computer lab or large gatherings with friends, even when he truly wanted Anne all to himself.

Mike had taken the timing of the game as a sign. He needed Anne to stay with him until he was ready to pop the question.

He just didn't want to do it in front of her parents—especially when the Yankees were down by one run.

Anne's mother, Hannah, leaned forward and put her hand on her daughter's knee. "What's the matter, sweetheart?"

"I'm just not feeling well enough to sit through a whole game," Anne said. "I'm sorry."

Her father, who'd been keeping score and noting the stats inside his program, looked up. "What's the matter?"

"Anne's sick. Maybe we should go," Hannah offered.

How could Mike say no and not sound like an insensitive clod? All his plans were falling apart.

Though he and Anne had been living apart for nearly five months, they'd somehow fallen into a comfortable routine, traveling between upstate and the city, sharing time at their apartment, or hanging out in Brooklyn with friends so that their separation hadn't struck them as keenly as her shift in work hours had a year ago. Of course, their relationship was no longer skating on new ice, but had solidified into an uncrackable bond nearly impervious to time and distance.

With confidence that their separation was just a temporary inconvenience, Mike had gone into his new job with determination. His Tourette's symptoms had returned to normal. Anne had thrown herself into her studies and was in the home stretch of grad school.

They were fast approaching yet another crossroads and more than anything, Mike wanted to merge onto that highway with Anne, not as his live-in girlfriend, but as his fiancée.

The path they'd traveled together had been rockier than some, but smoother than most. In his entire life, he never dreamed he'd find a woman who shared his love for his dog, great music, travel, baseball, and was Jewish to boot.

He was going to propose.

But to do it right, he needed her to stay at the game.

"Maybe you just need some fresh air." The minute the suggestion spilled from his lips, he winced at how stupid it sounded.

The evening was on the chilly side, but blue skies and a setting sun made it the perfect weather for baseball. The air couldn't get any fresher than it was in the lower reserve section behind the third base line.

The teams had been scoreless until the fourth inning, when Baltimore's Adam Jones had grounded into a double play, but sent Luke Scott home for the first run of the game. As a die-hard Yankees fan, Mike had not taken this as a good omen. Anne's sudden bout of ill health did not make him feel any more confident.

This weekend, for Passover, was going to be filled with family. He had to propose here at this game. And yet, asking her in earshot of her parents sucked out the romance. If only he could get her to go for a walk with him. If only he could get her to agree to stay.

"Why don't you sip some soda, honey?" her mother offered.

Anne nodded and did as her mother requested and backed off

on the idea of leaving. Silently, Mike promised never to make a single mother-in-law joke for the rest of his life.

Uncertainty suddenly flooded through him. It wasn't like him to do something this big without a specific plan.

"I'm in the mood for Cracker Jacks," he said when the third out retired the side and the teams changed places on the field, with the Yankees up to bat at the top of the fifth inning.

Anne made a face that told him sweetened popcorn with peanuts was the last thing she wanted to eat.

"Come with me to get some?" he asked.

He didn't want to wait much longer. It would be bad enough asking in front of her mother and father, but the Oriole fans who surrounded them had been giving his white with dark blue pin-striped jersey suspicious—and in some cases, hostile—looks. His proposal didn't need any negative energy.

Anne shook her head. "I don't feel like walking. The guy will come around soon."

And as usual, she was right. A vendor selling the iconic base-ball snack did indeed show up a few minutes later. Mike pur-chased a box and pretended he wanted to eat them, when in reality, he only wanted an excuse to get away from the crowd. As he poured the sweet treat into his hand, a square-shaped tempo-rary tattoo floated to the top of the caramelized popcorn. If he had a pen, he could scribble two words on the slick paper.

Marry me.

But what good was it if Anne wouldn't even look at the can-died treat?

He'd almost changed his mind and was seconds away from offering to take her home when the Orioles' third baseman made an error on a single hit by Chad Moeller, sending Yankee Robinson Cano to the plate for New York's first run. The score was tied. He risked cheering for his team, despite the unfriendly crowd, then decided this had to be a sign.

Standing, he made a show of stretching his legs and tugging at his jeans while he rolled his neck and shoulders. He watched the rest of the inning, his brain split between hoping for another run and trying to come up with some excuse to get Anne out of her seat.

He was heartened when Anne's father decided to make a bathroom run and hoped his wife would go, too, but she declined and for the hell of it, Mike went with David instead. He endured a couple of minutes of good-natured ribbing about being a Yankee fan and a historical reminder that in the early 1900s, the Yankees had actually been the Baltimore Orioles. After they stopped at a concession stand for a beer, watching the game's progression (or lack thereof, as no one else scored in the fifth inning) Mike realized he'd forgotten to do something.

"I'm going to ask Anne to marry me," he blurted out.

With a beer halfway to his mouth, David's bushy eyebrows arched upward. He set the drink down and stared at Michael without saying a word.

He didn't need to speak. Something in his expression made Mike replay his words in his head and then make a very important amendment.

"I mean," he clarified. "I want to ask Anne to marry me. If I have your blessing."

He hadn't really planned to ask permission. As traditional as both he and Anne could be in many aspects of their lives, Mike had the distinct impression that Anne might not appreciate being bartered by her father. On the other hand, she'd understand that her father would want to be included on the decision that would ultimately affect the rest of her life.

After his initial hesitation, David lifted his beer and took a sip, the foam clinging to his moustache before he licked it off with a quick swipe. "Think she'll say yes?"

Mike downed a good quarter of his beer. Was this why he was so nervous? Did he think that Anne, after living with him and sharing his bed and confessing her secrets, was going to turn down his proposal?

"Yeah, actually, I do," he replied.

"Then why are you so nervous?"

Leave it to David to cut to the chase. He was a numbers guy, an accountant, a man of few words but deeply held convictions. A cheer rose up around them that indicated the Orioles had scored, but David's eyes never left his.

"I love her," Michael replied. "I'd move the world to make her happy."

He didn't reply specifically to David's question, but his answer seemed to satisfy his future father-in-law, who lifted his beer in a toast and then took a hearty sip.

"Gonna do it now?"

"I've been trying all night," Mike said. "Anne loves the Orioles. I thought she'd appreciate a proposal while they were trouncing my team."

Another roar exploded through the stadium. They returned to their seats to find Mike's chances of getting a yes to his proposal had increased by five runs—so far—scored in the sixth inning. Though Anne still wasn't eating much, her mood had elevated to the point where she felt more than comfortable razzing him about how much her team was killing his.

But he didn't mind. Maybe the Yankees had to lose in order for him to win.

After the seventh-inning stretch, Anne decided she really wanted to go home. She'd been feeling woozy since the car ride and though she'd sipped an ice-free soda the whole game, she was desperate for a nap. Between her demanding schedule at school, preparing for the trip home, and getting ready for the holiday, she'd pushed herself to the limit. And no matter how far she went from Albany, she couldn't forget that her graduate project was due in less than two months. The upside of not having Michael around during the week was that she could work late. The downside was that she wasn't getting very much sleep.

And yet, even though the Orioles had scored seven runs, Michael still didn't want to go home. He insisted that Chad Moeller's homerun over the left field fence in the top of the seventh constituted a comeback, but she wasn't convinced. She considered taking the car herself and leaving him to go home with her parents, but she'd spent too much time away from him lately. She settled for remaining in her seat, occasionally putting her head on his shoulder until his enthusiasm or disappointment regarding the game sent her flying.

When the Yankees failed to score again by the ninth inning, the game ended. She mustered up enough strength to razz Michael about her team beating his, but her heart wasn't in it. Darkness had fallen and she just wanted to go home.

"Camden Yard is awesome," Mike said as they streamed out of the row and up the stairs.

The stadium was an impressive place, particularly at night when the lights sparkled against a crisp Baltimore sky. Her parents had parked at a different entrance, so they left, but Michael lingered behind, wanting to look around.

"I don't know when I'll get a chance to come again. Can we just walk around once?"

The crowd was thinning. Anne didn't feel one-hundred percent, but she understood that while the Yard was nothing new to her, Mike was a baseball fan of the first order and poking around the stadium was just the sort of thing he'd enjoy. Their shared love of this sport had been yet another tick in the tally list of their compatibility. They both liked hiking. They both enjoyed yoga. They adored basketball and had similar—his Phish obsession notwithstanding—taste in music. She could no more deny him this chance to explore the home of her beloved Orioles than he would say no if she needed extra time at a knitting store to pick a new pattern.

By the time they reached the section between center field and the bullpen, the stadium was mostly empty. Mike walked to the railing, leaned over as he gazed across the sea of green grass and bright orange clay. The scoreboard had frozen with the game's final score of Orioles 8, Yankees 2. She took the opportunity to tease him a bit about the lopsided win before pointing out the two orange seats in the sea of dark green that filled the stadium.

"That one," she said, pointing to a spot in right-center field in the Eutaw Street Reserve seats, "is where Eddie Murray's 500th homerun landed back in ninety-six."

"And that one?" he asked, pointing to the orange spot in left field.

She smiled. "That's where Ripken hit his two-hundred and seventy-eighth home run, the highest any shortstop had achieved since Ernie Banks."

He turned and grinned at her. "You do know your baseball."

"One of my many charms," she replied.

He took her hand. In the space of a heartbeat, his expression changed. His bright blue eyes seemed to darken with sudden seriousness so much that her mouth dried and her blood thudded in her ears.

"Michael, what's the—?"

But before he could answer her question, someone shouted, "Hey, you two!"

They turned to see an ancient security guard toddling toward them.

"Game's over," he said. "Time to clear out."

Anne took a step toward the exit, but Michael, who'd snagged her hand, held her in place.

"We're just taking a look around," he explained.

She turned to him, perplexed by his obvious reluctance to leave. How much more of the park could he possibly see?

"We're clearing out now," she assured the guard.

"In a minute," Michael insisted, his voice low.

But the guard continued to amble over until he was right beside them.

"Great place, this is," the guard said, glancing around. "Old-style. Lots of character. Fan-friendly, but after a time, the fans gotta go home."

Anne couldn't help but agree. She looked at Michael with a silent insistence that they vamoose, and after an unexplainable hesitation, he finally moved toward the exit. The security guard followed them out, regaling them with stories about the stadium and the team that Anne might have found interesting if she hadn't just realized that Mike was acting very, very strangely.

He hadn't released her hand once in their walk and when they circled around the stadium to find their car, he stopped in front of the ticket booth.

"The car's this way," she said, pointing to the direction she was pretty sure they'd parked.

"I know," he replied, still holding tight to her hand. In fact, his grip increased. As much as she wanted to leave, he seemed to have an equal will to stick around.

"Mike, I'm not—"

"I want to marry you."

In the space of five words, her ears filled with cotton. Or maybe her brain just went haywire. But clearly, whatever ailment she'd suffered through all night had finally taken its final blow in destroying her ability to hear correctly.

"I mean," he said, taking her other hand. "I want to marry you, Anne. If that's okay with you."

The repetition broke through her shock and the words fell into her brain like gumballs down a novelty machine, clanging into the right pockets in a burst of sound and color.

He wanted to marry her. He wasn't asking—he was stating a fact.

At that moment, she understood how her Orioles had felt when the umpire called the third out in the top of the ninth. She launched herself against Michael and kissed him hard and long. He wanted to marry her. He wanted to bond their lives forever. He wanted her permission to want to marry her, and even as their lips pressed and their tongues clashed, she laughed in unbridled love for a man who truly understood her from the inside out.

When they broke apart, his eyes glittered. "I take it that means yes?"

"Yes!" she said at the top of her lungs. "Yes, yes!"

He opened his arms and she immediately fell back into them, the most wonderful place on earth. His muscles clenched around her, enveloping her with the full press of his love. She looked up into his face, about to ask if this was why he'd seemed so out of sorts all night when they were approached by an Orioles fan in black and orange who smelled as if he'd swallowed a brewery.

"Go Orioles!" he shouted, wrapping both of them in his sweaty arms.

The moment went from romantic to surreal in an instant, but all she could do was laugh.

Twenty-Three

"YOU KNOW WHY I DIDN'T GET YOU A RING, right?" he asked as they drove to her parents' house.

Anne reached across to Mike and stroked his cheek, still high with happiness. "Because you know I'd want to have a say in picking it out."

"Just wanted to make that clear," he said with a decisive nod. "I don't want your family to think I'm not serious about marrying you."

Anne frowned. God, she was going to see every single one of her local relatives over the course of this weekend—the very same relatives who had peppered her with questions about her unmarried state practically since her *bat mitzvah*. Okay, not quite that long—but close. She had visions of her aunts dragging out their wedding dresses, her married cousins bombarding her with definitive assessments about which florist had the freshest peonies, and her mother making a list of caterers that ranged from casual barbeque to the swankiest five-star restaurant in the tristate area. The impending onslaught of wedding wackiness turned her stomach back to the unsteady state she'd been fighting all night.

"Michael," she said, turning in the seat as far as her seatbelt would allow. "Do you think we could hold off on announcing our engagement? Just until I'm done with school?"

Disappointment skittered across his face. "But everyone is going to be together. Your side of the family, anyway. It's the perfect time."

"The perfect time for me to lose my mind," she countered. "There's so much going on right now. School. You living in New York City. My graduate assistantship and then looking for a job. It's just too much for one person to think about—particularly if that one person is me. My family is going to go nuts. Your family is going to go nuts. Shane, Adele . . . Nikki! The minute we make the announcement, they're going to descend on me with bridal magazines and start planning trips to the city to find my dress. I just can't handle all that now on top of school. Can't it be our little secret for a little while longer?"

Mike considered her reasons and then glanced at her with an indulgent smile. "You still want to marry me, right?"

She huffed impatiently. "You know I do."

They'd arrived at a stop light.

"I'll do anything you ask," he confessed.

"Anything?" she asked, wagging her eyebrows suggestively.

He laughed, then leaned across and pressed his lips to hers. Their long, luxuriant kiss lasted until the cars behind them honked when the signal turned green.

To make up for keeping their engagement to themselves for over two months, Mike and Anne orchestrated a Sunday afternoon outing in July at a Yankees-Mets game at Shea Stadium with twelve of their best friends. During the seventh-inning stretch, Michael took out the ring Anne had chosen and slipped it onto her finger. Despite their plan to announce their upcoming wedding to everyone in attendance, when the rousing rendition of "Take Me Out to the Ballgame" stopped, they sat back down, silently wondering if anyone would notice the ring before they had to say anything out loud.

At the top of the eighth inning, a foul ball arched in their direction. The crowd surged toward the out-of-bounds hit, but neither Anne nor Mike made a move.

"You could have had it!" yelled Ben, seated in the row behind them.

"Honestly!" Adele agreed. "You didn't even try for it!"

Anne gave Michael a knowing glance before turning around and holding out her ring finger proudly. "So sorry, but I was busy catching something else."

Ben continued to grouse until Nikki, who was seated two rows behind them, let out a scream that made the entire section and even a player or two on the field turn in their direction.

"I knew it! I knew it! I've been telling them forever that they needed to get married! Oh, my Lord, girl! Look at that rock!"

And with that, the party started. Cheering, clapping, hugging, and a round of beer topped off the next few innings. Despite the fact that the Yankees had trounced the Mets in the two previous games in the miniseries, Anne's preferred team (which was basically any team who opposed the Yanks) managed to eek out a three to one win over Mike's boys in pinstripes.

And yet, Mike couldn't bring himself to care. He'd hit a home run.

"What do you mean the rabbi can't come?" Anne shouted into the phone.

She hadn't meant to raise her voice. She hadn't intended to

send Sirus scampering off the couch and into her bed, where she pressed her head onto her paws as if she'd just been scolded for getting into the garbage. Anne winced and patted her thigh, calling the dog to her so she could soothe the pup's frazzled nerves. The dog didn't budge.

She supposed she didn't blame her. After what her mother had just told her, she was severely tempted to crawl back into her own bed and hide under the covers.

"His message said the date conflicted with a conference he was scheduled to speak at in Virginia. Apparently, he'd looked at the wrong calendar when he'd agreed to do the wedding. I'm sorry, honey. We'll find another rabbi."

"Really? Where? Because last time I checked, Rabbis R Us was fresh out!"

Anne glared down at the latest printout of her to-do list. It was going on thirteen pages long now. Immediately following their ball-game announcement of their engagement, her life had evolved exactly as she'd anticipated—every second of every day seemed utterly consumed with wedding plans. Friends and family bombarded her with advice, offers of help, and contacts to various caterers, venues, and bands. Their parents started making lists of people who absolutely had to be invited to the ceremony. Mike contacted friends he hadn't seen since his Phish days and Anne charted the names of friends from Albany whom she hadn't talked to quite so often since she'd moved with Mike to the adorable brownstone apartment in the Park Slope section of Brooklyn, but that she still wanted surrounding her when she and Michael exchanged their vows.

Anne flopped onto the deep purple couch she'd brought with her from Albany and dragged her computer off the stack of *National Geographic Adventure* and knitting magazines on the coffee table and onto her lap, then in deference to the fact that Mike would be home soon, she stacked the magazines neatly and even weeded out a few really old ones and tossed them in the recycling bin. After extracting a promise from her mother that she'd make a few more calls on her behalf, Anne disconnected the call.

She took a deep breath and with intense determination, decided to ignore the fact that with only six months to go until the wedding date they'd printed on their invitations, she still had no religious official to make their union legal either in the eyes of the state or God. Instead, she concentrated on a task that wasn't so daunting—like finding the right bakery.

She thought of the ricotta-cheese mice she'd brought to Michael's apartment on their first date and was glad they'd decided to do a dessert bar with a wide range of sweet delicacies. He'd taken charge of finding the perfect cookies. She'd decided to be responsible for the cakes.

By the time she'd set up tasting appointments, it was near dinner time. Anne decided to lose herself cooking, but the wedding plans had gotten in the way of shopping and the cupboards and fridge were bare. She improvised and whipped up pancakes. When Mike came home from work, he immediately sniffed the air and smiled.

"Either you had a really bad day and want to start all over again or I'm just a really lucky guy," he said.

She uncovered the batter and threw a pat of butter onto a pre-heated griddle. "Both. Do you mind?"

"I'll make coffee and change into my pajamas if you want me to."

"No need," she said. "But Sirus needs to go out. Then we'll eat."

When they returned, Anne stacked her infamously delicious

homemade pancakes high on Mike's plate and placed the bowl on the floor for Sirus to lick. The dog danced around for a second as if confused by the odd timing of her favorite treat, but in seconds, she was scooting the glass bowl around the kitchen while she licked away every last smear of sweet golden goodness. Though Sirus still adored Michael beyond any human on the planet, Anne's penchant for giving her the bowl to lick whenever she cooked had won her serious points.

"Want to talk about it?" Mike asked, swirling syrup over his pancakes.

Anne cut a triangle several layers deep. "We have no rabbi."

"Again?"

"We're cursed."

"We're not cursed," he assured her, moaning in pleasure as he demolished a quarter of his stack of pancakes in two neat bites. "Weddings are always like this."

"And you know this, how?"

He leveled her with an exhausted look. "You're not the only one at the receiving end of hours of unsolicited wedding advice and matrimonial horror stories."

"I can't imagine anyone can top the absence of a rabbi at a traditional Jewish wedding."

He reached across the table and though she thought he was going to pat her hand, instead he snatched the syrup for an extra drizzle. "We'll find someone. We'll tag team the entire Jewish community in the tristate area."

"We'll have to cast a wider net than that. We're getting married in Delaware."

They stayed up until midnight, but ended up with a short, but hopeful list of rabbis to contact on Monday. After collapsing together into bed, they spent an hour in the dark talking about their preferences for color schemes and which food items they absolutely had to have on the menu. By the time Anne's eyelids rebelled and forced themselves closed, she was ready to dream long and luxuriantly about anything other than cake styles and place settings.

Unfortunately, she was jolted awake only a few hours later by Mike's cell phone.

"Mike," she said, shoving him in the back so he'd wake up. "Mike."

Groggily, he opened his eyes.

"Your phone," she told him, aggravated that anyone who knew his number would think it acceptable to phone him before six o'clock in the morning.

He cursed when his sightless grab for the phone sent his glasses tumbling to the floor. Anne forced her own eyes open wider. Her heart thumped in her chest. If someone was calling at this ungodly hour, something horrible had happened.

"Hello?" Mike said finally.

A split second later, Mike sat bolt upright in bed. "No way! You're shitting me!"

That wasn't horror or sadness she heard in his voice.

It was abject excitement.

"Mike, what is it?"

"When?" he asked the caller.

She flipped on the light, momentarily blinding herself. She put her glasses on and Sirus, who'd been dead to the world at Anne's feet, gave a doggie growl that made it clear she didn't appreciate being woken up before dawn.

"Tell me about it, sister," Anne commiserated.

Mike's voice grew louder and more enthusiastic, but Anne was too sleepy to make much sense of his end of the conversation.

"What was all that about?" she demanded once he hung up.

"You're not going to believe this!"

He'd jumped up and was pacing the carpet in front of their bed as if Santa Claus had just arrived six months early. "That was Amy."

Amy. Amy. It was too early in the morning for Anne to place names with faces or even identities. She needed coffee. No, actually, what she needed was more sleep—preferably without dreams of her walking down the beach to the location of her *chuppah* and finding it held in place by three beach bums and a chef in a baker's hat.

"Amy. You know—she came to the game with us when we got engaged. Used to go to the Phish concerts with me," he prompted.

"Right," Anne said, not ashamed that she couldn't make the connection before caffeine. "Is she okay?"

"She's better than okay! They're getting back together."

Was it too much to hope that he was talking about Amy and a boyfriend?

"Who is getting back together?" she asked, though he was broadcasting the answer in the brilliant light flashing in his eyes.

"Phish!"

"Phish, the band?" she asked, not sure why she needed clarification. Probably because of dread. That emotion tended to clog up the brain.

He whooped, verifying that the band her soon-to-be husband adored, the band whose music seeped into his soul and made him dance so that he forgot completely about the twitches and tics that were a constant part of his life—the band for whom Mike had traveled thousands of miles and attended hundreds of shows—had decided to come together again for another tour.

Before their wedding.

She pressed her lips together, forbidding the grimace churning in her stomach from showing on her face. "Wow."

The delight on his face died slowly.

"You're not excited?"

"I'm excited for you," she said. "But I've got to be honest, Mike, I'm tired and overwhelmed with the wedding plans. This isn't exactly going to make my life any easier, is it?"

Mike frowned, but even her lukewarm reaction couldn't squelch his excitement. In less than ten seconds, he was grinning from ear to ear again. "This isn't going to interfere with the wedding. Their first shows will be in March and the wedding isn't until August."

Now wide-awake, Anne's eyes darted to the bookshelves where at least a dozen of Mike's scrapbooks, mostly filled with memorabilia from his Phish tour days, sat in places of honor next to her hardcover copies of *Pride and Prejudice* and *Kavalier and Clay,* her full DVD set of *Buffy the Vampire Slayer,* and the photo album Mike had started shortly after their engagement, complete with the ticket stubs from the Jeff Tweedy concert where they'd met.

Guilt nudged her between the ribs. This was important to him. She respected his obsession, even if she didn't fully understand it. The least she could do was let a little of his ebullient enthusiasm infect her. She had nothing to lose by being happy for him.

But first, she had to make one thing perfectly clear.

"Promise me, Michael," she said, holding out both hands in loving invitation. "Promise me that no matter when or where Phish performs, you will not miss our wedding. Or our honeymoon," she added, wanting to cover all her bases. "Or the birth of any of our children."

He took her palms in his and used the leverage to yank her into his arms and roll with her across the bed. Sirus, startled, barked and jumped off the mattress.

Anne could feel Mike's joy racing through his body and had a sinking suspicion that they were not going back to sleep anytime soon.

"I promise," he said. "Phish will not interfere with any important milestones."

Mike never made a promise to her that he couldn't keep.

Not until now.

Twenty-Four

"NO," ANNE SAID.

Mike stared at her, his jaw lax. Okay, so he'd made a vow not to allow the concerts to interfere with the wedding. He'd repeated that promise several times since March, right before he'd scavenged through their storage space for his tent in order to reunite with Jeff, Amy, and several other Phishhead friends for the first of three Phish concerts on the East Coast.

Anne had worked her Ticketmaster magic and scored him a pair of tickets for all three shows despite the fact that the 8,000 seat venue sold out in less than a minute. He'd declared her a goddess and promised to follow her to the ends of the earth.

Under any other circumstances, he never would have asked for a codicil to their initial agreement. But sometimes, situations arose that called for flexibility.

"Anne, honey, you've got to understand," he explained. "This is Red Rocks."

She glared at him, making it clear that if Phish were performing the first-ever concert on the moon, she wouldn't care. The shows he simply had to attend were scheduled for the week of the wedding. And if that wasn't insult enough, they were in

Morrison, Colorado, which wasn't exactly a hop, skip, and jump from their venue at Rehoboth Beach.

"I can't believe you're asking me this," she said, shaking her head as she walked into their kitchen and picked up her knife. The fact that she had been using the sharp implement to chop onions before he'd walked in didn't make him feel any safer.

Or any less conflicted.

He was entirely aware that making a request to travel across the country the week of the wedding to attend a concert by the band whose new shows he'd attended six times since the reunion tour began was pushing her goodwill.

In June, when the band had played in Camden, New Jersey, he'd brought her with him so she could fully understand the experience. And she'd enjoyed herself, even if she had stopped short of conceding that Phish was the best band in the history of music. During that trip, his friends had discussed the pact they'd made years ago to attend any show held at the spectacular amphitheater in Red Rocks. She knew he wasn't making that part up. She simply didn't seem to care.

He snagged his laptop and pulled up the venue's gallery of pictures.

"Look at this," he begged.

"No," she snapped.

"Just look at it," he insisted.

"What difference will it make, Mike? I can't move the wedding. I *won't* move the wedding. I wouldn't move the wedding unless there was a death in the family, which I suppose, under the current circumstances, is a distinct possibility."

She waggled the knife and it took all his power not to laugh. Anne was formidable, but it was hard for her to look menacing with her glowing cheeks and soft, round eyes.

"Killing the groom will not solve your problem," he said.

She glanced down his torso. "Who said I wanted to kill you?"

He winced. He'd walked right into that one.

"I'm not asking you to move the wedding. If I get tickets to the Thursday night show, I'll be back in plenty of time for dinner Friday night. Just look at the pictures. It's the most incredible—"

"Mike," she interrupted. "Red Rocks isn't a half hour by car from the beach. It's in Colorado. Anything could happen to keep you from getting back in time. After all we went through to get a rabbi, design a half-dozen cakes, including one with a edible Sirus on top, create our own invitations and hell, take the pictures of the dog with the tennis balls shaped like numbers to use on the tables so she could 'be there,'" she emphasized his words with the dreaded air quotes, "you want to put all our planning at risk in order to hear a band you've already seen six times this year? You're nuts."

He was nuts. Nuts about her and nuts about his band. Since their very first date, he'd tried to show her the depth of his Phish obsession, but she simply didn't get it.

"My friends are all going, Anne. Jeff, who is my best man. Amy. Ben, who was there the night we met. They're sticking to the pact. They've all promised to be back in time, but if I go, too, I can make sure they don't miss a minute of what is going to be the most spectacular wedding in this century."

Her eyes narrowed. "That's the lamest argument I've ever heard."

"Maybe," he said, truthfully. "But it's Red Rock, baby. I swear to you, I'll make sure every detail is taken care of before I leave. If something happens with the airline, I'll sell an organ and charter a plane back home. I made you a promise not to miss the wedding. I won't break it, I swear."

Anne set her knife down, which Mike took as a very good sign. Then after a painfully long minute, she sighed in defeat. When her soulful brown eyes met his, he saw myriad emotions swimming in their rich depths. Fear. Doubt. Confusion. But the one that skimmed to the surface when she reached across the counter to take his hand was trust.

"Don't let me down, Michael."

"I won't," he pledged, before quoting one of their favorite songs. "You can rely on me, honey."

Anne's gaze darted to the door of her hotel room. Her best friends in the universe, Shane, Adele, and Becky, whom she'd met back when they lived in Albany and who had hand sewn the *chuppah* they would use for tomorrow's ceremony, sat on the bed, toasting the upcoming nuptials with white wine in plastic cups. In between sips, they finished tying up the programs and pouring the candy store-worth of sweets—all with some significance to either the wedding or her relationship with Mike—into big jars and bowls for the reception.

She'd bought chocolate balls wrapped to look like baseballs, Jelly Bellies in coconut and berry blue to match the white and blue colors of her dress and Mike's suit and tie.

Then there were the blue and white gummy fish.

Or as Mike would call them, Phish.

On the dresser was the royal blue *yarmulke* she'd given him two years ago for Chanukah. She'd had the Phish logo silk-screened on the back in gold. She'd even agreed, shortly after their engagement, to let him wear it for the wedding.

Now, if he'd only show up, they could both say they hadn't broken their promises.

Becky grabbed the sleeve of Anne's pajama top and pulled her attention back to the group. "He'll be here."

"His plane should have landed an hour ago," Anne said, glancing down at the cell phone she'd kept by her side all day. "He hasn't answered the message I left him."

Shane waved away her concern. "He probably forgot to turn the thing back on. Sweetie, he'd never let you down. Not like this. Not even for Phish."

Anne wasn't so sure, but when a knock sounded on the door twenty minutes later, she leapt off the bed so quickly that an entire container of butterscotch discs went flying across the mattress and Adele spilled the last of her wine.

Anne wrenched open the door to find Mike standing there looking travel worn, but ecstatic. He took her into his arms, spun her to the side and not only dipped her halfway to the ground, but kissed her until she thought she might faint.

"You're back," she muttered once he finally set her upright.

He wiggled his eyebrows. "Of course I'm back. Do you really think I'd miss marrying the woman of my dreams?"

"Not on purpose," she said.

"Not even on accident. Now, let's get this party started."

That night, they had a cursory rehearsal, then met up with some of their wedding guests at the Dogfish Brew Pub. On Saturday morning, Anne and Mike stole away from the friends and family and hid themselves on the crowded beach, stretching a towel under the scorching sun with only the sound of the crashing waves and the laughter of nearby kids hampering their private conversation.

Avoiding everyone had been a handy trick, but Anne insisted that they spend some quality time together before the craziness truly began. Mike didn't argue. He seemed just as determined as she was to steal some time together before obligations divided their attention in a thousand different ways.

Now that he was safely back, Anne asked for the details about Mike's trip. For the rest of her life, she didn't think she'd ever hear anything more soothing than Michael when he was in the throes of enthusiasm for some topic, whether it was for music, politics, or especially, for her.

On Sunday, they had no time together at all. Anne wasn't even sure what Mike and his groomsmen were doing while she and her friends went into beauty mode, having their hair and nails done, slathering makeup on their faces, and ensuring that the robin's egg-blue bridesmaid dresses and her contemporary gown in pale white with swirls of azure were pressed and perfect. It wasn't until she tried to adjust her lipstick in a mirror that she realized the lighting in the hotel room was suddenly inadequate for the task.

She glanced out the window and her stomach dropped to her feet.

Clouds.

Smoky and ominous, they were rolling in from the horizon.

"No!" she shouted. "Not rain!"

Nearly an hour before, Michael had noticed the change in weather. As the day progressed, the blue skies that had made Saturday so magical had dulled to a murky gray. His best man, Jeff, a friend from his earliest days of following Phish, stepped up to the window beside him and laid a hand on his shoulder.

"Think Anne's noticed the change in weather?"

"I don't hear screaming from her room," he replied. His ears had been trained for the sound, or at least the ringing of his cell phone. She'd either remained silent because she hadn't noticed— or she was too overwhelmed with other details of the wedding to worry about the sky opening up and dumping their guests with sheets of soaking rain.

"This doesn't look good," Jeff said.

Mike flipped on the television, amazed that a day that had started off so gorgeous that he'd convinced both Jeff and his father to join him for a daybreak swim had devolved into disaster.

Of all the things Anne wanted most for the wedding, a beach ceremony had been her fantasy. Unfortunately, the weather report confirmed that the storm barreling toward them wouldn't pass until the prescribed ceremony time had come and gone.

"Crap," he said.

Mike's dad clucked his tongue dispiritedly. "Time for Plan B?"

"It could blow through," Mike argued, but even his well-honed debate skills weren't going to get them out of this one. He wanted Anne to have the wedding of her dreams, but while they'd micro-managed everything about this wedding, neither of them could influence the atmosphere.

"You can go for a rain delay," Jeff offered.

Mike shook his head. "No, the important thing is that we get married, not where. I'm ready to go."

"It's four forty-five," Dad announced. "The wedding is supposed to start at six o'clock. If you need to move everything indoors, the hotel has to know now. You could call Anne—"

Mike pulled out his cell phone and dialed. Though he'd taken care of every one of his responsibilities before flying off to Colorado for the concert, Anne had carried the bulk of the matrimonial burden up until now. He was glad to take his turn in making the best of this unexpected situation—but he couldn't make a decision this monumental without consulting the woman he loved. "I'm going to prep her for the possibility. Then, we'll wait fifteen more minutes. If the storm doesn't look like it's going anywhere, then we'll pack it up and move it all inside. Agreed?"

By the time Anne's father came to collect her, her blood was thrumming with a wild mixture of anticipation, relief, and peace. She tried to be upset about the cancellation of their outdoor wedding, but she couldn't conjure enough indignation to care. She loved Mike. He loved her. They'd sacrificed, compromised, and surrendered their way into a partnership of souls that she never imagined could exist, not even back when Anne was buying an extra bedside table for her bedroom.

Just when she thought she couldn't make another decision about anything, he took over. With his signature *joie de vivre*, Mike had made all the arrangements to transfer the wedding indoors.

The results were perfect.

In the room next to where their guests waited for the ceremony to begin, Anne, her parents, and her brother gathered with Mike's immediate family and their wedding party for the signing of the *ketubah*. After the rabbi explained the significance of the document to the party, emphasizing the history of the marriage contract, they both signed.

Once the rabbi and the witnesses added their John Hancocks, Mike's childhood friend, Matt, and his brother, Aaron, produced shot glasses and a bottle of Schnapps. They toasted their future before the wedding party and rabbi left with the *chuppah,* the traditional, four-pole canopy that Becky had sewn.

Anne held tight to her parents while Mike departed with his mother and father on each arm. He shot her one last look over his shoulder. Against his pale white suit and bright blue tie, his eyes seemed even more turquoise, even more intense—even more hypnotic and filled with unadulterated love.

In a matter of moments, they'd be man and wife.

His expression made no secret of his anticipation. She blew him a kiss to seal hers.

The ceremony was an eddy of emotion, tradition and laughter. By the time Michael turned to her to recite his vows, her entire body suffused with warmth. He took her hands and she couldn't help but notice that despite the crazy stress of the wedding, the weather, and the crowd, his touch was entirely steady in hers.

By custom, she recited her vows first. Thanks to a faulty computer, the words she'd slaved over for weeks were trapped in the circuitry, so she had to go entirely off the cuff. With anyone else staring at her, she might have been nervous. But with Mike standing across from her, unconditional love radiating off his body, she had no trouble putting together what she wanted to say.

"You might not believe this, but the first thing that comes into my mind when I look at you tonight is that time we went to Target together and you started playing basketball in the aisle."

The knowing laugh from the audience confirmed what she knew to be true: they'd gotten to this day because of how they complemented each other. His neat to her messy. His playful to her pragmatism. His crack organization skills with her boundless creativity. With these contrasting combinations, she knew they could face whatever curveballs life threw at them, from rainy weather to neurological disorders to deciding whether or not Sirus slept on her side of the bed or his.

"So on that note," she said, taking his hands in hers. "I want to promise that I will always try to find you entertaining and I promise that I will always try to keep my sense of play because that's what you bring out in me and is one of the greatest reasons that I love you."

Despite the catch in her throat, she reached into the depths of her heart, remembering the moments when she'd leaned on him the most. "We've been through so much together. I had a profession that I loved that ended up not being a good fit anymore and

I quit and went to grad school. You were there for me in ways I never imagined anyone ever could, so I promise that I will always do the same for you."

She swallowed thickly, fighting to contain her emotion. She needed to lighten things up, so she decided to make a promise that Mike might not entirely believe, even if it was coming straight from her heart. "One of our biggest challenges we've faced was moving in together. Our styles are," she said, aware of the increasing chuckling in the crowd, "different. So with everyone here as my witness, I want you to know that I will do my best to make our home as neat and as clean as I can, even beyond my abilities."

As the crowd laughed, probably in disbelief—especially from her side of the aisle—she thought of the poem she'd selected to recite, but for the life of her, she couldn't even remember the title. She focused on Michael, on his comfortable, casual smile, and said the most important part of her vows. "I just want to say thank-you for loving me the way you do and I promise to always, always love you."

She was on the verge of tears, but luckily, Mike launched into his vows so that she didn't have time to cry.

"Anne, in addition to the traditional promises that I have made today, I have three promises to make to you. First, if you promise to make the pancakes, I promise to always make the coffee."

Anne laughed, but couldn't cover her mouth because Mike was holding so tight to her fingers.

"Second, I promise to always put you ahead of everyone and everything in this world."

Her eyes watered and at that moment, she knew that if she would have insisted, he would have skipped the concert in Colorado. But she was incredibly glad that she had not taken away his joy out of nerves or fear or selfishness. Instead, she'd earned another sliver of his love. She couldn't ask for more, yet he went on, "Not even the forlorn eyes of a four-foot-tall Weimaraner can steer me wrong, with God as my witness."

Anne's eyes misted. All because he'd told her she was more important than a dog.

Weddings really were a torturous business. Beautiful, but torturous.

"And finally," he said, giving her hands a tentative squeeze, "when you and I first moved in together, I knew that this was a huge decision. I also knew right then and there that I was not going to want to ever go back to being alone. So to paraphrase the great philosopher Homer J. Simpson, I'm gonna hug you, and kiss you, and then I'll never be able to let you go. But I was afraid that you would not let me do so, but not only did you, but you have returned that feeling each and every day. So if you will let me, I will hold you, hug you, kiss you, and never let you go for the rest of our lives. You are my soul mate."

The rest of the ceremony was a blur. The circling. The breaking glass. The shouts of *mazel tov*. Before she knew it, the DJ had turned on the Wilco song that she and Mike had chosen for their exit entitled, "I'm the Man Who Loves You."

And now the world knew that he was—and that she loved him just as deeply in return.

They were married. Husband and wife. With each step they took toward the *yichud* room where they would, by Jewish tradition, spend the first few moments of their married life in seclusion, Anne realized that her entire life had changed—for the better.

They entered the same room they'd used to sign the *ketubah*, only now it was empty of everything except a table, a small tray of food, two wineglasses, and a bottle of her favorite red. After promising to return for them in ten minutes, the rabbi left.

Anne couldn't help but think of the line from one of Mike's favorite films, *The Candidate*.

"So, what do we do now?" she asked, smiling.

Mike's breath eased out of his lungs like a long-held sigh. "Well, I'm no Robert Redford, but we've just made it through the campaign of our lives. Kiss me."

Without hesitation, she did exactly as he asked.

Epilogue

"SIRUS, SIT!" MIKE ORDERED.

The dog wiggled her way into her best impersonation of obedi-ence, her mouth open and panting. He was holding her absolute favorite treat in the universe, which luckily, was easy to find in their Brooklyn neighborhood.

"Mike, stop torturing the dog and give her the ice cream," Anne said, swiping a lick of her own confection.

He set down the cup of soft serve and the dog immediately dug in until her muzzle was covered in creamy goodness. He joined Anne on the step outside their nineteenth century brownstone and enjoyed the cool chocolate on his tongue and the feel of his wife sidling up closer to him. The tree-lined street brimmed with activity, not from cars, but with children dashing along the side-walk ahead of their mothers' strollers on the way to the park or to the main drag only a few blocks up where he'd purchased their ice cream.

"That's going to be us someday," Mike said, eyeing a father across the street who had his son perched on his shoulder.

"I don't think I could carry you on my shoulders," Anne teased.

He nudged her ice-cream cone so that a smudge of white cream tipped her nose. She protested, but wiped it off and smeared her hand on his shirt. Only fair, he supposed.

"I meant the kids," he said.

"I know," she replied, hooking her arm in his. "I hope they have your eyes."

"I hope they have my sense of neatness."

"So do I," Anne agreed. "Then they can do my share of the cleaning."

He chuckled, turning so that he could wrap his arms completely around her while they finished up their frozen treats. Sirus had already demolished hers and was nosing around for a taste of his, which he denied. Luckily, the little girl from down the block appeared and Sirus decided that allowing the child to pat her head was more interesting than begging for more ice cream.

Mike waved to the child's mother and then settled into holding Anne. He remembered the time when he'd thought a moment like this would be impossible—when his Tourette's would have made him a hard man to hold.

Apparently, all he'd had to do was find the right woman because at this moment, all he wanted to do was hold her for the rest of his life.

Submit Your Own True Romance Story

"The marriage of real-life stories with classic, fictional romance—an amazing concept."

—**Peggy Webb,** award-winning author
of sixty romance novels

Do you have the greatest love story never told? A sexy, steamy, bigger-than-life or just plain worthwhile love story to tell?

If so, then here's your chance to share it with us. Your true romance may possibly be selected as the basis for the next book in the TRUE VOWS series, the first-ever Reality-Based Romance™ series.

- Did you meet the love of your life under unusual circumstances that defy the laws of nature and/or have a relationship that flourished against all odds of making it to the altar?

- Did your parents tell you a story so remarkable about themselves that it makes you feel lucky to have ever been born?

- Are you a military wife who stood by her man while he was oceans away, held down the fort at home, then had to rediscover each other upon his return?

- Did you lose a great love and think you would never survive, only for fate to deliver an embarrassment of riches a second or even third time around?

Story submissions are reviewed by TRUE VOWS editors, who are always on the lookout for the next TRUE VOWS Romance.

**Visit www.truevowsbooks.com
to tell us your true romance.**

TRUE VOWS. It's Life . . . Romanticized

Get Ready to Be Swept Away...
By More *True Vows*™
Reality-based Romances

Code 533X • Paperback • $13.95

Like many high-school sweethearts, Ted Skala and Erika Fredell spent plenty of time in parked cars making out under the stars, but it was an unlikely courtship between a college-bound beauty and a free-spirited jock. By graduation Ted was talking marriage. Erika, however, was ready to spread her wings. She broke his heart and sailed the world. Fifteen years later, when fate intervenes, Ted and Erika meet again in Manhattan. But Erika once ravaged his heart. How can Ted ever trust her again? And now that he's involved with another woman, how can Erika hope for a second chance with the man she should have never let go?

www.truevowsbooks.com